Women Of Note

M.J. BUCKMAN

UpLit✦Press

Copyright © 2025 by M.J. Buckman

All rights reserved.

No portion of this book may be reproduced in any form without written permission from the publisher or author, except as permitted by U.K. copyright law.

Contents

1. Helena — 1
2. Nefertari — 17
3. Cynthia — 30
4. Trung Tac — 44
5. Clare — 51
6. Mawia — 62
7. Lily — 68
8. Theodora — 77
9. Carol — 87
10. Wu Zhao — 98
11. Ende — 105
12. James — 118
13. April — 123

14.	Hildegard	133
15.	Christine	146
16.	Alice	166
17.	Alex	174
18.	Dido	193
19.	Amy	197
20.	Mary	208
21.	Constance	212
22.	Dorothea	226
23.	Jean	239
24.	Susan	249
25.	Rachel	260
26.	Edith	274
27.	Nina	285
28.	Gertrude	304
29.	Lilly	313
30.	Dorothy	330
31.	Paula	350
32.	Joan	362
33.	Helena	372
Author's Notes		383
About the Author		386

References	388
UpLitPress.co.uk	406

Chapter One

Helena

Helena winced as she deposited her bag and struggled with the stiff lock mechanism. *I'm going to have to get that looked at.* She knew, even as the thought crossed her mind, that the chances were extremely slim. She turned away from the locker, and sighed as she hung her coat on one of the wall hooks and put on the lanyard. The name on it was already fading. She got her hair tangled in it. Typical.

'Penny for them,' said a friendly voice from behind another locker door.

'Oh, sorry Chris, I didn't realise I'd made a noise,' said Helena, still battling with the lanyard.

'No need to apologise. Well, once more unto the breach. Shall we?' Chris opened the staff room door and gestured Helena through with a sweep of his hand and an elaborate bow.

She wasn't working in a war zone, didn't have to make difficult decisions, didn't really have much responsibility, yet the start of every shift brought with it a familiar sinking dread. Walking through the door with head bowed, Helena massaged her aching wrist in preparation for the onslaught of repetitive activities it was about to perform. This was a pointless exercise; shooting pains along her arm would inevitably start within five minutes. Certain sections aggravated it further. Crime Fiction was the worst; the size of those books was ridiculous.

It was lazy, shoving lines of books sideways, but she did it anyway. Every member of staff was reminded every day that everything always had to be in exactly the correct place. Carol the library manager said this was to avoid criticism from senior management and the public. God forbid you put a McCreary before a McCready, or didn't arrange the spines precisely two centimetres back from the edge of the shelf. Crime Fiction readers in particular were not at all tolerant of those kinds of misdemeanours. Tuts would be heard, followed by mutterings towards whichever poor soul was on the information desk. Helena complied with this regime mainly to avoid criticism during Carol's regular inspections, although inwardly she conceded there was an element of satisfaction in having stuff tidy and sorted. If she thought about it, which she did often because there was little else to think about, not much else in her life was at all tidy, and all she had to show for nine months of working as a library assistant was a bad wrist. It probably wasn't as painful as nine months of pregnancy, labour and childbirth, but it was inconvenient all the same.

She loved reading and liked the concept of free access to books for all, therefore imagined a job at the library would suit her. But the way it was run didn't suit her at all. The first job of each day was to check the rota. Staff weren't aware from one day to the next what they would be doing, and it seemed to Helena that Carol allocated tasks completely randomly. Everyone had to learn every section of the library and be able to do every job, whether or not it played to their strengths or preferences. Helena's aversion to the Crime Fiction section was partly because of the size and sheer number of the books, partly due to the customer type who read them, and partly because she didn't enjoy the genre. Other sections and duties she didn't mind quite as much. Reference section duty for example, was ok as it merely required keeping the place tidy and keeping the people quiet. It was the only part of the building where silence was demanded. Tidying took very little time at all as the books were rarely disturbed, and only the daily newspapers required regular reorganising. At the beginning of the day, certain customers raced up the stone staircase to reach their preferred daily first, leaving the papers lying in disarray once they had devoured the contents. Anyone who dozed off had to be woken up, and persistent offenders had to be asked to leave; this library, the same as all others in the county, had a zero tolerance policy towards slumber. Situated at the quiet top end of the High Street in a precinct area, the building attracted people who had nowhere else to go and nowhere else to sleep, especially in these wetter, colder months. But rules were rules, and they had to be moved on. Helena hated doing that.

Thankfully, the first half hour stint was in her favourite section. It was nestled in a far corner, one of the few areas that still had the original dark wooden shelves. The people venturing over there were mainly nerdy enthusiasts who left the section as neat as they had found it, which meant she could usually shelve and tidy before the allocated half hour slot was finished and have a sneak peek inside one or two books until she needed to move on to the next task. She wheeled the trolley into position and shelved ten books. One shelf was half empty and books had toppled over in the gaps. This was against Library Law, so she shoved all the books to one side, and bookended them with another wince. Once the tasks were done, she considered what to read about, or rather, where to escape to. Sometimes she'd let her eyes find a book at random which caught their attention, and other times she had a particular person or topic in mind. Today, she was drawn to American History. She settled on a book written from the perspectives of Indigenous peoples, women, and slaves rather than the men who came, saw and conquered. She preferred these books – the ones depicting history from a range of personal viewpoints.

Helena was generally awkward around people. She favoured this section also because she might bump into one particular customer, who always had interesting things to say, and who always made Helena feel comfortable for reasons she couldn't quite identify. After several minutes of reading, she heard a distinctive cough and peered over the top of the book to see the familiar pair of oversized *Dr Martens* boots, the long brown woollen coat falling to the floor with its partially undone and frayed hemline, and the long wisps of white hair flowing out from underneath a large orange bobble hat. Never mind American History for now. Helena put the book back in its place and approached the older woman.

'Hello Cynthia,' she said. 'I hoped I'd see you today. How are you?'

'Oh, hello, dear,' said Cynthia, turning slowly to greet Helena. She appeared to be even smaller than usual, swamped by her clothing. Her hair, never sorted into the tidiest of arrangements, was decidedly dishevelled, limp and lacklustre. Helena glanced down at herself: non-descript beige jumper and baggy black trousers with scuffed brown shoes and hair which hadn't been cut for two years dangling aimlessly around her shoulders. She was in no position to judge.

'Is there anything specific you're looking for today?' enquired Helena, deciding against asking anything personal.

'Here's the thing, dear. I haven't a clue where to start.'

'Isn't that the great thing with history, though?' Helena said. 'You can dive in anywhere, any time and be transported. Erm, I think so anyway,' she added, shifting her weight from one foot to the other, suddenly self-conscious at her level of enthusiasm. Cynthia didn't look to be in the mood for it today.

'Yes, I would normally agree. But there are simply so many.' Cynthia stared ahead of her, as if she were gazing through the books rather than at them. Helena was unclear what there were so many of and decided she wasn't being of any use. She said, 'Well, let me know if I can help.'

Helena pretended to be busy, fiddling with books for a few minutes, taking volumes out and replacing them in precisely the same place, careful to line them up. Her mind wandered, and she began wondering what her parents would make of her life. Her mother had persuaded her to take a vocational course rather than study for her preferred option of a history degree that wouldn't guarantee a job on completion. So, nursing it was. She had been interested in some of the lectures but didn't feel she had the patience or bedside manner to be a nurse, and despite her mother's disapproval, she abandoned nursing, ending up in admin. It suited her to file and record things, and it gave her life some structure. She worked in various charities and managed to land a project officer job in her late forties where she derived pleasure from carrying out desk-top research and writing reports for the project managers. Once that contract was over, a library assistant post became available, which she took as a temporary measure. It wasn't the pinnacle of achievement for a woman in her mid-fifties, but she wasn't ambitious, and it was better than doing nothing for a lifetime as her mother had done. God only knows what her dad would have thought. He would be turning in his grave, wherever that was, to see she'd ended up in admin and then a library, saying it was a waste of her abilities. He must have been dead for years by now.

Helena surfaced from her meandering mind and peered over towards Cynthia, who appeared to be lost in her own daydreams. Helena decided wisely or otherwise to try again.

'What was the last thing you read?' she asked. 'Maybe something else from the same era would be interesting?'

'I was reading about the ancient Egyptians. One era in particular.'

'Oh, you can't go wrong there. There's so much fascinating stuff.'

'You see, I can't fathom where to begin, and yet here I am, hoping I'll find the proverbial needle.'

It took Helena a moment.

'Ah, right needle in a haystack. I see. Well, we don't have much on the ancient Egyptians, but everything we've got is here.' Helena gestured towards a collection of books on the lowest shelf, mainly consisting of large glossy volumes heavy on picture content.

'Thank you dear. I'm afraid I can't get down there. Would you be kind enough to see if there is anything on Nefertari?' asked Cynthia.

'Nefertiti? Yes, I think there should be.'

'I'm interested in Nefertari, wife of Ramesses II,' replied Cynthia.

'Great,' said Helena, unsure which one of them was pronouncing the name incorrectly.

Helena shuffled through the tomes, but drew a blank.

'I'm really sorry, we don't seem to have anything. Maybe she appears in one of these books, though. We could search the indexes?'

'Yes, if you think so.'

Bending to find a book, Helena noticed Cynthia's unmatched socks, and felt a rush of protective sympathy. *She must lead a tough life. I hope she's got somewhere decent to sleep.* Both women fell silent as Helena flicked through a few index pages.

Suddenly, Helena had a thought. 'Have you done an online search?'

'I wouldn't have a clue how to,' said Cynthia, with a weak smile. Helena was surprised to see the smile lines were many and deep, indicating this was a face that must have smiled a lot at one time. 'I'm eighty-six years old, continued Cynthia, 'and I've never switched on a computer in my life, let alone searched for anything with one.'

'Would you like to try now? We've got a new young volunteer with us today and she's helping us on the computers, you know, showing people the ropes.'

'I'm sorry, I don't have much money with me,' said Cynthia.

'Oh, it's ok, you get half an hour free for your first session. Shall I go and check if she's got a slot?'

'If you think it could help.'

'Nothing to lose, is there?' said Helena, her eyes flitting around to locate Lily. But instead of seeing Lily's fresh face, it was Carol's glare she caught. There she stood in the centre of the room, arms crossed, lips tight, head tilted and shaking from side to side ever so slightly. Who knew it was possible to see nostrils flare from twenty paces? This familiar patronising and impatient stare meant only one thing: Helena was about to run over time in the History section as usual.

'Just what I admire,' said Carol as Helena walked past her to the computers. 'Library staff standing around chatting. Here's the rota in case you've forgotten where you are supposed to be.' Carol waved a sheet of paper at Helena as she walked past.

Helena had always hated sarcasm, having grown up in a household full of it. She had learnt to avoid Carol after trying to engage in chit-chat in the staff room over lunch one day, sharing how she was trying to lose weight. Recalling the conversation still made her uneasy.

'My mum always said no-one would want me,' she had joked.

'Mmm, I don't eat much, it's why I am slim I suppose,' Carol replied.

Helena surveyed the size of her lunch.

'I felt fat when I reached ten stone,' continued Carol. 'I always remember the old advert which said you should watch your diet if you could pinch more than an inch.' Carol lifted her blouse and pinched the taught skin on her ultra-flat tummy. Helena surveyed the spare tyre round her middle. Was Carol being deliberately bitchy, or was she merely oblivious?

Helena knew she worked harder than some staff who spent much of their day hiding in quiet corners doing nothing whatsoever chatting amongst themselves. At least she'd been chatting with a customer.

'Thank you, I'll be right there,' Helena said to Carol, as she continued to walk over to the computers ignoring the sheet of paper being shaken at her. She'd check the rota sheet when she had done this. These sheets were Carol's way of telling people their place, literally and metaphorically, and Carol could wait a minute.

As luck would have it, Lily's ten-thirty hadn't shown up. Helena gestured affirmatively to Cynthia, and Lily smiled politely as the hunched and diminutive figure hobbled slowly towards them, weighed down by the tatty briefcase she carried.

Helena hurried towards Cynthia, passing Carol's glare again. Why did that woman work in a library for goodness' sake? She didn't appear to be keen on books much or people at all, the very things you are most likely to encounter in a library. Helena held Cynthia's arm as she helped her over to the computers, aware of more staring, and perversely relishing it.

'Lily, meet Cynthia.'

'Hi guys,' said the teenager. She had a carefree manner Helena assumed only young people with no real life experience could muster.

'Cynthia would like to learn about an Ancient Egyptian Queen called Nefertiti,' said Helena. 'Could you help her with an online search? Sorry to dash, but I'll have to leave you two now. I need to go to my next job. Where's the sheet? Ah right, Crime Fiction shelving.'

Helena supported Cynthia's arm as she lowered into the chair, then left this mismatched pair of a teenage girl with perfect make-up, perfectly tied back hair and matching socks under her jeans, and a tatty old woman who appeared utterly bemused as she stared at the computer screen in front of her. Cynthia sat on the edge of her seat. This was due, Helena realised, to her crooked spine rather than any sense of anticipation. With considerable effort, Cynthia pushed her belongings under the chair.

'No worries,' said Lily. 'Ok, so, er, Neffie?'

'N-E-F-E-R-T-A-R-I.'

'Okaaaay. Yes, here she is. Let's see… Oh wow, she's beautiful! Let's scroll down…oh yes, there's loads on her. What shall I click on?'

Helena watched from across the library as Cynthia took a breath which caught in her throat, resulting in a long bout of coughing. As this subsided, she laid her crooked little hands in her lap and seemed to study them, fingers clenched tightly together. Helena asked herself if she'd done the wrong thing. She'd more or less forced Cynthia into this alien experience and maybe it wasn't what Cynthia wanted. Thankfully, Cynthia lifted her head and began to speak.

'I have the transcription of a letter written by Nefertari to her husband Ramesses II on her deathbed. I am trying to find out if anyone else is aware of the letter's existence.'

'Ok, lovely. Here we go then. I'll search for letters by…'

'Nefertari.' Cynthia coughed again.

'Yes, lovely,' said Lily, moving her chair ever so slightly away from Cynthia's.

Half an hour later, Cynthia gingerly stood up, armed with several pages of printed documents. Helena left Crime Fiction and dashed over on her way to reception desk duty.

'Did you get anywhere, Cynthia?'

'No, I'm afraid not. But we found some interesting articles on her and Lily has printed those for me. She's a sweet girl.'

Helena took Cynthia's arm again and led her towards the imposing main doors beyond the reception desk, noticing from the corner of her eye that Carol was scowling again.

'Do you mind me asking why you're particularly interested in Nefertari?'

Cynthia regarded her with eyes expressing thanks for finally getting right the name of this great queen.

'As I said to young…'

'Lily.'

'Yes, I should remember. It's similar to my mother's dog's name. Oh, does that sound terrible?'

Helena shook her head and smiled.

'Anyway, I have a letter written by Nefertari. I assume many people aren't interested these days in ancient history but…'

'Oh, I am! Honestly, I am. That's why I am always hanging around in History whenever I can. Oh, sorry, I interrupted. Do carry on.'

'That's ok dear. As I say, I don't think many people are terribly interested, but my daughter was a historian, and she collected letters written by historical figures. This one from Nefertari is I think the oldest one.'

'How fascinating!' said Helena.

They arrived at the reception desk. Cynthia heaved the tattered briefcase she'd been clutching onto the desk. With a satisfying clack, clack of the fasteners, she opened it and lifted the lid.

'How amazing,' said Helena, peering inside to see roughly two dozen papers, all apparently typed in the same font, and all housed inside individual plastic punched pockets.

'My daughter's work,' said Cynthia. She typed out the letters on our old typewriter. I found them all after she…well I have been going through her things.'

'I see,' said Helena, unsure if she should ask any more and quickly deciding not to.

Cynthia lifted a few of the plastic pockets, several of which slid over one another and fell from her grasp onto the worn blue carpet. Helena picked them up, and read the words "My dears William and Lucretia" as she gave them back to Cynthia.

'Ah, here it is,' said Cynthia. She placed the other letters back in the suitcase and held on to one, hesitating as she stared at it, tracing her fingers over the plastic cover. After a few seconds she gazed at Helena with watery eyes and said quietly, 'Would, would you be at all interested in borrowing it?'

'Oh Cynthia, I'd love to. Are you sure?'

'Yes, yes. It would be lovely to share it. I haven't shown them to anyone. You can give it back to me next time I see you. I'll be coming in regularly to try and establish what I can, while I can.'

Cynthia held out the plastic pocket to Helena, who reached out to take it gently from her, aware Cynthia was passing her a piece of her daughter's memory, a piece of her daughter. At the top of the letter she read the words, "Beloved husband."

'I'll guard it with my life,' she said.

Cynthia allowed the letter to slip from her hand. She closed the case and lifted it with effort off the reception desk. As she turned away and, head bowed, began shuffling towards the exit, she raised her free hand to gesture goodbye, before facing the bitter cold outside.

Helena watched as she paused in the doorway to cough heavily, retrieve a hankie from her coat pocket and wipe her mouth. She slowly crossed the precinct and headed towards the bus stop, her demeanour suggesting that even the smallest whisper of wind would send her flying.

A couple of hours later in the library staff room, once she'd eaten her lunch of processed cheese roll from the library café, Helena went to her locker, where she retrieved the plastic pocket and gave herself the luxury of sitting in the only comfortable chair. She pulled out a neatly typed letter which was stapled in the top left corner and began to read. The type was quite small, and she had to hold it a distance away to read it properly.

Chapter Two

Nefertari

Beloved husband,

Know that I, above all others, love you in this life and for evermore. It will be painful to let me go, but soon enough the time will come for me to begin my journey to the afterlife. Once there, I will wait for you until we are reunited and shall live with the gods for eternity. Now my Lord there are matters to discuss, plans to make.

First, I must journey to see the two temples that you are building at Abu Simbel and witness for myself the masterpieces being created there in the rock face. Though the temples are far away at Nubia, I will travel there to honour them and bless them and honour you and bless you, my Lord. I have seen the plans and listened with great keenness to your descriptions. Your enthusiasm is infectious as you talk of creating a temple for me as your Favoured Wife alongside your own great temple. I am honoured to know that for my Temple of Hathor, statues of me are being made in size equal to your own, standing tall beside you. It is the greatest monument ever bestowed upon a Queen by a King.

I await to see depictions of me beside my beloved goddess Hathor, blessed goddess of love, mother of the sky and the sky-god Horus, mother of the sun-god Ra. Mother of the pharaohs, creator of femininity and procreation! You tell me I am shown wearing the cow horns of Hathor and the sun disc of Ra. I must see this! I must witness also the inner pillared hall, where I stand with you before the barque of Amun, playing the sistra. I long to see the scenes where I make offerings to Hathor, Khnum and Mut. There, we are all connected forever as equals. I will witness the dedication you have made to me, proclaiming that I am "the king's great wife Nefertari, beloved of Mut, forever and ever, Nefertari for whom the sun does shine."

At your own magnificent Great Temple, I will bless the four great seated statues of you along with the statues of me and our beloved children. Inside the temple I will seek out the depiction of myself on a pillar in the great hall worshipping Hathor, and I will pray there for safe passage to the afterlife. I must travel there soon, my Lord. Please have it arranged.

Second, I make solemn requests for you to consider until you join me with the gods.

You are a warrior, and your masculine power, fearlessness and strength are essential in defeating current or future enemies. Continue to celebrate your victories with great temples that are bursting with statues, writings and pictorial depictions of your great life. In the temples at Karnak and Luxor, I wish for you to add greater monuments than your predecessors, particularly the Queen Hatshepsut. At Karnak, the great Hall will rival anything ever built by mankind. It will stand for eternity; hence our names shall live for eternity. Have a colossus built, the biggest statue ever created. It will signify your strength and will influence our beloved kingdom for thousands of years hence as you peer down on all who come after you.

You have other wives, and you will marry yet more. But I am your Great Royal Wife, a title well-suited for I was born of noble blood being descended from the boy king Tutankhamun, and from Nefertiti herself. Ours is the greatest partnership. For twenty-five years we have reigned, and been married many more. I request that no other will take my place as your Favoured Wife, and trust that you will make it so. Our bond is eternal. While I wait for you and watch over you, our devotion will always steer you.

One of many titles you bestowed upon me is "the one whom beauty pertains." My beauty is enhanced by the adornments you bestow upon me, and it is celebrated in many poems. I am known too for the way that I have run the Royal household as a Great Queen should. But I am more than my beauty and my position as a Royal Wife. I have been involved at every level of ruling our great kingdom. No Queen prior to me has done so. As your Queen, I am known as "Great of Praise" and "Great of Favours" for my important contribution. Always remember my Lord how we have done things

Remember too how I have stood with you at many official ceremonies, such as the elevation of Nebwenenef to High Priest of Amun at Abydos. I made great speeches, including at the Festival of the Mast when I proclaimed to the gods that you, Lord of Both Lands of Egypt, had come to them and erected for them the great Mast, so you might be granted eternity as King, and victorious over all who might rebel against you. As high priestess, I led ceremonial prayers and appeased numerous gods with offerings. I took active part in ceremonies that no other Queen has done, including the annual festival of Min. At the Royal Court I served as a political expert, and had no fear of any aspect of rule, travelling widely with you, including into battle. I earned titles that no other Queen has earned, such as the title of Mistress of Two Lands, the Upper and the Lower Kingdoms of our united Egypt. To honour me, please Lord, never forget my skills, celebrate my achievements and preserve my memory.

Remember the power of negotiation, especially through the written word. Rare among women, I can read and write our great language. I have combined my skills to become a great diplomat for you and for our Kingdom. After we made peace with the Hatti King, I wrote letters of reconciliation and sent gifts to the King Hattusili and his wife the Queen Puduhepa. I called them brother and sister. I gave a necklace of pure gold and many fine linen garments. This helps maintain peace, and exemplifies our greatness. I beg you, continue to promote the importance of diplomacy with our neighbour countries.

You and I are favoured by the gods. As would a King, I satisfied them. We achieved balance and harmony between earthly life and immortal life. In death, I wish to be remembered for my intellect and my achievements, as much as for my beauty. I know, my love, that you will preserve evidence of my achievements and will not pretend them to be your own. You are a great and unusual man for this. Having me by your side signals to our people and those of other lands the stability of our dynasty. Long may this stability continue.

Please, my Lord, ensure the law continues to respect and protect women, regardless of pressure from outside influences. Even the Greeks do not have laws such as ours. The balance of what men do and what women do is crucial for the success of our society. Only we observe ma'at without which there is isfet, chaos. Ma'at makes us the most civilised nation. Other countries have come to regard us for our superior governance and society. Lord, I implore you always to observe ma'at, as I have shown you, in all aspects of society: in art, workmanship, construction, worship, and in government. After I am gone, as mediator between the gods and the people, you must continue that which we started, to achieve balance and harmony in every part of life. We personify ma'at through our marriage and how we rule equally, each with our own strengths. We have no equals, in Egypt or any other land. Long may you continue to live how we have lived. Long may our dynasty reign.

I bore you wonderful children alongside the others you fathered, and you will father many more yet. I raised our children to be noble. I wish for them to hold excellent positions in government and the priesthood, and remain loyal to you, supporting you throughout your reign. Choose wisely who will become the next crowned King of our great dynasty. Most important is that our dynasty continues.

Our dynasty is our destiny. You rule a united Egypt, Lord of both the Upper and Lower lands in this great nineteenth dynasty. Dear husband, it is your destiny to lead this thriving dynasty to greater and greater things.

Do all that I request, and your reign will be long and fruitful. Your kingdom will go from strength to strength under your firm hand. Your empire will expand to cover new territories, and you will be remembered as the greatest ruler that Egypt has ever seen. Your name will be immortalised as the Ramesses The Great, Usermaatre Setpenre, Ozymandias!

Last my Lord, we must confirm the funerary arrangements. As I await my journey to the afterlife, I ask you to begin overseeing preparations for it. In my tomb I ask for these things. I wish to have buried with me the white transparent dress, your favourite, showing glimpses of my naked flesh behind the drapes. With it, I will have a red sash and a necklace of gold, faience, carnelian and turquoise, and fine blue and white bracelets. And my twin-plumed headdress. I will have my favoured sandals. They show signs of wear, as they were worn at the most extraordinary occasions in this life. Accordingly, I will require them for the most extraordinary occasions in the afterlife. In paintings of me around the tomb, show me wearing these favoured items that the gods may know me when they meet me. Show me too wearing gifts from others, such as my Greek earrings, to indicate our success in diplomacy.

I have read your plans for my tomb. According to your wishes, I proclaim that I am in favour of all you propose.

The tomb shall be located near to that of the pharaoh Hatshepsut in the Royal Valley, but it will be the largest and most beautiful tomb ever created for a queen, greater than hers which has stood for 200 years now. It will outshine hers, as we outshine her. There have been other noble and deserving queens prior to me, Nefertiti is one, but we must show to the gods that no queen has ruled as I have ruled with you.

It will be the most magnificent of architectural endeavours, consisting of many chambers through which I will travel as I begin my personal and special journey into the netherworld. Resembling our great river Nile, the tomb will run north to south and, like the sun god Ra's journey across the sky, the course of my passage through the tomb will run from east to west.

The tomb will be lined with the finest new carved plaster, onto which the decorations will be added. Every part of the tomb, every chamber, shall be decorated in the most beautiful way by your craftsmen from the village of Deir el-Medina. On the ceilings everywhere, painted blue for night, stars will fill the sky, and the walls will be filled with exquisite paintings using the greatest multitude of colours. The pigments for the paint must be mixed with the exact right amount of water and gum arabic to produce the brightest colours. Once painted, the images will be covered with tree resin and egg white to preserve them that they may last forever. On your insistence, only the best artists will be employed to depict me.

I will first appear on the stairs descending into the tomb, and then reappear throughout the chambers as I proceed, as a goddess on my voyage to the afterlife. The gods will guide and protect me as I make that journey, and I will stand alongside them in death as I stood alongside you in life – as an equal. There will be many writings from The Book of the Coming Forth by Day, also known as The Book of the Dead, to guide me on my journey of transformation. It will be complex to navigate through the tomb, with its many atria and corridors, reflecting the arduous nature of my journey. Do not make it too easy for me; it must be difficult for me to obtain eternal life. I must face many tests as I travel through, and only then can my body be restored by Horus to arrive in my rightful place united with Osiris. The complexity of the journey is reflected in the complexity of the paintings and writings I will pass as I progress.

Entering the tomb, I will be greeted by many gods and goddesses, giving me comfort and strength. Serket and Isis will urge me forwards, taking my hand to lead me. Isis will introduce me to Kheperi, the god of morning light, who will support my transformation. Horus, son of Isis, will lead me and present me to Ra-Horakhty and Hathor. The vulture Nekhbet will protect me from above as I pass through the chambers. Ma'at, the goddess of truth, will observe me and offer me protection, health and joy. I will make offerings to Ptah, the god of truth. The creator God Atum will be there, along with the ocean god Nun, the air and light god Shu, and the moisture goddess Tefnut. The next generation will be there, the earth god Geb and sky goddess Nut, and also their children. As the gods guide me, writings will name me as your Great Wife, mistress of two lands, possessor and mistress of charm, sweetness and love, hereditary noblewoman, lady of Upper and Lower Egypt, beloved of Mut and justified before Osiris.

Descending into the lower chambers, I will be addressed by Anubis and Isis who will confirm my place in the sacred land. Statues of my essential servants in the afterlife will be placed with my funerary barque, my chariot, and the other goods necessary to transport me safely. Neith and Selkis will welcome me into the vestibule, confirming there is a place for me in heaven with Ra. I will make offerings to them and to Isis, Nephthys, Ma'at and Hathor the Mistress of the West. In there too I shall meet the jackal-god Anubis, embalmer god of the sacred land. He will proclaim, "I have given you the appearance of Ra in heaven so that you may sit upon the throne of Osiris."

Inside the sarcophagus chamber, I will continue west towards Osiris. The sunken sarcophagus, surrounded by my belongings and canopic jars, will be carved of my favourite pink granite, adorned with writings and drawings of the gods. Above my face will sit the goddess Nut, who says "Ra himself has purified you. Your mother Nut is pleased to lead you towards the horizon, you are justified by the great god." Only the finest materials will be used and only the most honoured craftspeople will touch my body as they prepare it for my journey. While I await resurrection, I shall be wrapped in the finest linen and embalmed with cattle fat. The linen shall be decorated with funerary jewellery to indicate it sheaths the Queen. It shall be placed in coffins that will shine as if pure gold, and finally the coffins will be placed in the sarcophagus. My organs will be preserved in the canopic jars standing inside niches in the walls protected by the four sons of Horus. The goddesses Nephthys and Isis will be beside my body, with the benu bird for resurrection and the water god for longevity. I will be surrounded by magic bricks. There will be writings of the domain of Osiris, for that will be my domain.

I will be named "The Osiris" as I become one with the divine and make the transition to deity and immortality. To succeed I will proceed through the portals of His realm denouncing my adversaries, the keepers who will block my way. I will name them all. "Downward of face," "Eavesdropper," "Loud of voice." When they hear their names, they shall let me pass to the next portal. "Opener of the forehead," "The burner," and "The one who eats the excrement of his hind parts." Thus, it will go on. I will pass through each portal saying prayers and surrounded by deities.

Finally, I will be prepared to meet Osiris in the West, where I will be reunited with my organs and complete again, my body prepared for resurrection. I will experience no fear as my journey reaches its conclusion. Osiris will welcome me and assure me of my place alongside him for eternity. I will pay homage to him and to Hathor, and Anubis as Thoth the recorder of events and Ma'at the truth will bear witness. I will make offerings to Osiris the saviour and to Atum the creator who wears the United crown of the Two Lands. Four pillars hewn from the rock will be decorated with the most sumptuous design and will show the priests performing their rituals with Hathor, Isis and Anubis observing. The priest, wearing a leopard skin draped over his shoulder, will perform the final rites. Ma'at will declare that I have a place in the House of Amun on Earth, at our great Karnak.

I will emerge from the eastern horizon as does the sun, and Isis will take my hand and lead me to the sacred land. The beetle-headed Khepri, god of renewal, will say, "I give to you eternity like Ra, I give to you the appearance of Ra in heaven, I give to you a place in the sacred land." Then, I will prepare for my journey on the water to Abydos, home of Osiris. Ra will steer me with steering oars and none of my enemies will be able to touch me.

The detail of your plans my Lord is beyond anything ever seen. I am honoured that you will honour me so. The time draws near, therefore the many craftsmen required should come together in haste, to plan, dig out, plaster, carve, draw, paint, write and gather everything. I know you will spare no expense my Lord for my House of Eternity. It must remain locked forever, its treasures intact for me alone in the afterlife.

I remain for eternity your companion, beloved of the Goddess Mut, whom you call the one for whom the sun shines. As your Great Wife I am a Bride of God, mistress of all mankind and the Lady of Two Lands. In death I will become immortal, and will await your arrival once your work on Earth is done.

All will be well with you, my Lord. May the sun god Ra shine upon you.

Your beloved Queen Nefertari Merytmut

Chapter Three

Cynthia

No longer in the staff room of a twenty-first century library in a town not far north of London on a cold damp day, Helena was immersed in a sumptuous ancient world of mystery and enchantment, revelling in the heat of a brightly coloured underground chamber crammed full of the most sumptuous decoration and the most beautiful objects. She was wearing a white semi-transparent dress festooned with jewels and was surrounded by strange and spectacular animal-gods as she wafted through chamber after chamber, preparing for her death and the journey to the gods that she was to encounter.

How did Nefertari feel? Was she excited or nervous, and did she believe she would become a goddess, and that her mummified body and organs would be reunited? Helena knew a little about the ancient Egyptians but hadn't appreciated the extent to which they worshipped gods representing what they could see and feel around them, gave them life, and was important for their well-being – the sky, the sun, the animals, the air, and the river. She had never heard of ma'at, but it sounded similar to Gaia, the Greek mythological concept of mother earth where everything is connected and balanced. This concept, she knew, had inspired the pagans. *Imagine how we might live our lives nowadays if we revered nature in that way. How different might society be. Would we fight less over things such as religion and politics…*

'Helena!'

Bam. She was back with the peeling magnolia paint, the cracks, and the musty smell defeating even the strongest of perfumed room sprays. It was an environment that reflected how little senior managers cared for the well-being of their staff. She sighed, hauled herself up, and carefully returned the letter to its pocket, before placing it in her locker. As she forced shut the locker door, she tried to shut out dreams of a life more interesting and exotic, a life of devotion, such as the one Nefertari must have led.

When Lily the volunteer joined the library staff as a library assistant a few days later, Helena was assigned to be her buddy, which involved showing her the various elements of the job. For Helena, this was another opportunity to reflect on the mundanity of the role. *This job, with this manager, in this place, it's not much to show for my life*, she thought. It covered the rent, and it allowed her to be among books and meet a few interesting people. But there was no ambition, no direction. Where might she progress from here? She certainly didn't want to be a manager, if Carol was the kind of manager the council employed.

'This, by the way, is not how you're supposed to move the books,' she said, demonstrating her shoving technique. 'I've managed to hurt my wrist doing it, but you're young so you'll probably be fine!'

'No worries,' said Lily. 'I couldn't do that anyway as I've got a mild hemiplegia, but I'm sure I'll be fine.'

Helena felt the blush rise from under her jumper and cover her neck and face. She put her hand to her mouth and then to her chest, consciously trying to hide her scarlet appearance, subconsciously comforting herself. She had assumed Lily's slight limp was due to a sports injury or something. She didn't quite understand what hemiplegia was, but she understood damn well it was more serious than a sore wrist.

'I'm so sorry, Lily. How clumsy of me. I didn't realise. Is there anything I can do? Do you need any help? Sorry, I'm babbling.'

'It's no problem, honestly. They've explained the physical side of the job. The only thing I've got to avoid is heavy lifting, but we're not s'posed to do that anyway, right?'

'Yes, that's right. I feel incredibly silly moaning about my wrist.'

'Honestly, I'm fine', said Lily. 'I've got mild cerebral palsy, that's all. And I can tell your wrist is uncomfortable.'

Helena's blush deepened. *You idiot.*

'We'd better get on', she said, glancing over to Carol. 'The boss doesn't approve of us chatting on the shop floor.'

'Sure,' said Lily. 'Oh, isn't that your friend?'

Helena followed Lily's line of vision and saw the familiar coat and boots. She darted across the floor to History, aware of Carol's prying eyes following her every move.

'Hello, Cynthia, how are you?'

'Oh, hello, dear. Not having such a fantastic day I'm afraid. Bit of a struggle getting here. I simply don't have the energy I used to. Oh goodness, sorry…telling you all my woes. Typical old woman being a burden. I'm sure you have better things to do than listen to me moaning.'

'It's no burden at all,' said Helena. She took a folded piece of paper from her trouser pocket and read the rota sheet that she'd photocopied. Staff weren't allowed to do this as it was a waste of paper; they were supposed to go to the places in the library where they were pinned up. Well, sod that.

'I'm sorry, but I won't be able to chat to you as I'm not in the History section or on the computers at all today. I do have the letter to return to you though, if by any chance you can wait til my lunch break. We could have a chat then, maybe? I wanted to ask you more about the letters.'

'I have nothing else to do, dear. I'll amuse myself in Ancient History for a bit.'

Helena studied the rota again.

'Oh hang on, Lily has a slot on the computers in half an hour if you'd like to try searching again.'

'Yes, I suppose I could. I'd like to try and research an aspect of Vietnamese history. And I remembered to bring in the money today.'

'Perfect, ok. Lily can help with that I'm sure.' Helena felt guilty taking the cash from Cynthia, and hoped she hadn't had to go without something else to pay for this.

Cynthia and Lily had their second session and from what Helena could see when she glanced over, the two seemed to be getting on a bit better, at least if their proximity to one another was anything to go by.

Helena suggested they sit in the library café at lunchtime. It was run by the council and offered volunteering and catering training opportunities via the local learning disability service. It was a lovely idea, but unfortunately it was grossly under-funded, and the food was often terrible as a result. Nevertheless, eating an awful lunch from there was preferable to preparing anything herself.

They sat in a corner and ordered soup of the day: mixed vegetable. Helena insisted on paying. It was a bright enough space, having recently had a lick of paint. On the walls were photos of smiling volunteers and trainees working hard in the kitchen or serving customers or holding their certificates. All the tables and chairs had been donated or bought in charity shops and were in various states of repair and stability. Helena tried to select one for Cynthia that didn't wobble. Despite genuinely liking Cynthia, Helena was nervous. Something seemed significantly wrong and she was useless at emotional stuff.

'So, you said that you're not great,' she began. That, she felt, was a decent opener.

'Oh, it's just my old age I suppose. I find it harder to cope with things these days. Everything is more arduous than it used to be.'

'I'm sorry to hear that, Cynthia. I hope you don't mind me saying, but I had noticed you appear a little less spirited lately.' *This is going well.*

'I don't mind at all. Oh dear, I really don't want to complain.'

'I asked you to have lunch with me. That means I want to listen.' Helena was pleased with herself. Then she saw that Cynthia's eyes were brimming with tears, which spread across her swollen red lower lids, hovering momentarily then spilling over and falling onto the laminated gingham tablecloth. Her expression reminded Helena of an animal caught in barbed wire, at that moment when it begins to stop struggling and starts to give up. Helena was stumped, couldn't envision what to do or say. So she didn't do or say anything. Remarkably, Cynthia didn't seem to notice her awkwardness. After several seconds, Helena pulled a napkin from the little silver coloured dispenser on the table.

'Here take this,' said Helena, placing one hand on Cynthia's shoulder as she handed her the napkin. She could feel Cynthia's shoulder blades through the threadbare coat.

'You are so kind,' Cynthia said after blowing her nose loudly and coughing. A few people in the café turned and stared. Someone in the corner opposite whispered audibly how it was selfish risking other people's health, what with covid. Thankfully, Cynthia didn't seem to notice that either.

'The truth is,' Cynthia continued, 'I've recently had a bit of news. I found out that my COPD is winning and my lungs are losing. It's my own silly fault. A lifetime of smoking. I don't particularly mind about me. I've had a long life. But most upsetting for me is… it's so unjust. My poor daughter Clare. She was full of life and healthy; did all the right things: ate healthily, exercised all her life, had a great career. Then cancer took her, out of the blue, just like that.'

Cynthia's head was bowed to such an extent it was almost touching the table. Helena searched for a response. Thankfully, they were interrupted.

'Oh, here's our soup, Cynthia.'

Cynthia gathered herself and they began their lunch quietly. The wetness of the tasteless soup contrasted with the dryness of the stale roll that accompanied it, and as they ate lunch their conversation mainly centred on trying to identify vegetables. They ordered coffee and while they waited, Helena tried, and failed, to work out what to say next. Thankfully, Cynthia saved her the worry.

'As I mentioned, Clare was a historian and must have collected the letters over the years. I've only in the last few days been able to start going through all her things. After… well after it happened, I had to sell her flat, and that's when I found that she had all these boxes. I couldn't bear to open them, so I had them brought to my place. I don't have anyone else, which means I must decide what on earth to do with them before it's too late.'

The coffee was as watery and indistinguishable as the soup. They sipped it anyway, and Helena soon forgot the insipid taste, transfixed as Cynthia began to describe Clare's life and work. It was exactly the kind of life she would have wanted, except for the terrible ending. Clare had studied history at Warwick University and then become a museum curator. She had planned to do a PhD.

'In addition to completing her doctorate, she wanted to write a book. I expect this was all part of her research,' said Cynthia.

'Sorry to interrupt you guys, but your lunch hour is over. Helena, Carol's looking for you.'

Helena glanced up. 'Oh god, Lily. Thanks for that.'

Helena took the lunch things to the counter then returned to Cynthia, who was still easing herself out of her chair. Once she was as upright as she could get, Cynthia turned to face Helena, her eyes still reddened, but brighter. Helena noticed a faint but discernible smile emerging.

'If you're not too busy, would you like to come round one day to see the whole collection of letters?'

'Oh, I'd love to!' said Helena. 'I'm not busy at all. Literally, I've got nothing in my diary. Would tonight be ok…oh sorry, is that too soon?'

'No dear, not at all. I'll leave the door on the latch, just let yourself in.'

After work as Helena went to get her coat, she reflected that she hadn't been quite as bothered or irritated as usual. Even sitting in the back office sorting out damaged books to be deleted from the system didn't drag on quite as long as usual. Her wrist remained painful, but it didn't matter as much as it had. Could her mood have lifted simply because she had something pleasurable to do at the end of the day?

Cynthia had written down her address. Helena tapped the postcode into her phone, and read out the street name.

'Chestnut Walk. Mmmm, not sure where that is. OK, let's check. Erm, hang on, that can't be right. Well, that's where she said, so I guess that's where I'll go.' She spoke out loud as she often did when alone. Did everyone do that? She'd done it since she was a child, pretending to be a history teacher to her motley assortment of mostly second-hand teddies and dolls.

She headed out of the library and over to the bus stop. The bus took her to a part of town she didn't recognise, north of the main hubbub and into leafy suburbia. In four short stops, she was deposited into a street straight out of a tourism advert depicting a typical English idyll. Tree-lined and quiet, Chestnut Walk was full of detached houses set back from the road with neat lawns and well-tended flowerbeds containing manicured conifers and evergreen shrubs to maintain winter interest. The ornate black lampposts cast a warm glow, and gave the impression they'd grown there rather than been built. It was all rather different, to put it mildly, from her shared house on a main road in town with its municipal lampposts and constant traffic, with its rusted gate and patch of mud and weeds that she passed to get to the dirty uPVC front door. As she walked towards the red dot on the phone marking her destination, Helena tried to imagine growing up here, and how she might have turned out.

When she arrived at the location marked by her phone as the correct address, she approached with caution. The street was eerily quiet; even the squeaking gate disturbed the peace. Still unconvinced that she was in the right place, Helena approached the front door slowly and touched it gently to see if it would yield. It did.

'Cynthia, are you there?' she called as she peered round the door and entered a large hallway. She glanced around to see paintings hung in gold frames, a Persian rug on the wooden floor, and a slim dark wood table decorated with a lace tablecloth, on which sat a loudly ticking clock. The hall was lit with a chandelier that cast delicate shapes around the walls and floor. She waited a few long seconds and was turning to retreat, when she heard a familiar sound. Cynthia's cough.

'Is that you dear?' said a small voice from far away. 'Come straight through. I'm in the dining room.'

Helena walked along the hall and saw rooms going off in all directions. The house smelled of old smoke but also of natural things, of wood and linen, and it had the rhythms and sounds of a proper home, with its peaceful ticking and gentle creaking as she walked over the floorboards. All the doors were opened. She spotted the corner of a wooden table and headed for that. As she approached, she heard more coughing, and the sound of papers being moved.

'Hello dear,' said Cynthia, and before Helena could respond, she continued, 'I'm so sorry about all the mess. I'm rather ashamed of it, but I can't manage as much these days.'

'It doesn't look too messy at all,' said Helena. 'It just looks as though you've been very busy.'

Cynthia was sitting at the far end of the huge table. On the floor beside her was an empty-looking cardboard box, labelled "Letters" and scattered on every surface and across the floor were papers, some in plastic pockets, others loose. Cynthia seemed flustered as, blushing, she hurriedly put the lid on the box.

Helena scanned the room. The furniture wouldn't be out of place in a stately home. A silver candlestick stood in the centre of the highly polished wooden table. Around the table was a set of upholstered wooden dining chairs, and along one side of the room ornaments were displayed on a dark wood sideboard with intricately carved doors.

Near to a pair of doors leading outside, a standard lamp was positioned to shed light on an armchair facing the garden. Beside the chair was a small table. On this table were a dainty cup and saucer, one of the letters, and a single framed photograph of a young woman, beaming at the camera and holding a degree certificate.

'Here we are then. This is the collection.' Helena followed Cynthia's gaze as she gestured around her to the mass, the mess, of papers.

'I've been trying to organise them, but I'm afraid I've got a bit bogged down. Why don't you have a peruse, and I'll put the kettle on. One thing though. I'd rather you didn't open these two boxes, if you don't mind.' Cynthia pointed towards the box marked "Letters" and then to another in the corner behind the standard lamp. As she peered down, Helena could just make out what was written on top. "Diaries etc."

'Of course,' said Helena.

'I haven't been brave enough to open that one yet. I'm unsure I ever will be.'

'That's completely understandable.' Helena sensed she should change the subject. 'Cynthia, you have such a beautiful home, and such lovely things.'

'It's not what is used to be. I've been selling quite a bit of it. I was lucky I suppose, that's all. Born into a family with old money,' replied Cynthia as she glanced towards a painting over the carved marble fireplace. 'My mother and father, with the dog Lulu,' she said. 'All long gone now of course. His family were lawyers. He was killed in the war when I was tiny. I was farmed out to an aunt and uncle in the countryside for a while afterwards, but that was fine. They were kind souls. And my mother there, she was at Bletchley Park in the war. She did her best. It can't have been easy being a single mother.'

Helena began fidgeting with a hangnail, embarrassed that she hadn't heard of Bletchley Park, and awkward because Cynthia was so forgiving. She really should cut her nails soon. Cynthia got to the door and reached for the doorjamb while she paused for breath. She turned back to Helena and let out a little sigh.

'You remind me of her. Clare, I mean, not my mother. Anyway, why don't you have a read through of that Vietnamese one?' she said, as she walked into the hall. It's the one I was looking at with Lily today. It's over on the side table. Take a seat there in the light, and I'll try to make tea with an element of taste to it. Milk and no sugar, correct?'

'Perfect, thank you.'

Helena sank down into the armchair and picked up the letter, careful not to disturb the photo. She began reading by the light of the standard lamp.

Chapter Four

Trung Tac

Trung Nhi,

Come quickly now, for together we face the gravest situation. Since childhood, we have shared the same challenges and triumphs, experienced together the thrill of joy and the despair of grief. We learnt strength, independence, honour and valour. Now we are called upon to deploy these qualities as never before. You have been my constant companion through conflict and victory. We must stand united side by side one last time. For the future of Nam Viet we are compelled to act in haste. Sister, join me so we may seal our fate. They may attempt to capture us, and kill us. I fear that this is the course they have planned. We cannot let them succeed.

While I wait for you, I look back on everything we achieved. I write this down for you in case I die at their hand before you reach me. I wish you to understand I am proud of you and to assure you our legacy will live on. This tale should be told to those who come after us, and who better to tell it than me!

We grew up under the rule of tyrants, those invaders in our own land for over 200 years, men who did not recognise or respect our way of life. Our noble and commendable father trained us well, as he did all his children, to love the martial arts and to be warriors, encouraging us to fight for Nam Viet against the Han. Fortunate to be born to a Lac General, we were destined for yet greater things, for he was governor of only one region. He knew we were capable of more and to honour him and our nation, we set out on our mission to meet his expectations, and to exceed them.

The Han tried many tactics against us…executing our men without trial, imposing taxes, bribing our noble families to accept their rule, and putting their own Chinese chiefs in place of our own leaders. Still, they endeavour to subordinate our women, claiming men to be superior. They dare to take away women's property and tell the men that women are their property. They brutally killed my dear husband Thi Sach, Lac Lord of Chau Dien and then wrongfully punished me under their ridiculous laws. They killed our Generals and our family.

Soon, no-one would be left to defend our land. They reasoned that issuing us with such warnings would stifle us, but their harshness and their atrocities instead drove us to rise up, inspiring us to fight against them. Our forefathers the Hung who founded Van Lang here thousands of years ago, would expect nothing less.

So, I put away my mourning headdress and, with you, began my revenge. This was not the time to retreat and grieve, it was the time to fight. I put on my golden battle dress patterned with birds, and adorned with belts, buckles and bells. It was my best armour, and I wore it to encourage our fighters and to diminish the enemy. The Han did not suspect two young women to be capable, and so we made our plans right under their noses. We gathered a great army, numbering into the many thousands led by generals, mostly women, including our own aging mother. Armed with many varied weapons, we co-ordinated our Army to seek revenge! We created battalions of men and women, armed with axes, spears, swords, bows and arrows. We recruited from across our society all people willing and able to retaliate, whether poor or rich, nobility coming together with those of low birth for the noble cause.

Our troops happily pledged their allegiance with the oath.

I swear, first, to avenge the nation;
Second, to restore the Hungs' former position;
Third, to have revenge for my husband;
Fourth, to carry through to the end our common task.

The sight of us riding triumphantly on our elephants stopped the Han in their tracks, so astonished were they by what they beheld! Surely, they had never seen anything as powerful nor beautiful. Though we were smaller in number, we repelled their invasions. And when together we stormed their citadels, our supremacy of mind and body prevailed over the enemy. We killed their leader Ma Yuan and took over their settlements. With support of our people, we overturned the Han rule.

Together, my sister, we created a nation! We awakened the belief amongst our citizens that Nam Viet could once again be independent and thus they acted, rallying round at our request and propelling us to victory. They saw that Nam Viet could have and honour its own monarchs, and that a woman could fit the role. And so, at the solar eclipse I was declared Queen, and you were my consort, but in truth you have jointly ruled with me, two strong and brave sister queens, she-kings ruling our land better than any Han. Our father trained us well! For three years we have reigned from our capital Mi Linh with no opposition, such is the love of our people for us, trusting us to rebuild our nation after all these years, and willingly paying us taxes to do it. We have achieved much, releasing prisoners and freeing soldiers from the grips of the Han, and giving aid to the poor.

But the Han Emperor Guang Wu Di has other ideas, determined to recapture our nation for his Empire. Unknown to us, the Chinese have been active at the border for many months, repairing roads and bridges, amassing fleets of boats, troops of foot soldiers and supplies including munitions and food carried on huge wagons. I am unable to organise an army again at short notice to defend against them. I fear the poor will not possess the means to fight again, and as I write, our own generals are now deserting us. Declaring that women cannot rule, the Han Emperor has turned a number of our own Generals against us. Without our army we are defenceless. The Emperor's army has descended upon us rapidly, arriving along the coastline and across the mountain paths and surprising us with their ambush when we were in a state of vulnerable unpreparedness. They are beheading our people, and yet they call US the bandits! In abandoning us as their rulers, our own Generals abandon the notion that our nation can be governed by its own people, at least for now. They abandon Nam Viet. Without them, we are doomed.

Assuming we can find the means, we must perform one last act of bravery together. We cannot let the Han capture us. We have endured too many battles, won too many times despite the odds against us, and been through too much bloodshed for them to finish us now. We must finish it before they get to us. Since we were little girls, our father trained us to win. But if the winning in this world is over, we shall never concede, never let them overcome us. We must do the deed ourselves. So, my sister, travel stealthily but speedily to me, and protect yourself from capture. I will gather the means necessary for our retreat and for our final journey together. You must trust me as you always did, my little sister, that I know what is best for us. I will go into hiding; you will find me in our place by the river Hat Giang, the place we always go to contemplate.

As we prepare to leave this world, understand that the Gods will not let us be forgotten. We will be remembered as the great Trung Sisters. When the people of Nam Viet prevail over China, as surely they will, they will build Temples and shrines to us. There, we will sit on our elephants with power and majesty. Should our beautiful and worthy nation ever be invaded again, the people will turn to us for inspiration and pray to us that they will be released from the tyrants again. And we will be there for them. We will ascend to the afterlife and continue to protect our people from there, the Two Ladies Trung preserved as martyrs and heroes in the hearts of our country for eternity, in which place our work will never end.

In death, we must continue as in life: fearless. Be brave, now as ever!

Your sister, Trung Trac

Chapter Five

Clare

Helena was finishing the letter when Cynthia returned. Helena was vaguely aware of Cynthia's movements as she set the teapot and its stand on the dining room table, left the room in order to find other tea-related paraphernalia, and returned again to gather yet more things more from the sideboard.

Helena eventually emerged from her introspections and peered up to see all the items placed meticulously on the table. Teacups and saucers, a milk jug, a sugar bowl and tongs, and small plates.

'Sorry, I should have been helping you. I was miles away, creating images in my head of these two sisters in all their regalia, parading around on elephants.'

'Not at all dear. It's lovely to have a guest. These days, I'm more likely to host the chiropodist than a tea party.'

'That's gorgeous china,' said Helena.

'Clarice Cliff. It was a wedding present to my parents. After my father's death, my mother kept everything just as it had always been. At the time I thought it maudlin, but when she died and I inherited the place, I did exactly the same. I live in a kind of shrine to the past. The only rooms I changed were the bedrooms. I wanted Clare to have somewhere bright and cheerful for her studies. Oh, and the summer house. We painted that too. She loved it in there. It feels so very empty now. Oh dear, I'm being maudlin myself.'

'Not at all. I think it's good you're talking. And I love to listen to you. You are so clever.' Helena was usually threatened when people talked of emotional matters, and by people who were clever, but there was nothing at all threatening about Cynthia and Helena was starting to feel more comfortable with her than she had done with anyone for as long as she could remember. There was no edge to her, only kindness and gentleness.

'That's kind of you, but Clare was the clever one, not me at all. I expect you've noticed the photo.'

Cynthia nodded towards the photo on the little table.

'I did, yes. She looks like you,' said Helena.

'Do you think so? How nice. As I say, she was much brighter than me. I never amounted to much. I often felt somewhat guilty because I lived my life through her. Everything she did I celebrated it with her. Her life WAS my life in many ways. I rattled around in this old house and earned a living of kinds as a piano teacher. I was fortunate too that my father had invested in property, meaning I had income from the rents. It was convenient: when Clare was at school, I could work from home and be there for her when she got in.'

'Well, she was extremely lucky to have a mum who loved her so much,' said Helena. 'Not all of us are as lucky.'

'Perhaps I tried to do it differently with Clare because of how I was brought up. There was no malice, just a lack of care. After my father died, I suppose Mother was rather lost. And she didn't approve of me having Clare out of wedlock. To her it was quite shocking, as it was to many in the 1960s. But as I said, she did her best.'

I wish I could say the same, thought Helena. She wanted to tell Cynthia about her mum, but couldn't find the words, and wondered whether Cynthia would even be remotely interested. She was an expert at creating awkward situations, therefore decided to stay quiet.

They were silent momentarily while Cynthia conducted the tea-pouring ceremony. Helena admired the way so much attention was paid to the details of it, turning a simple act into a ritual. The stirring of the tealeaves in the pot, the pouring with a strainer into the colourful cups, the setting down of the pot and the strainer, the addition of a splash of milk from the jug, and the dropping in of a sugar cube with silver tongs. Helena had never possessed a cup and saucer or a jug, let alone sugar tongs.

'Here, sit in the comfy chair,' said Helena, getting herself out of it and moving towards a dining chair. 'Let me pass your tea.'

'Oh thank you dear,' said Cynthia. She collapsed into the chair, breathless from her efforts. Helena noticed there was an oxygen tank and mask behind the chair. Cynthia gestured towards the table.

'I got these biscuits on the way home. They're nothing special, but do help yourself.' Helena took a couple of digestive biscuits and placed them carefully onto a delicate side plate. She offered the biscuits to Cynthia who shook her head. Helena picked up her cup and saucer as if she was an extra in a period drama. Some people who moved into old houses ripped out the interiors along with any memories of the past, to create a bland, minimalist, almost clinical interior. Cynthia wasn't like that. And neither would she be, if she could ever afford her own place.

'I must say, this is nice,' said Cynthia. 'I hope you don't mind me asking, but how would you feel about making it a regular thing? You could pop in every now and again and we can have a chat while we read a few letters.'

'Honestly? I'd really enjoy that, thank you.'

'I would appreciate your company, dear. And in all truthfulness, I would appreciate having your help sorting through them, if you'd be interested?

'I can't think of anything I'd rather do.'

'Really?' Cynthia seemed surprised that Helena would want to do this with her. 'If you're sure, dear. I'd be delighted.'

'Yes really. I'm fascinated. Take the Trung letter, it's amazing. I am clueless when it comes to Vietnamese history. I understand something of the ancient Egyptians. I guess we all grew up with the Tutankhamun story. But Vietnam I only know because of the war. I learnt a lot merely reading one letter. It's so interesting.'

'Clare would be delighted to hear this. It was her passion as well as her life's work to study history. She was widely travelled too. She went to Egypt, Vietnam, Germany, Ireland, Italy, oh all over the place. We'll probably come across more sites she went to in the letters. Goodness, there are a lot of them aren't there?' Cynthia cast her eyes around the room.

'There certainly are. But what an amazing discovery, Cynthia. I'm looking forward to reading more of them.' And she was. It was the first time she had looked forward to anything in years.

Helena settled back in the chair. 'Can you tell me more about Clare's travels?'

'Goodness, where on earth do I begin.' Cynthia stared at the red and gold patterned rug at her feet. 'Ah yes, I do remember her telling me of her trip to Abu Simbel. She went out to Egypt in the late 1980s, which happened to be during a pilot strike. The military took over flying the tourist planes, but everything was a bit chaotic and her flight to Abu Simbel was overbooked. They asked if anyone would travel in the cockpit with the pilots, and she jumped at the chance. She said they handled the plane as if they were on a military operation, banking sharply and taking off and landing at breakneck speeds. She loved it!'

Cynthia paused, and had a bit of a coughing fit.

'Sorry, dear, this happens often.'

'Can I get you some water?' said Helena.

'Thank you dear.'

Helena returned a couple of minutes later and saw the oxygen mask had been moved.

'Are you ok to carry on?' asked Helena.

'I think so dear. Yes. Where was I? Oh yes. Clare said when Abu Simbel appeared on the horizon it was a sight she'd never forget. They travelled south over the desert from Aswan following the river, then banked sharply. As they levelled off again, there, emerging from the sand in the middle of the desert were two magnificent temples set into the rockface. Despite the aircraft's speed, she said everything slowed down as she took it all in.' Cynthia stared at the photo on her little table, her lips pursed tight. She remained frozen for a few seconds, then shook her head and looked up, as if remembering she had company. 'She was fascinated by Nefertari, talked about her for hours, how her femininity was seen as a strength, and how she was hailed as equal to her husband. Clare visited all the sites; I have a photo somewhere of her sitting on the giant foot of Ramesses' fallen colossal statue. She said visiting Nefertari's tomb was one of the best experiences of her life, seeing for herself all the writings on the walls and the glorious painting, as fresh as if it had only recently been applied.'

'I love that she had all those amazing moments to savour. And I bet she'd be delighted you are trying to find out more.'

'Yes, I suppose she would. I've been reading the information from the search Lily did. I am flabbergasted at how much available is online. We believe Nefertari died in around 1255 BCE. Isn't it incredible, she died all those years ago and yet the letter brings her back to life? The references we found said conflicting things, such as how old she was when she married Ramesses, how long she lived for, and how many children she had. It hasn't been ascertained whether she lived to attend the opening of the Temples at Abu Simbel, but there is consensus she saw them.'

'What an incredible woman. And this letter she wrote to her husband. I guess it's really special.'

'I believe so, yes. It may be of interest to other historians. Unfortunately Lily and I didn't find any reference to the letter during our search. That's not a huge surprise. As I say, it was like looking for a needle in a haystack, trying to find any provenance. Perhaps more thorough research will provide some answers in due course. I do hope so.'

Cynthia was noticeably animated as she talked about Clare, and Helena sat back as she went on to detail her travels to Vietnam and her travels from Hanoi in the North down to Ho Chi Min in the south. Her favourite place had been Da Nang with its sweeping white beach and Lady Buddha statue standing majestically overlooking the sea, but Hanoi was where she did most of her research, as it was teeming with temples, including the temple for the Trung sisters.

'I wish I could've met her,' said Helena, as she put down her teacup and plate, and turned once more towards Clare's photo.

'Me too. I'm sure you would have got along. But she died just before her sixty-first birthday, the poor girl. Academically she was brilliant, but she never quite found her way in the world of relationships. She always felt different, an outsider. It took her until she was in her thirties to tell me she was a lesbian, although I had always suspected. Sadly, she never met the right person.'

Helena shuffled slightly and blushed. Sexuality was a subject she had never discussed, mostly because it was taboo growing up, but also because she was very confused about her own feelings, and had been too embarrassed to turn to anyone for support. She glanced over to the clock on the mantel above the fireplace.

'Goodness! It's nearly eight. I must be getting home. It's been lovely, thank you.' Helena jumped up.

'Oh yes, I see. I hope to see you again next week?'

'Yes of course. Oh, I hope you don't think I said I must go because of what you said about Clare being, you know, a lesbian? It's not that at all, I really do have to be going.' A pregnant pause and a brief intake of breath later she added, 'You're right, I am sure Clare and I would've got on well. I imagine we'd have much in common.'

Cynthia smiled and reached over to take Helena's hand. She squeezed it slightly, saying nothing. Helena had never felt safer with anyone than she did in that moment.

As she walked away from the house, Helena saw it was noticeably less well cared for than its neighbours. That made sense, confirming Cynthia was beginning to let go. Helena surprised herself, realising she was experiencing the opposite. For the first time in ages, she felt genuinely excited. She felt alive.

⟢✦⟣

When they met the following week, Cynthia had begun arranging the letters by date, spreading them out in rows across the dining room table.

'I've been meaning to do this,' she said. 'Now you're involved, I have a reason to get myself motivated and bloody well do it.'

'Oh, that's brilliant,' said Helena. 'And I've got a good reason to bloody well help you.'

They both chuckled, which unfortunately induced a severe coughing bout. Cynthia apologised repeatedly and asked Helena if she wouldn't mind getting her the linctus from the sideboard. Helena offered Cynthia the oxygen, hoping this wouldn't embarrass her. Cynthia accepted it readily.

Once Cynthia's episode had subsided, they continued sorting letters. Helena insisted on bringing the ingredients for a meal and appreciated the use of a full-sized kitchen to prepare it. She opted for something simple, a ready-made quiche with salad and new potatoes, followed by a sponge pudding.

'By far the best meal I've eaten in years,' said Cynthia. 'Thank you dear.'

Helena decided Cynthia should rest. As she rose to leave, Cynthia picked up one of the letters. 'This one must be next in line, from what I've read of it. Perhaps you could take it home with you and bring it back next week.'

'I'll do that, thank you,' said Helena. She wanted to dive into the letter immediately, but decided to wait until she was home so that she could savour it. She managed to save reading it until she was in bed: chores done, door to her flat locked and bolted, mascara off, nightie on, earplugs in to dampen noise from the traffic and pub-closing antics outside, and lights out, except for her bedside lamp.

Chapter Six

Mawia

A letter for the monk who goes by the name of Moses.

I am told you are a pilgrim of note, a spiritual Christian man respected across the land for your faith. Moreover, you are celebrated for your eloquence and your leadership skills, displaying both humility and strength. It is this combination of qualities I seek, and I need.

I ask for an urgent meeting with you to discuss a most important matter concerning the future of my people, of interest to you by reason of the potential benefit for your faith.

I am Mawia, Queen of the Arabs. You will have heard of my people. I have led them from the front and succeeded to this point. Now I enter a new phase of my leadership. To achieve my goal, I approach you with a proposal.

We live in an era of immense change. Recently the people have been shaken by witnessing great bloodshed, frequent shifts in religious affiliations, and multiple disasters, including drought, famine and plagues. In the past I inflicted pain on the Romans. Now my desire is to strike a deal, to bargain with them, and this is where you come in. It is time for stability. I believe I hold the solution to suit all parties. With your help, I can achieve it.

Many Romans are converting to the Christian religion, especially since their Emperor Constantine took that faith. They leave behind notions of many gods, and focus instead on the one god, but they deliberate and squabble over the details, such as whether Jesus is God's son or God himself. I use this infighting as my opportunity. I will speak to them in a language they comprehend. I will speak to that faith, reason with that ideology, and I will offer them you.

My plan is to place you in the midst of them, and in so-doing promise peace to Emperor Valens if he agrees to ordain you Bishop of my Arab people. He is a weak leader, an Arian Christian sent to govern us in the East of the Roman empire, but not fit for the job. He struggles presently to deal with the Goths. He will agree to this offer, I am sure of it.

My husband was King of our Saracen land and ruled with great authority. Yet under his leadership, our people were foederati of Rome, mere auxiliaries in their army, beholden to the Emperor and his wishes. This arrangement kept our people from being the targets of Roman oppression, but we were their puppets, a state of affairs continuing all the while my husband was alive. When he was murdered, the Romans assumed his successor would simply accept the same terms. They wagered if the successor refused, then our land and our people would become most vulnerable to further sanctions and attacks from them, and that any successor would avoid this. But the Romans made a grave mistake.

They failed to extend me the courtesy of requesting my agreement to the arrangements. I believe they assumed as a woman, I would follow meekly in my husband's footsteps. But meekness is not my way. With no such invitation from them, I seized the opportunity to take control. I set out to avenge my husband's death and to continue ruling as he did, but with one important exception. I had no intention of a foederati arrangement, no intention of fighting the Goths as a subordinate to Valens. I sought to be recognised as an equal.

Initially, the Romans did not take me seriously, and I used this weakness in their assumptions to my advantage. As for others in the past, so it is for me: my womanhood has been both a shield and a weapon. It has shielded me from being seen as a threat, and thus has enabled me to win at war and in society.

The people accepted me as Queen of our Arab tribes, witnessing and appreciating my strength and skill. I fought to retain and expand my territories, claiming back from the Romans that which they had taken. I ambushed them, directing my troops onto the battlefield. We scattered the opposition as we rode and marched through vast areas.

I led a major revolt, storming with my troops into Phoenicia and Palestine, and as far as the Arabian lands of the Nile, into Egypt no less. The Romans were completely unprepared for it. One or two local commanders called for assistance, sending word of my victories and the threat I posed, but their warnings were not heeded. Indeed, a Phoenician commander was foolishly ordered not to become involved in the combat. When we approached the General, he rushed at us and ran around among us, calling us Barbarians and shooting at our people. Inevitably, he failed to stop us, and we continued to seize back vast regions of the east for our people.

Now, the Emperor will do anything for peace, I am sure of it. You are a Nicene Christian, as are some of my people. They, and others of my people will follow you, I am sure of it, rather than follow the Arian Valens. If you accept my offer, it will benefit everyone.

Your assistance will give me leverage with the Romans. Additionally, I will be comforted by the knowledge my people are in safe hands. Furthermore, this deal will support the advancement of your faith, as you will be in a favourable position to spread your teachings. If you accept this offer, more of my people will surely convert to your form of Christianity. As long as this land and our heritage are protected, then so be it, I care little for the details of my citizens' faith. Valens too will be satisfied. We will enter into a truce agreement, and I envisage us going so far as to support him in his quest against the Goths, if provided he grants my wishes. This arrangement will appease him, and he will assume he is victorious against us, whom he dares to call the Barbarians.

Once all agree, you will be brought to Alexandria to be sworn in to office and then you will be free to preach, as the first Christian bishop of the Arabs.

I hear you live a pious life of quiet devotion, a solitary existence in the desert, and that you have performed miracles. You may protest you are destined for this quiet life or are unworthy of the office. But I have learned of your proclamations and speeches, and these make you more than worthy in my eyes. Rufinus himself, a monk who has witnessed the persecutions by Valens, has talked to me of your persuasive and rousing words. It is my fervent wish to persuade you. This offer is your calling.

I trust your wisdom and spirituality will serve me well personally. I am a woman who cares little for the gods or any singular deity, as my faith is in our land and its peoples. But I will listen to any man or woman who can offer me wise words on seeking and achieving peace for my people and offer comfort as I grieve my husband.

There are those who seek to diminish my role in defeating and influencing the Romans, describing my merits in terms of my fine face or my dress, or claiming my successes are false and unverifiable. They argue whether I am Arab, Ishmaelite, Roman or Christian, a follower of Syrian Orthodoxy or of Greek Orthodoxy. That is of no concern to me, as long as my land and my people are intact. This will be my legacy.

Delivered via messenger by order of Mawia, Queen of the Saracens

Chapter Seven

Lily

This was only the third letter she'd read, but she was seeing a pattern. All these letters had been written by women. And they weren't ordinary women. Apparently fearless and fiercely intelligent, they were women who became powerful and influential, who spoke their minds and garnered respect. Their lives and their worlds were the stuff of fables rather than history, and yet they were real historical figures. Helena was curious if all the letters in the collection were by women, and if they were all rulers. She read a couple of online articles about Mawia then lay down and switched off the light, picturing herself being the scribe as Mawia dictated this letter, in an elaborate tent in Southern Syria during the fourth century. Mawia was seated on a throne of sumptuous cushions, surrounded by bright hangings billowing in the breeze and servants who tended to her every desire. *I must do some more research into…*

BRIIIIING.

Helena awoke with a start. Incredibly, she'd slept right through the night. She hadn't tossed about with her head full of nonsense, getting tangled in the sheets waiting for the alarm to go off. She hadn't needed to get up for a wee. As a result, she felt rejuvenated and for once wasn't dreading work. She wanted to tell someone what she and Cynthia were doing, and as she worked in a place full of people who were interested in books, hopefully they'd be interested in this. Well, most of them.

One of the lotteries of library working was being unaware in advance who'd be sharing lunch breaks. Helena hoped it would be Chris, as he was the perfect combination for the chat she had in mind: approachable, a book nerd and a history geek. But during her break he was busy preparing for the afternoon Rhyme Time session. Helena had only done a couple of these, and they bothered her for several reasons. She found no pleasure in being the centre of attention, scrutinised by mummies, daddies and childminders who expected their little ones to be entertained. She didn't know all the rhymes, meaning she had the embarrassment of having to read them from a sheet. She hated hearing herself sing. Most of all, she wasn't keen on children. They were demanding, snotty, loud, unpredictable aliens. She was convinced all of these factors were obvious to the onlooking parents and carers as they scrutinised her feeble attempts to amuse their precious little bundles. Chris on the other hand appeared to love it; he was a hands-on dad at home, and at work was popular with the parents and kids alike; a natural.

Today, the rota indicated it was only Lily with her at lunch which was a bit disappointing. She was sweet enough but was lacking in life experience and would be too naïve to understand or be enthused by Helena's new-found interest. As Helena entered the staff room with her cellophane-wrapped mystery roll of the day from the library café, Lily was finishing a delicious-looking salad, evidently made at home by a person who cared about what she ate. Having no-one else to talk to, Helena reluctantly decided she'd broach the subject anyway.

'Do you remember Cynthia, the lady you helped on the computer?'

'Oh yeah, I like her, she's nice,' said Lily.

Helena hesitated as she hadn't expected this response. She had assumed Lily was a bit repelled by Cynthia.

'Yes, she's great. You know she lives in a detached house in the leafy part of town?' *What are you saying? What does that matter, and why did you say it? What will she think of you?*

'Oh, really? said Lily. 'Awesome.'

'Erm, yes, but that's not what I meant to say at all.'

'No worries.'

'Well, anyway, she has got lots of letters written by historical figures and I've seen some of them.' *You idiot. You're just coming across as boastful now.*

'Yeah, she told me a bit about it,' replied Lily, her tone and demeanour unfalteringly pleasant. 'I think she's very lonely. I feel bad 'cos the first time I met her and she was coughing, I moved away and I'm sure she noticed. I've got to avoid infection. But she said about the COPC and how I can't catch it.' Lily scraped round the bottom of the bowl to chase the last dregs of her lunch.

Helena recalled seeing Lily move away from Cynthia's coughing and how she'd judged her for it. Misjudged her. She wasn't great with young people. With any people. She decided to try again and not correct Lily with the name of Cynthia's condition.

'Well, I'm glad you two got along. There's more to her than her old, frayed coat and oversized boots.' *Now you're being patronising.*

'Yeah, and cos I'm a bit stiff on one side, even if I'm smiling, one side of my face acts like I'm not. I expect she thought I was being horrible. But I told her about me too, so we're good.'

'You had a lovely looking lunch,' said Helena, changing the subject in an attempt to stop embarrassing herself.

'Yeah, my mum makes them for me. I get a different thing every day. She left work to care for my nan who lives with us now, and she's watching all this daytime tv, 'specially all the cookery shows. So she's trying to get us all eating healthy. Otherwise, I'd be living off chips, doughnuts and crisps. No, I'm joking.'

'Pretty close to what I often eat,' said Helena. She wasn't joking.

'Shall I get her to make extra for you?' said Lily. 'She won't mind, honestly, she loves being mum to everyone.'

'She sounds lovely,' said Helena. 'But no, I'm simply lazy. Actually, I can cook, but I can't be bothered these days. I was just imagining what it would be to have a mum who was so, well, mumsy. I often ended up making my own food when I was young.' Helena surprised herself at how candid she was being with this young girl.

'My mum is the opposite, fussing a bit too much.'

'Funny, isn't it? I would have loved to be fussed over.' *Too much information?*

'She can be a bit over-protective. I get it though. When I was little they weren't sure how bad the brain damage was, so they had to wait and see how I turned out. I was lucky compared to some. It just makes me a bit weak and wobbly down one side. Mum wasn't sure I'd be alright to do this job, but Dad came with me to check it out and it helps that Aunty Carol's here too.'

Aunty Carol? Oh shit, what? Have I said anything awful about Carol to Lily? Think, think, think…

Lily turned to Helena and gave her a sympathetic nod.

'She's Dad's sister. She can be a bit harsh, but she doesn't really mean it.'

'Right, I see. Well, it's good she's here to, well…'

Fail. You stupid, stupid woman. Mum was absolutely right. You're hopeless.

'Yes, it's good,' said Lily, and her face broke into one of the kindest smiles Helena had ever received.

Helena watched Lily get up, wash her bowl and spork and replace them in her locker, and was impressed how deftly she navigated round the obstacle course of scattered chairs and coffee tables.

A weekly ritual developed. Two women from opposite sides of town, hailing from entirely different backgrounds, met in a suburban house and delved into stories from the past, collected by another woman and brought to life through a series of letters. As part of this routine, Helena took pleasure in preparing a home cooked meal each week to share with Cynthia. Whisking was tricky with her damn wrist, but after practice and several spills, she became fairly adept at using her left hand. It was a small victory, but it counted. And each week, Helena would recount to Lily in their shared lunch break what she and Cynthia were finding. Helena wouldn't go so far as to believe Lily and Cynthia were becoming her bosom buddies, but this was the closest she had come to forming new friendships in years.

After a few weeks, the letters were sorted more or less into date order, and two things became apparent. Firstly, as Helena had suspected, they all appeared to be written by women. And secondly, it looked like there was a large gap in the timeline. After the letters from ancient history, there was nothing much until hundreds of years later.

'I suppose it wasn't called The Dark Ages for nothing,' said Cynthia one afternoon as they sat together at her dining room table, polishing off portions of baked macaroni cheese. 'Life was all religion and power and little else. There was plenty of international travel and trade, but there was little in the way of creativity or culture as we would understand it, especially in Europe, and much of the world was dominated by patriarchal societies, where the voice of the woman wasn't recorded. The three big monotheistic religions…'

'Sorry, I don't quite…'

'Oh, do forgive me. I'm gabbling again.'

'No, you're not. It's me, I don't understand it all. Mono…what was that?'

'Monotheistic. One god.'

'Of course.' Helena pushed her plate to one side and placed her hands on the tablecloth in front of her. It was white linen, and had tiny yellow and brown age spots on it. 'Please, carry on.'

'Where was I? Honestly, I'll forget my head one of these days.' Cynthia tapped her forehead.

'Monothe… sorry I still can't say it.'

'Oh yes, the three one-god religions. Christianity, Judaism and Islam were spreading rapidly, with their theories of the one male god, the superiority of men, women being the property men, and so forth. Many women who succeeded were of noble birth, so they had an advantage. There were exceptions of course. Take this lady, Theodora.' Cynthia picked up a letter. 'She interests me because she was a woman who made it despite her humble background. Have you heard of her?'

'Cynthia, I haven't heard of most of these people, I'm not educated like you.'

'I learnt a lot from listening to Clare. Anyway, you're obviously bright.'

'Oh, I don't know about that.'

'You just weren't given the opportunities, dear. Clare would sit in that chair where you are now and talk through her research. It's so sad, so unfair she wasn't able to finish the work.'

'It is. Well, I am really grateful you're letting me see all of this. Can I read Theodora's letter next?'

Cynthia coughed for a few seconds and was breathless after the exertion of talking.

'Of course,' she said in a tired and hoarse voice. 'Here she is. Sorry, dear, but I think I ought to rest.'

Chapter Eight

Theodora

A warm welcome to you, great artists. Theodora complements you on your skill, your mastery of design and colour. Since Rome was at its height, your art remains famous and sought after. My husband and I thank you for what you are about to create and are most pleased that our likenesses will be captured at the splendid Basilica of San Vitale in Ravenna. This mosaic will be a thing of beauty and will be of great significance, marking an end to hostilities between us and your local rulers.

We thank you for travelling to our home to discuss arrangements. A scribe writes my words as a reminder of this meeting. We grant you this audience that you might know us and accurately represent us.

You may be surprised to hear I am the product of a poor family. My father was a keeper and trainer of bears in the Hippodrome here in Constantinople, and my mother a dancer and actress. Father supported the Green faction, but they turned their backs upon us when we needed them most. You see, we faced ruin when my father died. Mother remarried, but Father's role of bear trainer was not passed to her new husband. In desperation, she dressed my sisters and me in certain cloths, and paraded us around the Hippodrome for the pleasure of the Green faction. Even so, they rejected us.

Mother turned to the Blue faction who took pity on us and gave my step-father the bear-trainer job. To this day, I have sympathies for the Blue faction. This was my first harsh lesson in politics. The Blues and the Greens are both plagued by the presence of violent thugs whose only pleasure is to fight, but it is our tradition to align with one or the other, as they continue to wield great power in our city.

There was no money. Mother had little choice but to put us out to work as entertainers for the men and as actresses. This was lowly work. I quickly mastered how to please the men with my body and my moves. The more debased the better. Do you imagine I derived pleasure from lifting my garments to show them my breasts and my holes, and do you believe I rejoiced in letting birds feed on my naked body for the pleasure of leering faces?

No, I did not. I knew it was wrong, degrading and base. Thankfully I had my sister Comito by my side, giving me comfort and the strength to carry on. I was skilled with words, having an aptitude especially for comedy, and thus I could earn a living of sorts.

I knew I was capable of more. I yearned to travel, become educated and make something of my life. My fortunes appeared to change when I was invited to Africa to be with the governor Hecebolus in Libya, and I anticipated a good life with him. But he was cruel to me, and I had to flee, fearing that my life of being persecuted would never end. Those were immeasurably dark days.

To Alexandria in Egypt next I travelled, a city which opened my mind! There, you can see how the Greeks and Egyptians and Romans all came together. I was told of the great library there, housing all the knowledge of mankind. Picture such a place, where you could study the earth, read the poets and the comic and tragic plays of Greece, and see the words of the great philosophers and religious leaders. Under one roof you could come to understand law, history, medicine, mathematics, and science. It was the best place for scholars in the whole world; they say it had 700,000 books.

Inspired by this rich history, I stayed and studied a little there, and came to appreciate that I possess the gift of intelligence. Yet I was frustrated as there was no opportunity to use it. Learning is a mixed blessing indeed.

The more knowledge I gained, the more I understood that women are not valued in any way except as mothers and wives. Noble causes and vital work, but not the limits of what a woman can achieve. I knew there should be more than the existence forced upon the women in my family.

I heard of a city called Antioch, similar to Alexandria but favoured more because of its position. Upon arriving there, I found a place past its glory. But the trip was to prove most important and fortuitous, for it was at Antioch that Justinian and I first heard of one another through a mutual acquaintance. Guided by intrigue and ambition, I set out to meet Justinian back in Constantinople. I had travelled far to seek my place in the world, and after all my searching, found it back here, where my life had begun.

On returning to Constantinople, I took honourable work as a wool spinner. Justinian and I soon fell in love. He too, was born into a peasant family, and he too is aware of the hard work it takes to become a person of merit, even for a man. A Latin speaker, he was adopted by his uncle Justin who brought him to Constantinople and ensured he had an excellent education. He understands as do I, that an education can save a person. He worked his way through the ranks, eventually becoming a senator. As soon as he saw me, he appreciated I possess an intellect to match his and that together we could become exceptional. But for one problem. By law, as a senator he was not allowed to marry an actress, as these souls are held in such low regard.

Fortune smiled on us when Justinian became regent and could change the law for us to be married. I desired for us to visit Antioch together, but the great earthquake of 526 prevented this. It makes me quake that if I had stayed there, I could have perished. Destiny had different ideas, and when he became Emperor, I was crowned Augusta, Empress of the Eastern Roman Empire. From the start of our reign, I became Justinian's partner in all things. This, as you may imagine, is most unusual. It has been seen before, as I learnt when in Egypt, but most Roman Emperors would not allow or admit to their wives' involvement in state affairs. I had my own court, my own seal, my own entourage.

Many of the men did not care for it. Nor do they still. They call me vindictive, and say I instil fear without caring for the consequences. How they misrepresent me. I must assert my authority to be given any credit. I have done nothing to cause any shame. I earnt my money the only way I knew how, the only way I could. And it was mine to spend on my travels and studies. If they fear a strong woman, then that is their concern, not mine.

I believe in justice and fairness for the people and have persuaded Justinian to consider these matters too. We banned corruption, and our officials across the Empire are required to swear an oath to me as Empress and

Justinian as Emperor, committing to abide by our legislation. Magistrates are closely monitored to diminish unnecessary bureaucracy, and to ensure their proceedings are fair. Between 529 and 534 we produced our legislative Corpus Juris Civilis. This unique law consists of three parts. The Code contains our legislation amassed together in one place, The Digest contains essays pertaining to the law, and The Institutes are textbooks for students. I was compelled to compromise on several aspects, especially the laws regarding the Chalcedonian Christianity. I protect the oft-persecuted Miaphysite Christians, providing sanctuary in one of my palaces and a monastery at Sykae. Religion is the one area on which my husband and I disagree, but in general our beliefs align, and our differences prevent us not from ruling with strength. We believe in tolerance, and we work tirelessly to end religious frictions. We aim for a united church working with us, where Justinian has ultimate authority. Already they are saying our Law will be the foundation for civilisations to come.

I do more for women and girls than any ruler of our time. I free those women forced into prostitution, make sure they are clothed and funded and educated through the convents I provide for them. They are not being imprisoned as some would have you believe; they are being protected. I understand from personal experience the hard life they endure. They deserve better. Under my rule, women are given the right to divorce, the right to inherit and own property, the right to control their own body, and the right to care for their own children. No more is a woman killed for committing adultery, but instead, a man can be killed for raping a woman. No matter their position or status, everyone present during the rape is breaking the law, and the rapist's property will be handed over to the victim. There are those who say I favour women over men, but what I favour is fairness to women after centuries of oppression.

We have amassed a substantial army and at a moment's notice they can be galvanised and act as necessary to defend our great Empire. Meanwhile, I have done all in my power to keep the peace across the East, forging strong relationships with our neighbours in Persia and elsewhere. There have been wars, including wars with your people, but these were necessary to maintain the Empire. I take credit for holding our Empire together. During the riots of 532, the Blues and the Greens engaged in the most violent riot. All at once, they stopped fighting one another and began chanting in unison. "Nika!" they yelled. Reports came in they were heading for the Palace. We faced the possibility they might unite and attempt to overthrow us. Officials begged me to go into hiding, the Emperor too. Justinian was all for it. But I was swift to act, forced to break protocol and speak at the government council, although it was forbidden for a woman to do so.

I gave them my opinion, and clearly. Flight was not the right course, even if it got us to a place of safety. I refused to become a fugitive, to forfeit my royal purple robe, for which I had worked relentlessly. There was still much to be done, and it would be impossible should we retreat into exile.

Justinian and the men knew I was right. The official, Joannes Laurentius Lydus declared me superior in intelligence to any man. And Justinian did what was required to quell the riot. Those 50,000 lives lost bear heavy on my conscience but they were rebels and had to be stopped. We could not risk being perceived as weak leaders, or they would find a crack, and enter it, forcing it wide open, resulting in a giant chasm of chaos. For the stability of the empire, this could not be allowed. As it was, they managed to burn and destroy much of our beautiful city in the space of a single week, including the Hagia Sophia.

We are already rebuilding the city. Magnificent new centres have been erected for pleasure, worship and study. The Hagia Sophia will be better than before. The Imperial Library rivals the library lost at Alexandria and we are ensuring all texts are gathered there, building on the work begun by Constantius. The great city of Constantinople has become again a thriving metropolis because of us, and we will make it the greatest city on earth. To pay for our programmes we tax the rich. They can afford it, the poor cannot. But all will be richer through our programmes.

I appreciate the importance of international relations. I have personally made alliances with the great families of our Empire, and forged friendships between them. I receive foreign envoys in person, and corresponded with leaders from many nations.

Ah, the time, gentlemen. I must hasten. And so, let us turn attention to the mosaic you are about to create.

I wish you to show me in my portrait as you see me standing before you. Show my age; I am late forties not a young girl. Show all I have been through. Perhaps in my eyes portray a life that has not always been easy. A frown may be added, depicting the weight of responsibility I bear and how I toil tirelessly. I wish to be portrayed in full face, not the side view favoured by the Egyptians and many of the Romans and Greeks. You will see I am thin these days. Something eats at me from inside. Show it.

Note what I am wearing. This is how I wish you to represent me. I am an Empress with my fine headdress, my jewelled earrings, necklace, cuffs and shoulder adornments, but I remain a hard-working woman from a poor background, denoted by the dark colour of the cloak. It is adorned around the bottom, but much of it is plain. If you so desire, the background could resemble a halo to reflect my status. Yes, depict me if you will, making an offering, perhaps holding a fine chalice, with my ladies in waiting on one side, my men of the court on the other.

The man Procopius, in his work The Secret History, paints me as a vindictive slut who is only interested in power and self. He is jealous of a capable woman, and distorts the truth for his own amusement. He would have me go down in history as a harlot. He dares to insult my husband also, and calls us the worst Byzantine Empire officials ever. His account should not prevail. If you do as I ask, you will show me as I truly am, a woman of intellect and spirit, a woman of strength and determination, a woman of the people. I desire an honest representation. Accordingly, those who see it in the future will see me, and will know me.

Justinian will be here soon. You will note when you meet him how the Emperor and I dress in a similar fashion. He too has the jewels associated with his status. He too wears a dark garment. This is how we shall be shown together to reflect our partnership, how we rule, and how we will be remembered.

I trust you will be faithful to all that is required of you. I trust you will employ the finest craftsmen from the local area to help create the tiles and form the image. If there are any women or girls who wish to train in your great art of mosaic, I ask you to involve them as apprentices and assistants so they may learn the craft.

He is here. I present my husband, the Emperor, Justinian.

Chapter Nine

Carol

Helena guessed Cynthia had given her Theodora's story deliberately, with its message of a woman achieving great things from difficult beginnings. She was sure Cynthia meant well, but reading these letters was beginning to make her feel inadequate. Unlike Theodora and the other women whose letters she'd read, her life, her contribution to the world amounted to nothing. Nevertheless, she was intrigued enough to find out more and it was her day off, so she spent it researching Theodora. As Cynthia had found with Nefertari, she came across conflicting opinions from scholars and authors regarding Theodora's life, including her religious beliefs and the exact nature of her work as a girl. Actresses were banned by the church and an "actress" could be anything from a burlesque performer to a prostitute. Helena agreed that Procopius, author of Theadora's biography during her lifetime, was merely mean and jealous. What a woman though! Not that you'd gather this from the *Wiki* page on Justinian which hardly mentioned her.

The next day, Cynthia found Helena in Fantasy, a part of the library she'd never entered.

'It's a different world here,' said Helena. 'Well, lots of different worlds. I prefer the real one, don't you?'

'Absolutely I do,' said Cynthia as she peered quizzically at the colourful book covers featuring mystical creatures and swirly patterns. 'Each to their own though. I can understand why people enjoy escaping into other realities.'

Helena finished shelving and turned to face Cynthia, who was wearing a black punk-inspired coat, full of rips and tassels and bedecked with safety pins. 'One of Clare's from the 1980s,' she explained.

'I love it,' said Helena. It suits you!' I'm really glad you popped in. I wanted to tell you…I read about Theodora last night. I get what you're saying, you know how a lot of men who wrote history ignored women altogether.'

'Yes,' agreed Cynthia. 'Perhaps that was a wrong Clare was trying to right. She wished to highlight these women's achievements in the context of the world they lived in. By the way, did you know Theodora is a saint now, in the Orthodox Church?'

'I did, yes. And those mosaics. They are still there! I saw pictures of them online. They exactly match how she describes herself. I wonder if she knew she was dying and wanted to leave a true record of her life, including her illness.' Helena hesitated. 'Oh, I'm so sorry Cynthia, I didn't mean to… I didn't think…'

'Don't worry, dear.' Cynthia leant against the Fantasy shelving, and paused for breath. 'And yes, I suspect you may be right about her intentions. I've realised too, Theodora was making a speech rather than writing a letter. But it served the same purpose, preserving her history in her own words. Perhaps Trung Tac did the same when she wrote details of her life to her sister. These women possibly wanted their words found, their voices heard, their stories told in their own words.'

'But how on earth did Clare come across this? All the sources I found say there's not much information on Theodora, especially her early life.'

'I really can't say, dear. It's truly incredible, all she did. Now then, what did I come in for today? Oh yes, the Chinese Tang Dynasty.'

'I'll help you look,' said Lily, as she passed them whilst heading over to History.

The following morning, Helena's wrist appeared to be slightly better. She'd bought a strappy wrist support online and worn it overnight as recommended. However, after only an hour at work the intense pain started darting along her arm again. She spent her coffee break waggling it around as it felt in need of a click, but that only aggravated it further.

Lily wasn't in as she had a hospital appointment, and Carol was taking over her rota. Maybe she should make a bit more effort with her. If she was Lily's aunt, there must be a bit of decency there.

'Do you remember Cynthia?' she asked as they sat together for lunch.

'The woman you talk to a lot? Yes. Why?' Carol bit hard on her celery, which sounded as brittle as she did.

'Well,' said Helena, unsure whether this was worth continuing. 'She's become a bit of a friend and I've been visiting her house.'

'Oh ok. I assumed she was a complete recluse.'

'I think she is, mostly. But she's trying to sort something out. Her daughter was a historian and collected letters. Cynthia is going through them all and she's got me interested. Actually, it's really fascinating. The last one I read concerned Theodora.'

'The Byzantine Empress?'

'The very one.' Maybe this effort was paying off after all.

'I've read about her. Fascinating woman, quite controversial though.'

'Oh, why is that?'

'There are those who claim she was one of the first feminists. I'm not so sure. Oooh, right, here I go.'

Carol's face reddened and she began waving one hand frantically in front of her face as she reached for her handbag with the other and started searching.

'Where did I put the bloody thing?' she said.

'Looking for one of these?', said Helena, reaching in her own bag for her fan. 'I never go anywhere without one these days. Here you go.'

Carol took the fan and began wafting it around frantically.

'Thanks. I usually carry one too. But we're packing up the house at the moment, and I keep putting things in places then don't recall where they are. Make sure I give this back, I'm likely to walk off with it.'

'I'll try to remember. I have the same problem. So, you're moving? Anywhere nice?'

'Quite the opposite. All I can afford to buy is a small flat on the south side of town. It's so grotty there.'

'Hmmm,' said Helena, hoping they wouldn't be neighbours, doing the same commute. The bus journey was when she got her head ready for work, and she didn't relish the prospect of having to share it in work mode with the boss.

'I've no choice. Divorce,' said Carol, interrupting Helena's internal monologue.

'Oh dear, I'm sorry.'

'It's for the best. Anyway, I was meaning to try and catch you.'

'Oh, sorry, have I done something wrong again?'

'No, Helena. Everything isn't… the thing is, what with my disastrous home life and my raging hormones, I am aware I've not been terribly pleasant to be around for the last few months. I find myself getting rather snappy.'

'Oh, I hadn't noticed anything,' lied Helena. 'Anyway, I've been a bit preoccupied too, immersed in my own problems, reaching this part of my life and wondering what on earth I'm doing. And I've got this painful wrist. It sounds silly, but it's getting me down.'

'Chronic pain isn't silly. I met many people in pain during medical training.'

'You're a doctor?' Helena was astonished.

'Oh, no, no. I had to pull out. I drifted for a while doing this and that while the kids were at home. This job seemed suitable when I applied, mainly I have to confess, because it's so local. But I'm not comfortable around people, especially these days. And I am livid about all the cuts. There's no budget for anything. The state of this room for one thing. What does it say to new staff?' Carol waved the fan around the room, pointing at the damp patches and flaky paint.

Once again, Helena chided herself for being judgemental and for her own lack of empathy. Who would have guessed she and Carol had both done healthcare training? And that they'd bond over the menopause? It was an experience they shared, but plenty of women didn't discuss it, even with other women. It was the same with periods. All women had them, but they rarely compared notes. Not in her experience anyway. At school with her best and only real friend Sue, they had used a code name for the event. "I've got Duffy visiting this week." That was it. She'd never discussed the emotional roller-coaster, the monthly cramps, the excessive bleeding, the laser treatment for pre-cancer cells, the bulky womb and the polyp removals with anyone except doctors and nurses.

'It must be difficult,' said Helena, trying to sound understanding.

'It is. And I can't stand all the bureaucracy. I get too angry.'

'I'd be the same.'

'My problem is severe depression. I've had it my whole adult life. It's at the root of all my behaviour.' Carol blurted this out so unexpectedly that Helena needed a moment to gather herself and form a suitable facial expression. It was a shame she didn't have the fan to hide behind.

'Oh… it's fine,' she said, then quickly added, 'No I mean, it's not fine at all. It's horrible. I mean, thank you for telling me.'

'It's why I had to drop out of medicine, why I struggle with relationships. And why I get livid about things which shouldn't matter. I find it hard to control my emotions.'

Before Helena could answer, Carol spoke again. 'I see you've given up on the café's attempts at nutrition.' Helena noticed she wasn't the only one to resort to this tactic of changing the subject.

'It was Lily who inspired me actually. Her lunches always appear really appetising.'

'Her mum puts the rest of us to shame. Anyway, about your wrist. I've been checking the annual leave, and you're due a week. Senior management are on at me to make sure everyone takes their holiday through the year, to avoid it getting bunched at Christmas and in the Summer, when we're at our busiest. Why don't you take a week off, try and rest it?'

'That would be great. And, thank you. It's been nice to chat.'

Arriving at Cynthia's after work, the low late winter sun shone through the trees enough for Helena to see remnants of thoughtful planting in the front garden amongst the weeds and overgrown shrubs. Helena's mother had never tended to the yard at the back of their rented terrace, and from memory there wasn't a pot plant to be seen, let alone a flower bed. It had been a place to hang laundry and dispense of broken things. The idea of having a garden was both alarming and interesting: a big responsibility, but something to care for. When she went inside, she asked Cynthia if it would be ok to explore the back garden too.

'If you wish, my dear,' said Cynthia. I am ashamed to say I hardly ever venture out there anymore. I have a person in to tidy a couple of times a year, and that's all the attention it gets these days.'

Helena stepped out of the dining room and over the threshold into the cool space. As she had guessed, it was large, and yet felt cosy, zoned into different areas. She walked across the semi-circular stone patio, down the stone steps and onto to a lawn, soft with moss and lush because of the recent rain. Several trees were planted in the lawn and in the middle of it was a bed full of, what were they, roses? It was hard to tell, with no gardening experience, with all the weeds, and with it being nearly dark and winter. The lawn had a paved path curving through it, leading to a narrow space with tall hedges on either side. Helena walked through the space, under a rickety metal arch, to discover a second lawned area. In one corner stood a large wooden summer house, whitewashed with traces of pink paint showing through. More beds lined the sides. Red brick walls marked the boundaries with the neighbours and fir trees lined the bottom of the garden, providing shade, security and privacy.

'I love it!' she said, as she came back inside.

'I used to love it too, so much. I was quite a dab hand in my day. I'd be out there in all weathers, with my trug, secateurs and trowel. Weeding, planting, pruning, planning. It was such therapy, Helena. Clare loved the summer house best. I painted it pink for her, much to my mother's disapproval. As it turned out, Clare wasn't fond of the pink, bless her. She painted it white when she was a teenager. She would be in there for hours. Did all her A' level revision in there. And in recent years she'd go down there to use my old typewriter. She said it was the ideal place to study, even when she had her own flat. Oh, my poor Clare.'

'You must miss her awfully. I can't imagine. Well, when the weather improves, maybe we could go down to the summer house together. I'd like that, if it's ok with you.'

'I'd like that very much too, dear.'

'In the meantime, Carol has encouraged me to take a week off. She's been quite decent actually. We can use the time to read through loads of letters. If it's ok with you. I feel I'm being a bit pushy.'

'Of course it's ok. I love having you here, you bring the house alive again, and I am so touched you are interested in this. As for Carol, we're each on our own journey, aren't we dear?'

Cynthia always knew the right thing to say.

'Yes. We are. I should keep reminding myself this. Ok, well, I'll bring my laptop over so we can do some research too – as you did with Lily at the library.'

'Ok, but I don't have any way to connect, no wiffy, or whatever it is.'

'It's not a problem, I can use my phone as a Wi-Fi hotspot.'

'I haven't a clue what you mean dear, but that sounds fine.'

'We could get you a mobile phone,' suggested Helena. 'I've read they're phasing out landlines soon.'

'Oh, there won't any need for that, dear. Right, we'd best get started I suppose. I've found another letter for you to take with you tonight. This lady was very creative, a genius perhaps.'

Chapter Ten

Wu Zhao

I, Empress Wu Zetian, recognised also as Wu Zhao, Holy and Divine Emperor of China in the Second Zhu Era of the great Tang Dynasty, in this year 698, hereby announce that you Zhongzong are my favoured successor, on condition you prove you are now worthy of this great honour. Examine everything I have achieved and how. Then show me you are capable. If you succeed, I will bequeath to you our great Empire and in so doing, trust The Golden Age of China will be safe in your hands.

At a young age, I was already astute. You did not possess this quality, but you must attempt to master it, and develop skills in taking advantage of any situation. Seek out opportunities and grab them. I made sure to catch the eye of the Emperor Taizong at fourteen, when he made me fifth-rank concubine. He saw me not only as another of his many concubines, not only the maid who changed his bedsheets. He saw in me a spirit and intelligence beyond my years, such as when I impressed him revealing how I would tame his wild horse. Soon, he employed me as his secretary, and I quickly learned affairs of state. With his other consorts, I entered confinement respectfully after his death, but never intended to live out my days as a nun. The weak Emperor Gaozong came to visit on Taizong's anniversary to pay respects, and immediately I seized the opportunity to impress him as I did his predecessor.

I stopped shaving my head and demonstrated to him all my charms. Not long after, I was back in the Imperial court, elevated to second-rank concubine of Gaozong. I made sure to be noticed, and to remove anyone who stood in my path. Gaozong soon came to appreciate he needed my counsel and began to sit me near him when he gave an audience. From this position, I whispered instructions to him from behind a screen. In due course I became the new Empress and insisted I had a throne at equal elevation to his. As Gaozong became ever weaker in body and mind, so I became stronger, and as Gaozong increasingly relied on me, so too did the people. They trusted me at court and came to me and I delivered for them.

When Gaozong died and you made a claim to the throne, I roared with laughter. You were utterly ill-prepared, and I arranged for your departure and sent you into exile. Son, I did this for you and for China. You were weak, immature and unworthy of any kind of senior position. You were an embarrassment to me and to China. I am still to be convinced that you are deserving.

You were angry, you silly boy, when briefly I installed your brother, Li Dan. The people were angry too, for they wanted me, as they demonstrated with their petitions demanding I take the throne. I had been ruling for decades behind the scenes and they knew it. They longed for this to continue, but in public. I did that which they desired, and declared myself Holy and Divine Emperor. I have ruled outright these past fifteen years and done it in the most excellent manner. I rule China wisely but strictly, with both a diplomatic and a forceful hand, as a mother rules her children.

Heed my words: I created the most cosmopolitan culture, at the centre of the world. We outshine the Europeans who live in comparative darkness. They learn of our superior silks, spices, skills and society through our trade routes with them. They marvel at how we produce such beautiful things. We do not share our secrets. Tell me, son, will you be able to continue this?

We have built wondrous temples where the people may give thanks to me, Celestial Empress and Mother, and to our ancestors. I am a reborn Buddha. So great am I that I tolerate different religious factions so long as they do no harm to China. The Daoists, and even those religions claiming women to be subservient - the Confucians, the Christians, and the followers of Mohammed – I allow them all. Do you have the same strength of character required to lead all these various factions? Confucius says a woman ruler is as unnatural as a hen crowing like a rooster. He has not met the Tang women. We are as strong as men. We choose our own husbands; we excel at every aspect of life. But I am the strongest, I am the most excellent! I have uplifted the position of women, the mothers of the nation, and ensured we record their achievements. I outshine everyone. I dress as a man and I perform as a man, and I am strong as a man. But I possess a woman's mind. Those stupid men say I am a wicked woman. You will have heard all the lies they spread. You are lucky. As a man you are immune to all that.

Can you care for all of your citizens? I care for the peasants as a mother cares for her weaker children. When they are in need, I provide, and am so gracious that I cut taxes for them. I arranged education for the farmers and under my leadership, farming and food production have improved. I moved the capital and the court to Luoyang near the farming regions, as a mother moves her family to the best sources of food. Inevitably the people periodically squabble, as all children do. So they may enjoy a sense of being heard, I installed copper boxes in the capital where they can post grievances against one another. If the grievance is justified, action is taken. Thus, increasingly I gain their trust. You must show me that you can display such temerity. In spite of my greatness, there are men who continue to begin petty revolts, led by those old fools who served under Gaozong and resented me. I became tired of it. Now, there are no real rivals left.

Can you keep the officials in line? All my appointees are examined on my Rules for Officials. I choose them wisely, those who will be loyal to me, and those who are intelligent, educated and capable. It matters not their birth rank; what matters are their qualities, just as I became Emperor because of my qualities. Although I am a descendant of the ancient Zhou kings, your grandfather was a merchant, a minor Duke, not a senior nobleman. As Mother to my nation, I recognise and reward ability across society. I created Scholars of the Northern Gate for the promotion of literature. Being a great poet myself it is fitting. I am a defender of all our great arts.

As any excellent parent should, I ensured relations with the neighbours remained satisfactory. Under my lead, we co-exist peacefully whilst expanding Tang territories, and we are the most dominant force across nations. I do not waste money or men's lives on futile wars. Instead, I have unified my family, the Empire. I did all this to get where I am, I had to work years for it. You are having it handed to you. Do not dare to diminish my achievements. My multitude of successes will pave the way for you to maintain our dynasty. I have done much of the hard work for you.

Now, again, the mob are descending. Foolish men continue to criticise my way of ruling. What they object to most is that I am a woman. They force me to defend my authority because of my sex. If I were a man they would praise my valour, my strength of character, my fearlessness, and for surrounding myself with young fresh concubines. This behaviour is expected of a man, but is shocking for a woman. The hypocrisy. You will not have this issue because you were born in the male form.

Now I am of great age, and must consider the future. I scrutinised all options from within my own family and thought none strong enough to succeed me. I once favoured the handsome young Zhang brothers, but they have been executed, so I am forced to choose you. I do what is right for China as its Imperial and Holy Mother, and as your mother.

You will be brought out of exile and will meet me here at my palace. I will teach you everything, and I will test you. If you fail, you will force me to seek an heir elsewhere, but the clock is ticking, and you may be my last hope. Do not let me down. Do not let China down. Be the same as me. Be a Father to your Empire.

I have erected a memorial stone which I expect to be adorned with beautiful words and motifs celebrating all my successes. You should lead the way on this. Ensure history remembers all my wondrous achievements. Start on it now, spreading word of my greatness.

Your Mother, Emperor of China.

Chapter Eleven

Ende

Helena put the letter back in its plastic pocket and felt the heat rise from her chest and travel right through to the tips of her ears. She frowned as she put the pocket on the cluttered kitchen surface and put the kettle on. How could Cynthia possibly presume she would appreciate this story and this ruthless woman who was so full of self-aggrandisement. And such an awful mother. Helena had told Cynthia she was estranged from her mum. Surely Cynthia could appreciate the enormous strain this still put on her. Didn't Cynthia realise, a woman who treated her child this appallingly would upset her? She began to question whether Cynthia understood her at all. She slept fitfully, her head full of negativity and angst. She was consistently wrong about people. She was on her own and always would be.

However, she needed to return the letter, so the next day she visited as promised. She had begun walking across town to Cynthia's for the exercise, and had started enjoying it, but on this day she trudged along brooding that she'd wasted time yet again on someone who wasn't as pleasant as they first appeared. She was cross with herself for believing that Cynthia was becoming a friend, a confidante even. She supposed they weren't friends at all. Best get this over with promptly to prevent any more pain. She'd be as polite as she could manage in the circumstances, then make a quick getaway.

'Morning, Cynthia, only me,' she said as she pushed the door open. A wall of thick smoke hit her as she walked in, and she followed its trail to the dining room to find Cynthia sitting in her armchair in the corner. She was drawing heavily on a cigarette and beside her on the little table was an ashtray full of stubs. Her lips disappeared and her wrinkles deepened even further as she pulled on the cigarette, its tip glowing and crackling. Also on the little table was a large glass of whisky and the bottle from which it had been poured. There was no space on it for anything else. By contrast, the dining room table was tidy and empty, except for the tea things and a plate of battenburg cake slices. There were no papers to be seen.

'Morning, Helena. Come and take a seat.' Cynthia hardly moved as she spoke. Maybe Helena had done something to upset her, though she couldn't imagine what.

Helena put her bag on the floor and pulled up a dining chair to sit opposite Cynthia. They both stared out onto the garden for a few seconds.

'Before I say anything, could you open the window? It must be suffocating in here.'

Helena got up and opened one of the little windows on either side of the garden doors. A waft of smoke flew out. She sat down again, worried that Cynthia was gearing up to give her a lecture about something. She'd listen, then make her excuses and leave. There were things about Cynthia she didn't admire: the smoking, the daytime drinking. Maybe all the kindness was false. Maybe the cracks were beginning to show. It was all awfully familiar.

'I owe you an apology,' said Cynthia. Helena lifted her head and shook it slightly, pretending everything was fine. 'No, no, let me finish, please. I feel wretched. And I can see you are upset.' Cynthia balanced the cigarette on the ashtray and leaned over, reaching for Helena's hand.

'When I gave you that letter last night, I was muddling it with another one. I felt so stupid realising I'd given you the wrong one. I should have rung to tell you, but I don't have your number. Honestly, I feel very foolish. I put everything away because I assumed you wouldn't wish to visit me anymore. I thought you would be so exasperated with me. I am so sorry.'

Helena laughed with relief, and then the laugh suddenly turned into a little cry. 'Oh Cynthia,' she said.

Cynthia held onto her hand, saying nothing while she sniffed, and a few tears fell into her lap.

'I was supposing all sorts of stupid things,' Helena said. 'I can see now it was a misunderstanding. It's all ok, honestly.'

Helena squeezed Cynthia's hand gently to reassure her she meant what she said. It took a degree of self-control not to tell Cynthia she really shouldn't be smoking or drinking at her age and in her condition. She resorted to her default position: change the subject.

'So, you were saying, there was another letter?'

'Ah yes, the letter I DID intend you to read. It's a bit religious; they all were in those days in one way or another. I'm not sure if that's your kind of thing?'

Helena shook her head slightly in a non-committed kind of way, not wanting to offend Cynthia in case she was a believer.

'I am not religious at all, especially these days,' continued Cynthia. 'I respect people who are religious, who have faith. I see philosophy and religion as very similar, searching for answers. Philosophy is like religion, but without any gods. Clare and I agreed on that.'

'I wish I could have listened to you and Clare talking together. I would have loved it.'

'Thank you dear. Yes, we did have some very interesting conversations. Oh goodness, where was I?'

'You were saying… about another letter?'

'Ah yes... Anyway, this one was an artist. We only know of her because she was allowed to sign her name. It's over a thousand years old. Clare attached pictures of the art referred to. It's quite something. Her name was Ende. You could read it while I fetch the tea; it's very short.'

To the Abbot Dominicus in the Monastery of Tabala,

It is a great honour to work for you.

Here enclosed is the finished Gerona Beatus, the manuscript you ordered. You will see it contains 284 pages in miniature for your pleasure. I painted the 115 miniature images inside the book, and it is my only wish for them to meet with your approval. If I have done my job properly, the manuscript will satisfy you as you view the fine work.

Your generous commission allowed me to use the finest materials and purchase bright colours to create the boldest of images, bringing the holy passages to life. The paints enable me to show the full glory of the sumptuous buildings in reds and blues and browns with fine yellow drapes and ornate arches.

I depict Christ and the winged angels in flight as He addresses the flock below, and embellish the top of the picture with clouds in blue and white. If I may be so bold, my favourite work is The Alpha, the Maiestas Domini, and the Portraits of the Authors. Here, I created the most intricate design on the Alpha letter, and contrasted the green of the letter with the brightest most detailed gold patterns. Inside the Alpha sits Our glorious Lord Christ in His Majesty. Authors surround him discussing their business and are tiny in comparison. In painting this work I experienced the Holy Spirit traversing my body and flowing onto the page, as if the Lord himself was guiding me.

I have been made most welcome here in the Monastery. This place offers considerable peace, and has been a most excellent location for contemplation and creation of the paintings. According to your instruction, I include my signature in my own hand.

Ende, painter and helper of God.

Cynthia returned with the tea things.

'Oh no, dear, now you're crying again. I am sorry, I am making a mess of everything. I've been far too prescriptive, arrogant in presuming I might decide myself what you'd like to read.'

'It's not you at all,' said Helena. 'It's me. My hormones probably. My mind jumps around and gets up to all sorts of nonsense. Sorry, you've got enough on your plate without me blubbing. I should have realised there was a simple explanation.'

Helena lifted the letter from Ende, and the attached images. 'Those paintings are gorgeous; I love all the colours.'

'I expect they've been very well preserved. I thought you could do with a break from all those ruthless rulers. I meant to show you not all the letters were the same. And then what did I do? Give you the most ruthless of them all!'

'Honestly, don't worry. I understand.' Helena paused. 'I s'pose the Wu Zhao letter highlights something I was starting to wonder with all these women rulers. Maybe they felt they had to behave in a manly way to be taken seriously?'

'I believe they probably did, yes. Female rulers were forced to resemble men in order to succeed. Not just the women in these letters here, but even the most famous of rulers, such as Elizabeth the First. She gave a famous speech. I learnt it off pat when I did history at school. Let's see… "I know I have the body but of a weak, feeble woman. But I have the heart and stomach of a king, and of a king of England too." That says it all to me. Now, shall we do a bit of research on Wu anyway, as you've forced yourself to read her letter?'

'Good idea, yes, absolutely.'

Helena poured the tea and as they sipped, she searched for articles on her phone. Once more the references contradicted each other, for example on the role of women in ancient Chinese society, who it was Wu favoured as her successor, and the extent of her cruelty. In a centuries' long game of Chinese Whispers, it was impossible to find the empirical truth. Perhaps this letter was the key to unlock that truth once and for all.

'The biographies written shortly after her death depicted her as a murderous self-serving sex maniac,' said Helena. 'And the fact they didn't inscribe anything on her memorial stone despite her wishes, speaks volumes.'

'Absolutely. It's only more recently historians have been kinder to her. Rather impressive all she achieved but you wouldn't wish to get on the wrong side of her.'

'I was interested to read she wore men's clothing,' said Helena. I wonder if that was her preference, or if she felt forced.'

Cynthia glanced at Clare's boots in the hallway. 'Quite possibly. My Clare liked to dress unconventionally as you've probably gathered from the coat of hers that I wear. She went through a punky New Romantic-y phase back in the eighties. I wear her stuff now to feel closer to her, such as those boots, those big clompy, oh what are they called?'

'*DMs?*'

'Yes. I imagine I am walking in her footsteps, and it helps keep her memory alive, daft old thing that I am. Although I must say, they are surprisingly comfy.'

'Well, for what it's worth I think you look great in her things. And keeping her memory alive is lovely. I could take a leaf out of Clare's book and start to dress a bit more, well, imaginatively. I've never had the confidence.'

Cynthia stared out onto the garden for a few moments. Then, she gestured towards the box of letters.

'Would you mind picking that up?'

Helena lugged the box onto the table, her wrist reminding her this was not the kind of thing it should be doing.

'When I thought I had upset you, I assumed they'd never see the light of day again.'

'Oh dear, how sad.'

With effort, Cynthia stood and slowly opened the lid of the box. She leant over it, her hands placed on either side of it as she gazed inside.

'There's something I wish to tell you, dear. I feel silly now that I didn't say anything earlier, but I wasn't sure what we were going to do with all this. In each plastic cover, included with the letter, there was a hand-written note from Clare. Every single letter had one. I removed them all when I knew you were coming over the first time, that's why the letters were all strewn everywhere, as I'd only just finished when you arrived. I am sorry but I couldn't bear the idea of anyone seeing Clare's handwriting and touching her things, let alone allowing her notes to leave the house.'

'You've got nothing to feel silly about, Cynthia. Honestly, I love how close you and Clare were.'

'But you're not merely anyone. I wish for you to see Clare's notes. Some of them are simply the name of the woman who wrote the letter and her dates, and others offer more detail. I haven't read them all, I got too upset. But I would like you to, if you think you'd be interested.'

With great care, Cynthia gathered a bundle and placed it on the table.

'Here they are.'

'Oh Cynthia.'

Helena peered down at the stack of torn off lined notepad pages, envelopes, scraps of paper and old receipts with scribbled notes all-over them. Clare apparently wrote in haste on whatever was to hand.

She looked back over to Cynthia, noticing her breathing was becoming increasingly rapid as she steadied herself against the side of the box. Helena, worried that Cynthia was on the verge of another attack, looked around for the linctus.

'Let's write the book!' Cynthia said, her face suddenly animated and bright.

'I'm sorry?'

'The book! Let's sort these letters properly and match them with their notes. That'll help us with the research. Then we can select our preferred ones to include in a book.'

Helena paused as she tried to find the right words. 'It's a lovely idea, really it is. But Cynthia, I wouldn't have the first clue. And I don't really have…'

'The time? We must make sure you do. I'll pay you. Yes, that's it, I'll pay you to do the work, and we'll get in an editor or a historian or whoever we need to help. The salary you get at the library, I'll match it, and more if necessary. I'm sitting on all this money and all these things. I can sell the art and the ornaments. We can get you enrolled in classes on writing if they would help too. Oh, please, dear, do say you'll consider it.'

An idea had apparently popped fully formed into Cynthia's head. It was quite a sight, watching this woman in her eighties, normally pale and frail, all at once talking at speed and full of verve, as if an energy pack inside her had been switched on. Helena tried to choose her words carefully, to let Cynthia down gently.

'It's a wonderful suggestion Cynthia, and I'm flattered, honestly I am…'

'Lovely. That's settled then.'

Helena gave up. Cynthia seemed so enthused, she decided she may as well play along while she was on leave. The idea obviously delighted Cynthia, plus this little hobby was a welcome distraction from her life of emptiness. She would come clean and turn down the offer. But not yet.

Over the coming days, they managed to finish collating all the letters into date order, and began matching Clare's notes to them. There were over a hundred and fifty altogether – of different lengths and spanning thousands of years.

Because Cynthia tired easily, they divided their days between working, leisurely lunches and quiet moments, during which they read, sat listening to the clocks, or put on one of Cynthia's classical records. She had quite a collection.

'I haven't listened to any music for a while. Since Clare,' said Cynthia. 'It didn't feel right. But now it does, because you are here, dear.'

Each afternoon when Cynthia had a nap, Helena amused herself. She loved mooching around and Cynthia was glad to let her explore. In the lounge, between an upright piano and a pile of photo albums stacked high on the floor, there was a glass fronted wooden cabinet with a sunrise pattern on the front. Inside was a collection of assorted glass vases and dishes of many shapes, colours and sizes. She preferred those with iridescent purples and greens, with detailed carvings, and with hand-painted details. One afternoon she carefully opened the cabinet and read the names carved on some of the pieces. Lalique, Lotz, Galle, Moorcroft. Many more similar items were dotted around the room on bookshelves and on the mantelpiece, on every available surface. And on the wall were dozens of paintings and pictures. It was similar to being in a museum.

On the Friday afternoon of her week off, Helena finished pairing Clare's notes with the letters, only to find she had one letter and one note left over which didn't appear to match. This particular letter had caught Helena's eye while she was sorting, because of the name at the top. She opened the plastic pocket to find there were, in fact, two letters inside.

Chapter Twelve

James

To the Directors of the Medical Board
Sirs,

I have been informed of your plans to relieve me of my duties under the new Medical Act and I am writing to explain why this is a preposterous and unjust idea. I am healthy in body and of sound mind. My many accomplishments over fifty years of service are evidence of my abilities and I have an unrivalled breadth and wealth of experience. I attach for your information the *Memorandum of the Services of Dr James Barry Inspector General of Hospitals.* In it you will see a list of my accomplishments from the age of fourteen when I first entered service. There is simply no valid reason why I should not continue with my most important duties. My skills as a surgeon in the British Army are unparalleled, and have been required across the Empire, from South Africa to Jamaica and from Malta to the Crimea. Outside my duties as an Army Surgeon, I achieved many more significant successes. For example, in 1826, I developed new techniques resulting in the first caesarean surgery where both mother and child survived.

My attributes extend far beyond medical expertise. Achievements in the many communities I served include campaigning for improved sanitation, improving access to clean water for rich and poor, developing rules for the humane treatment of patients, demanding improvements to the living conditions and diets for soldiers, and working to secure them recreational facilities and libraries.

Am I therefore not a man worthy of more respect? I suspect Miss Nightingale or one of the other young ladies who have taken exception to me may be behind this, badgering you to force my resignation. They conceive and circulate inaccurate and inflamed accusations concerning my personage.

I accept you must remove any doctor who is not fit for the job but to imply I am one who fits that criterion is a great insult to me, and is not in the best interests of medicine.

I strongly advise that you reconsider your position.

Yours,

Dr James Barry.

'Hang on a minute, what's going on?' said Helena to herself. 'Why is there a letter from a man all of a sudden? Ok, let's read the one with it and then see if it makes any sense. Did these people know each other or something?'

Dear Arthur,

I hope you are settled in Spain, darling. That ghastly trial is long behind us now, and I am writing to see if we might possibly be friends again.

You knew my history when we met, but the pressure got to you. This was even before we were married, when the Sunday People outed me so unceremoniously. I have always blamed the Mirror group takeover you know – they were desperate for a bit of juicy gossip to boost their sales, and boy, did they find it.

Darling, we were in love once upon a time, weren't we? I believe with all my heart you loved me. We had such contrasting pasts, me a Liverpool lass, doing my stint in the navy and then becoming a model, while you were born into aristocracy, a Baron no less! But in the early days you loved me for who I was. I was different. I was completely honest with you concerning everything I had gone through physically and mentally to get where I was. Who I was.

And then it all got incredibly ugly. It's a paradox, isn't it, that when well-meaning folks work hard to openly discuss "issues" so they become more acceptable, the reverse can be the result, as more controversy can be created instead. That's what happened to us. People like me were thrown into the spotlight, suddenly scrutinised. I became an issue. And because I was married to you, dear, we were prime headline fodder. I do appreciate how it all got too much.

Honestly, I considered it fair I should receive a little income from you after our marriage ended. I still believe we could have settled privately. But no, the solicitors on both sides had a field day with us, didn't they? And, of course, my name got dragged through the mud in the process. I still stand by what I said then - that I was treated in a degrading and inhumane way – they set out to humiliate and discredit me entirely. It triggered my nerves again, I can tell you. I went to a tremendously dark place emotionally, as I used to in my youth. I watched with horror afterwards at how our case acted as a catalyst for such hatefulness and ignorance. I felt powerless to do much, and I simply wanted to retreat, get on with my life, try and put it back together.

You know, if we had waited a few years, we could have had a divorce by mutual consent, which might have saved us both a lot of heartache. Anyhow, it was all long ago as I say, and life has been much better on the whole. I'm still friendly with my second husband Jeffrey, and I thought, wouldn't it be nice if we could be friendly again too?

I always say, if you can be anything, be kind. And if you can't be kind, be silent. It's my mantra if you like, darling. Maybe it's because I am a Liverpool lass through and through.

My life is full and pleasurable these days. I've been writing and have started getting involved in politics. Yes, me! There are a few LGBT groups now and I want to use my voice where I can, if it will help anyone. One day we might even get legal protection. Wouldn't that be marvellous?

Hope you are living it up. Viva Espana!

All my love,

April xxx

Chapter Thirteen

April

'Nope, still completely confused,' said Helena to herself. 'Thank god for Clare's notes.'

Clare's note on April must have gone unnoticed by Cynthia when she'd gone through removing them all, as April's letter was underneath James in the same pocket. Helena read the note on James first.

Born Margaret Bulkley. FTM. Father a grocer. Evidence suggests he lived as a man his entire adult life in public and private and therefore was trans rather than dressing as a man to succeed as has been claimed. Some co-workers were suspicious, including Florence Nightingale. Fascinating, but do NOT include in a book about women. Use James as reference point only. Save instead for a project including other trans men – Anne Lister etc.

A row of red asterisks had been penned across the top, written with such force they had dented the paper, as if Clare had drawn them a moment ago, and would be back soon to resume her studies.

Helena opened her laptop and searched for James Barry. She learnt it would have been inconceivable in eighteenth century England for a woman to become a doctor, as women were deemed incapable of mastering the intellectual and physical challenges required. Their minds were not considered suited to the rigour of academic study, and their bodies were not thought strong enough to hold patients down and perform the brutal act of surgery without anaesthetic. James Barry had succeeded despite being born female. Some sources suggested that James was trans, as Clare had concluded. FTM stood for Female to Male. Others claimed "she" was just a woman in disguise who wanted to do a man's work. Had James' wishes been granted, his secret would have died with him, as he requested to be buried wearing the clothes in which he died. But his wishes were not granted, and when the truth emerged, it became headline news across the Empire.

Clare's note on April read:

April Ashley. Pioneer trans woman in the 20th century. Successful model and socialite. Fucking gorgeous. Had full *surgery – one of the first – performed by Georges Burou, French gynaecologist in Casablanca. Hence the phrase "Going to Casablanca," which sounds exotic but the procedure was incredibly painful apparently and left her suffering for years. This letter was to her ex-husband the Hon Arthur Corbett: Eton-educated and son and heir of Lord Rowallan. She went on to campaign for queer rights and the environment. Worked for Greenpeace, an art gallery etc. Awarded the MBE. Wish I could have met her.*

Helena found photos of April online, including one from the 1960s, a black and white image from her modelling days presumably. Clare was right, she was fucking gorgeous. Eyes to become lost in, and perfect skin waiting to be explored and caressed. Helena hadn't explored or caressed anyone for a long time, or had the same done to her. She was resigned to the fact no-one would find her the least bit desirable now anyway. She stared down at her ageing body. Everything had gone decidedly south and saggy over the years, and she'd passively stood by and let it.

Helena felt a flicker of emotion, and decided to say out loud words she'd never spoken. She rehearsed how she might go about it. "Cynthia, there's something I want to tell you..." "Cynthia, I think I might be..." "Cynthia, how would you feel if I was to tell you..." "Cynthia, can I ask you about Clare?" Yes, that would be a satisfactory way in.

When Cynthia woke from her nap, Helena had returned all the letters to the box and made tea, serving it with squares of home-made flapjack.

'Delicious as always, thank you,' remarked Cynthia.

'I like making things for you.' Helena sat forwards in her chair and gripped her arms around her chest as she leaned closer to Cynthia. 'Erm, may I ask you a bit about Clare? If it doesn't upset you?'

'No dear. It might upset me but it's good to talk, and it's so nice you wish to ask.'

'I am really interested in her. It's, well it's… I wanted to ask you… it concerns her personal life.'

'Go ahead. It's alright, Helena, you can ask me anything.'

'Thank you. Yes. It's um, it's…I remember you telling me Clare was a lesbian.'

'Yes, she was. But as I say, never found the right partner. There were one or two flings, but no-one to settle with.'

Helena shuffled on her chair, aware of her clumsiness. *Come on, you can do this, you're safe.*

'Well, the thing is, I've always been a bit confused regarding my own sexuality.'

'I thought as much, dear. But it wasn't my place to say anything until you were ready.'

'You did?'

'Call it a mother-figure's intuition.'

They both laughed. Helena suddenly knew exactly what it was she needed to say, right here, right now. At the age of fifty-five, she was going to do it.

'As a girl I always wore boyish clothes and still do, as you're well aware. I've never talked to anyone about my sexuality though. The thing is, I think I like men and women. I think I might be bisexual. But I'm not sure. I've been too inhibited to delve into my head or the internet to find out more, and I haven't ever had a partner I could trust to explore and share those types of feelings. I've kind of shut that aspect away all my life. Isn't it ridiculous?'

'No, not at all. Clare was the same, and she had a loving mother. Sorry if I am speaking out of turn, but it sounds as if your mother didn't treat you very kindly, dear.' Cynthia's genuine expression of concern was a huge comfort, giving Helena the strength to carry on talking.

'No, it's fine. I have kept it all bottled up long enough. Yes, my mum wasn't great. She never physically beat me, but hit me with her tongue. She could say extremely cruel things. Told me I'd never amount to anything, said I'd never find a man with my mousey appearance and drab clothing, that kind of thing. She could be really sarcastic too, saying things such as, "Oh look, here she is, my beeee-oooo-tiful daughter." And she was drunk a lot. I learnt at a young age my feelings didn't matter. I learnt to shut up. I more or less brought myself up.'

Helena worried she'd gone too far. She'd never talked about her upbringing and wasn't sure whether it was appropriate to talk about. Also, she might upset Cynthia by mentioning the drinking.

'It appears from what you've said you absolutely did bring yourself up,' said Cynthia. 'It's no surprise if you struggle, if you are inhibited, after such a childhood. It's prevented you from giving yourself the time and space to consider your own needs.'

Helena hadn't consciously ever been aware there was weight holding her down, but she could sense it was lifting. She was no longer being crushed under it.

'I can't tell you what a relief it is telling you this.'

'We are building trust, dear. It's to be treasured. It marks true friendship.'

'Absolutely. Erm, I hope you don't mind me asking, but I noticed your photo albums in the lounge. I'd really like to look through them with you... Would that be ok? I'd really like to get to know Clare, if you would trust me?'

Without speaking, Cynthia heaved herself out of the chair. Helena guessed she'd pushed too much again. Cynthia walked to the door and gestured towards Helena to follow her. Into the living room they went.

'I hardly come in here these days, said Cynthia, as they sat on the generous leather sofa. 'This room was always where life really happened for Clare and me. The piano, the endless talks we had in here. When I was a child, this was the room for reading and quiet. While Clare was growing up, it turned into her playroom. My mother disapproved of too many toys out at once; I had to bring down the things we'd play with each day. When I was teaching and she was still alive, Mother would retreat to the dining room. That's where I have retreated to now I suppose. As for the photo albums, I haven't so much as peeped inside them, haven't been able to. The one photo I do display, the degree ceremony one, it's part of the furniture really, it's always been there. I should have brought more out.'

'Maybe you weren't ready,' said Helena. Cynthia nodded. 'Might you be ready now?'

'With you here, yes, I believe so. You've been kind enough and brave enough to share your personal life with me. It's appropriate I should do the same.'

'Thank you. Thank you so much.'

'Let me think…' Cynthia's thin and shaky index finger guided Helena to find a particular album. Helena found it and brought it back over to the sofa. It opened out like a book. On either side, photos were slotted into transparent pouches which could be flipped over, allowing notes to be written on the back.

'Ah yes, this is the one. Oh, look at her. Never happier than when she was travelling, or regaling me with stories of her travels, or writing about them.' Cynthia flipped through a few pictures.

'Here she is, sitting on the foot of Ramesses II in Egypt. Can you imagine how tall the statue must have been when it was standing, with a foot that size? She loved it there. Ah, see this one? It's inside Nefertari's tomb. Those colours! And here, these ones are in Spain. I remember now, she went to see the works by Ende. I expect she wrote on the back. …yes look, here we are. There's a picture Ende describes in her letter, the miniature.'

They pored over the pictures and remarkably, Cynthia could recall where nearly all of them were taken. It was bitter-sweet to watch her as she relived these moments from her daughter's life. They were close, shared joyful memories, and now Clare was gone. In stark contrast, she and her mother were never close, and yet she was still alive. She may as well be gone as far as Helena was concerned.

They had read quite a few of the letters properly by now and it was clear many of the photos were associated with the women Clare had been researching. Some, such as the picture by Ramesses' giant foot, were of Clare smiling for the camera.

'She'd ask people to take her photo. Always travelled solo.'

'How amazing!' said Helena when they had finished looking. 'I wonder if she travelled to see where the letters were written, or whether she found the letters during research on her travels.'

'Interesting question. I'm afraid I don't know the answer. Or can't recall. Either way, I imagine Clare conducted very thorough research. She used to save things on a laptop but I'm afraid it got sent to a charity to be reconditioned. Oh, I probably shouldn't have done that, should I?'

Helena put the photo album back in its place. As they returned to the dining room, she speculated to herself what might have been on Clare's computer. Perhaps she started writing the book, explaining how she discovered all the letters. Hey ho, it was too late now.

Cynthia sat down at the dining table and gestured to the box of letters. 'Perhaps you could take a handful home to read at the weekend? From now on, you must choose whichever letters you wish to read and research. After all, this is your project now. You have sorted all Clare's notes I believe? Take those too. You'll need them for when you start writing.'

'Thank you. I will cherish the chance to read them. But Cynthia, I'm afraid I must say, I don't think of it as my project. I'm sorry if this disappoints you.' Cynthia's face fell. *You stupid woman. How clumsy can you be? All Cynthia wants is for you to share in her enthusiasm and you've spoilt it.*

'I'm sorry Cynthia, that came out wrong. Can we talk more next time we meet, is that ok? I can see you're tired after this week. We've done a lot. And I've so enjoyed it. I'll take a few, and come back in a couple of days, alright?'

'Yes dear. I have loved having you here this week. Have had a good weekend.'

Helena collected a selection of letters from the medieval period, aware that Cynthia watched her every move. Cynthia had been accepting and open when they'd discussed sexuality, but remained unusually and unnervingly quiet as Helena put the letters carefully in her bag and gathered her coat and scarf. For Helena, there was no project, other than one of reading through a bunch of fascinating letters. She supposed Cynthia was disappointed in her. It was going to be extremely difficult to tell her she wouldn't be writing the book. It was a ridiculous idea. She hadn't written anything since she was at school, apart from nursing exams and reports for project managers. How on earth did that qualify her to write a book? Her aim was simply to read the letters for pleasure, with no pressure. Surely Cynthia would come to understand.

After an emotional Friday, Helena retired to bed with a medieval maiden, hoping this would distract her from her own thoughts.

Chapter Fourteen

Hildegard

I see you slumbering, your little body resting after another day of study and prayer. But your mind is toiling, always at work even as you sleep. I have known you all your life and yet you have never met me in your ten years on the earth. You hear this message clearly though you may not comprehend it all as yet. You are the seer of visions and a conduit for messages from the angels and from the Lord himself, and I travel as if an angel into your soul to deliver important valedictions. Heed my words, dear child and all will be well.

Hildegard, you have been at the monastery of Disibodenberg for two years, and you are naturally curious where your life will lead you, what God has in store for you. Sent as a tithe by your parents to study under the watchful guidance of Jutta, you already discern that you are different. You are doing admirably child, listening dutifully to Jutta and the noble womenfolk who care for you, and not questioning your parents' wisdom in surrendering you to this life.

By day, I see you sitting in your tiny sparsely furnished room with nothing but your studies and Jutta for company, being fed meagre meals through a tiny hatch. One meal a day in winter and two in summer renders you and Jutta frequently ill and malnourished. You have only a chink of outside light and you barely keep company with others. Your life is dominated by prayer and reading the Psalter, the book of psalms. Your mind is further nourished through studying Latin and music. All of this prepares for you for the life which is destined. By night, I watch you sleep, aware of your every dream. Your dreams are vivid and, so far, make little sense to you. Fear not, as all will be revealed.

You wonder why you possess little, when other girls of your standing live as princesses. But this is all to your advantage. With no worldly distractions, you are beginning to see the light within you. This light-force will guide you. Listen to the voices you hear, and take heed of the visions you see, dear child. Be not afraid of them. They are the foundations of your life.

The adults around you are not ready to comprehend the depths of your spirituality. To them, you are but a child. Tis true they observe you are special, but many young girls are sent on a similar path by their families, who believe their children are better cared for this way, and will be favoured in Heaven. Your parents believe it proper to sacrifice one tenth of their possessions to the Church, and as tenth child, it is you. But they know not who you are and the significance of your life. Only God and I hold this truth.

The number four will have great significance to you always, and it begins now. Tonight, as you lay alone in your bed, listen to these four lessons.

Here is the first lesson. You are born in the body of a girl. Accordingly, it will be harder for you to do all God has planned. Learn who to trust and your destiny will be secure. Jutta, Volmer the monk and Gottfried you can rely on. Volmer will be the first you will entrust with the truth of your visions, and he will support you to share them wisely. But not all men are to be trusted. Most consider themselves the superior sex, believing that only they are capable of achieving greatness. They will assume you to be frail in mind and in body, for so they have been told, taught as they are tis unacceptable for women to achieve status. To them, twould be impossible for us to concentrate in the presence of status, our cravings would overcome us so. They think us wicked, and temptresses. You shall develop the ability to steer your way through men's misunderstandings, to use your inner powers, strengths and senses until they listen. You must be meek to them, show humility that they may grant you opportunities. Though you perceive well the right course, and understand well the answers to questions you ask, you must seek their counsel. Write to the Popes for spiritual guidance, and write to the Kings and the Emperors for political advice. In the future, your Divine Feminine Wisdom will be accepted, but this will not be for many a year hence. Do as I advise, and you will make a difference for all women.

The second lesson is that there is more than one mission for you in this life, for you are destined to achieve greatness in many fields. As you grow, make sure to pursue many disciplines. Your study is presently limited to Jutta's offerings, but increasingly, you will learn to listen from within and from above. The studies you do now will form the beating heart from which will grow many channels of communication. Your soul will surely rise up and you will see right into the vaults of heaven. You will come to rely less and less on the teachings of others, and even on your own five senses as you develop the faith to listen only to your soul and to God.

When tis time, you will become a religious leader. Jutta will be prioress, and after her death, you shall take her place at Disibodenberg. Later, you will receive a calling to create and lead as abbotess a monastery for worship and education at Rupertsberg, overlooking the Rhine near Bingen. It currently stands ruined after the Norman destruction. The Abbot will obstruct you, preferring you to remain in his presence and under his jurisdiction, but you will prevail by going to the Archbishop and obtaining the necessary permissions. You will receive criticism and ridicule from plenty of men and even from your own nuns. You will be called a foolish uneducated woman, and they will accuse you of being inhabited by evil spirits. Undeterred, you will act consistently and with strength until they come to believe the words you speak are derived directly from the Holy Spirit.

Once at Bingen, you will shine as a feminine religious leader, and your followers will love you for it. Your nuns will have the freedom to celebrate their femininity, wearing their hair long and flowing if they wish, and adorning themselves with decorations such as tiaras of flowers in their hair as emblems of blessed virgins in Heaven. They will enjoy the same freedoms and liberties as men. Eventually, your community will grow large which will necessitate the building of another place of worship, at Eibingen. Once established as a trusted religious leader, you will go on four great journeys of religious importance, sharing your wisdoms across the land and becoming a leading light across Europe, not only in the Rhineland or Franconia. You will be recognised widely as a seer and as a leader, respected far and wide for your visions and your many achievements.

Your creativity will extend to all the arts. Notably, your musical talents will be towering. You will write songs for your nuns which sound as if the angels themselves created them. The sublime notes emanating from your mind will soar and spiral, their complexity unrivalled. They will free the minds of anyone who hears them. Your songs will be sung far beyond the boundaries of Bingen. Poetry will flow out of you resembling a river of divine ecstasy gushing forth. Your eighty chants will celebrate the Lord's creation, and will be used for meditation and healing, for prayer and enlightenment, delighting all who hear them. Each will be given a musical setting composed by you, in your collected "Symphonia Armonie Celestium Revelationum." You will create great artworks to illustrate your many talents. These will not be limited to religious iconography, but will include depictions of the cycles of the seasons, even the whole universe. You will depict many of your visions with your glorious art in order to preserve them forever.

You will become a great scholar across a wide scope of disciplines. You will study science, becoming an expert in natural history, especially botany, and you will further the advancement of knowledge in medical practice. You will offer healing through your combined skills in medicine, the power of plants, and the strength of your spiritual energy. You will be celebrated for your expertise in natural healing. You will help others appreciate the importance of the sun and of all nature, and realise that without it, humankind would surely perish. You will consider how all the world is connected, and you will make great advances in the study of patterns in nature, especially through the number four. You will forge hitherto unknown connections between the four cardinal humours of blood, phlegm, choler and melancholy and expand on the understanding of them. You will study the four elements of earth, air, fire and water and interpret how these connect to the humours. After your many years of near starvation at Disibodenberg, you will teach the people how to live a more healthy life through adequate nutrition. You will show how a balanced life of herbal remedies, cleanliness, diet, proper sleep and a healthy mind will keep the bodily humours in harmony, leading to healthier outcomes.

You will hail the awakening of "greening power" as the basis for humans to protect and care for the world. You will teach that greenness is the cosmic life force, the Divine in nature. And you will show how music and greenness are intertwined as your music elevates the soul in praising the source of life. They will mock you, not comprehending what they see. Be patient. Eventually, you will be revered for teaching that nature and science can live agreeably with the Church, and that nature itself is a life force.

You will become a philosopher and a visionary, spreading wisdom from your prophetic visions. You will introduce the Feminine side of divinity and reveal how the Divine is both feminine and masculine, and how both sides are essential for wholeness. You will confirm that God resembles a cosmic egg, both male and female, pulsing with love. In your philosophy "Liber Vitae Meritorum," the book of Life's Merits, you will expand on the theme of the human struggle between virtue and vice. You will show how God's presence and love is expressed in many ways including through female sexuality, where the female orgasm is a spiritual force holding the man's seed. You will explain the merit of women when those around you doubt it. You will challenge men when necessary.

The people will be left in no doubt you are a woman of distinction.

The third lesson is that your life and your teachings must be preserved. At first, you will resist your visions, but after your Great Vision - of which I shall speak more - you will have a change of heart. You must write profusely. In generations to come, your words will endure. Volmer, the trusted monk, will become your assistant and scribe. He will travel alongside you faithfully and compassionately, and will ensure your life's work is captured in the written form. After him, Gottfried will scribe your dictations, including your "Vita" in later life. All your work will be written in the most beautiful of languages, the Latin tongue, as befits their majesty. You will create books on theology, medicine and the natural world, and you will write letters, hundreds of them. You will become immortal through your words, in character with all the great scholars of history.

You will write "Physica," a scientific and medical encyclopaedia including many of your herbal remedies, and "Causae et Curae" concerning the diseases of body and mind and their cures. You will write on all aspects of human life and wellbeing, and will not shy away from sexuality in your theories, a subject seldom addressed, particularly the sexuality of women. You will create your own alphabet (Litterae ignotae) and vocabulary (Lingua ignota) to demonstrate your versatility and your humour, and moreover to quickly record in note form your concepts and visions before they are fully transcribed in the Latin. The music and poetry you create must be written down, that it may be shared now and forever.

Finally, and most importantly, **the fourth lesson** tonight concerns your visions. For now, you must keep them secret. Though they be mighty powerful in light and immeasurable in scale, the world is not yet ready for them. You must be strong, girl. Let them in, embrace their power, and remember them. They frighten you with their intensity, but fear not; you are chosen as a messenger on earth. Know that your fear will be rewarded, however much the visions trouble you. Tell no-one what you see, what you experience. They are to be shared only once you are established as a great woman. If you declare them too soon you will be dismissed as a mere girl and more tragically you will be branded a witch with visions deemed black magic or maleficium, presented to you by a demon or the Devil himself. Your life would be ended before it had barely begun.

Wait until you receive your Great Vision. There will be a blinding light, different from, and fiercer than all preceding it. The strength of the vision will overpower your body causing an affliction lasting many days and nights, and your body will burn. You must not be afraid. As the Virgin Mary did when the Angel Gabriel came to her, open your body and soul completely to its message. Everything thus far beheld will lead to that moment and in that moment, all will become clear. You will receive profound insight seldom bestowed onto any man or woman. Be reassured as you receive this wisdom, although your body will be in pain, you will not suffer the indignity of ecstasies. Instead, you will receive the Lord calmly and wholly.

After the Great Vision, you will seek the advice of the Archbishop of Mainz, and a committee of men will confirm the authenticity of your visions. This is when Volmer the monk will be appointed to help you write.

Oh, and write you shall! In addition to all the writings aforementioned, you will write a work based on 26 of your visions and will call the work "Scivias." In it, you will impart the way, the path to the Lord. Word of this great work will reach far and wide, to the Pope himself, who will send for a copy. Once you receive his endorsement, your place as a woman of great substance will be secure and you shall be known as The Sibyl Of The Rhine. "Scivias" will take you ten years, and after its completion, your writings will become prolific. Your brain and your heart will be inflamed with creativity. To celebrate the opening of your convent, you will write a play with music more magnificent than anything heard before. "Ordo Virtutum" will be its name and it will teach of the struggles of the soul. It will depict the virtues by which you live your life, and rejoice in the defeat of the Devil. He will be the only who does not sing, being incapable of producing music, as it is the true praise of God. Your final volume of works based on your visions will be a trilogy: on the activity of God "De Operatione Dei"; on divinity "Liber Divinorum Operum"; and on books of the Bible.

You will oftentimes become bedridden by your visions, but you must not let this deter you, for tis when you are sick you shall receive the greatest visions. They will become part of your life as a Leading Light, and from them everything will emanate, dictating how you live. You already envision yourself to be different. Your destiny is to remain so.

I know all of this to be true because I have seen it with my own eyes. Your future is glorious. If you heed my words, everything I tell you will transpire, but only if you listen to me and do it all at the pace I dictate for you. You must learn to reign in that steely determination and singlemindedness, otherwise you will be perceived as arrogant or mad, and they will not listen to you. Be humble, be gentle, and all will be well.

The Bible says no woman is to teach or have authority over men. Wretched as you are to bear a woman's name, those words do not apply to you as you will not be teaching from books; you will be teaching directly from the word of God. No man will be bold enough to challenge the word of God!

Hildegard, this vision is near completion. Through my umbra viventis lucis, the reflection of the living Light, I come to you. I am old, nearing my eightieth year, and residing in Bingen as I have for many years. Still, the multitudes flock to me, seeking my prophesies and prayers. They say I possess rare gifts never before seen, and I am the first woman since the Virgin Mary to have these gifts bestowed upon me by God. Still, I blush at their proclamations.

I will travel to your mind often dear child and reside there as do the angels and the Lord himself. I will guide you and protect you, always, as will they. You will not remember all the words I give you now, but fear not, I will return to you throughout your life and guide you, that you shall follow the light.

   Hildegard

Chapter Fifteen

Christine

The next morning was a bleary one. All her life, Helena had wrestled in her head and with the bedclothes as she tried to get to sleep and then to stay asleep, and lately it was getting worse. Reading occasionally helped, but after reading about Hildegard, her mind was too busy buzzing to rest. Did Hildegard actually believe she was able to communicate through the power of her mind? Did others from her era claim to have such powers? And quite apart from that, how on earth did she manage to do so much with one life?

Helena knew little of medieval history, and with nothing better to do, decided to spend her Saturday morning doing research. First, she read Clare's note.

Hildegard of Bingen (1098 – 1179) Sainted in 2012. Lived during the Holy Roman Empire, when very few women were afforded any status. Hildegard was a polymath comparable with da Vinci, but was largely forgotten until her writings, art and music were rediscovered. Letter implies she didn't 100% believe her visions were from God. Reflection of the extremes women had to go to in patriarchal societies to stand a chance of being noticed. Her visions could have been migraines, according to notable scholars and medics.

It was easy to find examples of Hildegard's music, art and writing online. Helena listened to a piece of music as she re-read the letter. It was achingly beautiful and gave her goosebumps. Helena appreciated how people might believe sounds this magical had to have come from a divine place rather than the mind of a mere mortal, especially a woman. She felt sure she had seen a few of Hildegarde's pictures in Clare's photo collection. Like Ende's, they were full of detail, colour and life. They reminded her of works by Gustav Klimt, one of the few artists she knew. "The six days of creation" for example, featured an abstract sun, stars of differing sizes on a lined black background, and intricate patterns around the border. Yes, it was remarkably Klimt. No. Klimt was remarkably Hildegard.

Later that day, Helena arrived back at her little flat after stocking up on food shopping. The area was still grotty. The flat was still small and remained stubbornly on the top floor of the house. But as she entered her little space and shut the door on the world, she appreciated at least she had this. She could come and go as she pleased, and could keep it as she wanted. Scanning the space, she realised it was pretty dirty and really rather messy. The walls could do with a lick of paint. Funny how she'd noticed the library staff room's shabbiness but never before considered the appearance of her own home. She found her old hoover at the back of the cupboard, wedged in behind unpacked boxes of books and the few ornaments she possessed. *Maybe I should get round to putting those up. I've got a few shelves. Apart from a lamp and the remote control, all they've got on them is nearly a year's worth of dust. Oh my god, there's a duster hanging off the hoover handle. It must be a sign!*

Over the rest of the weekend, Helena amused herself with doing a bit of cleaning, and reading the other letters she'd brought home from Clare's medieval finds, continuing her own basic research just out of interest.

Matilda of Flanders was William the Conqueror's wife, and of more senior rank birth wise. When William was preparing to invade England, Matilda spent money from her own wealth to prepare a ship for him. After the conquest of England, she was crowned alongside him at Westminster Abbey but spent most of her life in Normandy. The letter was to her son Robert giving him money and imploring him not to tell William.

Margaret I of Denmark aimed to unite Scandinavia. She was married at ten years old and for part of her life effectively ruled solo, in the same way as Wu Zhao. She started a union between Denmark and Norway which would last four centuries, and gained notoriety for suppressing the church in order to maintain royal power. The letter from Margaret was to one of her court officials, and was business-related.

Isabella I and Ferdinand II of Aragon were the first joint Spanish monarchs, reminding Helena of Nefertari and Ramesses in Ancient Egypt. Isabella's letter referred to the explorer Christopher Columbus, to whom she had offered finances for his 1492 voyage. Helena worked out this was probably Columbus' maiden voyage to America. In her letter to a family member, Isabella predicted Columbus would fail.

Helena was interested to read the letters, and they were obviously great women, but there was a little niggling notion in the back of her mind. A lot of the letters were from queens and women of high status. Helena was more drawn to the ones from women who were not born into privilege or who found an alternative way to be successful. Women such as Theodora, Hildegard and Ende. Attached to the letters from these three queens, Clare's notes were annotated with red question marks. Maybe she felt the same. Helena was intrigued to read Christine's next, whose note had a big green tick at the top.

'Thank you, Clare,' she said as she pulled the letter out of its pocket.

To Thomas Montague, most honourable patron,

I, Christine de Pizan present humbly this most recent book penned by me entitled "The Book of the City of Ladies." You will observe straightway it is a departure from my earlier works. Being self-taught in the art of writing and being a woman, it has taken a while to establish a following who would welcome works more erudite, philosophical, and literary. You are one of the worthy people who has helped it to be so.

In truth, I never intended to be a writer, though I was well-read in numerous fields including history, science and philosophy. I was young and content to be wife and mother. Fortunes changed when my dear father died and my beloved husband Etienne was taken by Plague, leaving me without the financial means to support my family. Etienne was a decent man and encouraged me to read and study, unlike many husbands at the French Court, but he left me with no access to income. For thirteen years I fought for financial compensation, but was ignorant of all my husband's arrangements and was beaten by bureaucracy. To this day I am angered to think on it. I began to write poetry and found it a great comfort.

It was fortuitous for me when my poems proved most popular at Court and, soon enough, they were earning me sufficient income to support my children, mother and niece. Gradually, I learnt to think as a man, to be a man, and this helped them accept me the more. I came to understand the frivolous ways of Court and how to make my place. Yet in my heart I longed to write works of more breadth than those lamentations on the loss of my love, and I yearned to be accepted as a woman capable of such.

I taught myself how to manage my affairs and how to progress with the craft of writing. I produced for them that which they yearned to read and did this for a while longer earning money and respect. A woman poet was such a novelty! I gained notoriety, enabling me to find honourable patrons such as you, kind sir. Like most artists, I need my patronage to survive. Though a foreigner in France, I have been accepted and presented at Court, and am most gratified to benefit from the Court Library. In my home country we are but a land of small city states; there is no Royal Court as befits us here in France or over in your England. Once accepted graciously and fully, I began to write more important works, and was humbled when they were well received, even by your own King who was impressed by my "Letter of Othea to Hector" sent to him in a special edition.

Hence to this my most recent book. I mused about it as I wrote my last, "The Tale of the Rose," in response to Jean de Meun's offering. His views of women I could not let stand without repudiation. He calls us vile temptresses and the source of all evil in the world. I once believed I would have to be a man to compete with men, but now I realise it is not so, and I demonstrate how women are as worthy.

My new book is written as allegory. In it, I come to the aid of three women who are named Reason, Justice and Rectitude. Together, we build a city. I use the method of loci to place the reader in the story as I lay forth the tale of how women can achieve anything they seek if they receive the same opportunities as the men, in particular education. I present a logical argument that women are to be appreciated and defended, and I recall past achievements of women to illustrate the points made. To quote from the book, "Neither the loftiness nor the lowliness of a person lies in the body according to the sex, but in the perfection of conduct and virtues." I do not shy away from criticising and holding to account those men who have throughout history condemned women as inferior, wicked and lacking ability. I poured everything into writing this volume, and wonder often if I will ever write again!

Yet, even now, the three women speak to me, urging me to write another volume for women, to instruct them how to care for themselves in all respects: their families, their homes and their business affairs. I would use my own experiences and bring all my learning to it. As one of my faithful patrons, would you see fit to support such an undertaking?

I am greatly unsettled by the unrest in France and the continued war between France and England, and fear the spread of war into Europe. I do not know what I would do if matters were to become even worse. I hope things fare well for you and your wife, the Lady Eleanor, in England after the death of your father, and that you succeed in becoming his successor as Earl of Salisbury if it is your wish.

Your humble servant,
Christine de Pizan

Other letters had impressed Helena, but this one left her dumfounded. She read it out loud again to absorb its contents further. "Neither the loftiness nor the lowliness of a person lies in the body according to the sex, but in the perfection of conduct and virtues." Inspired, Helena wrote this quote down and pinned it onto to her bedside table before reading Clare's note.

Born in Venice, Italy, late fourteenth century. Often referred to as the first woman of letters, and considered by many to be the first to write about feminism. Certainly one of the first European women to earn a living from writing. Her body of work provided unique insights into women's lives in medieval Europe.

Married at 15, widowed at 25. Earlier love poems include Alone am I. Progressed from these, which read like greetings card sentiments, to literary masterpieces – because she was given the opportunity. This letter would have been written in 1405. She did write again – her famous "Book of the Three Virtues" was written later that year. And she remained prolific. "The Book of the Body Politic" was published in 1407 where she set out a political treatise analysing late Medieval customs and governments. "The Book of Peace" was written for the French Dauphin in 1413, during the Civil War, on how to govern. Wrote too the only book written on Joan of Arc in Joan's lifetime. A poem about a woman leading men.

Christine was acutely aware she lived in a period atrocious for women, yet she managed to become one of the most successful writers of her era. She didn't have any one patron – sought patronage from French royals but also elsewhere. Thomas Montagu did become 4th Earl of Salisbury. Got very involved in Hundred Years war and spent years in France, killed at the Siege of Orleans.

As the Hundred Years war intensified around her, Christine retreated to a convent. She managed to gain acceptance but had to really work for it. Could compare with the way Judy Chicago was treated on completion of the Dinner Table.

Helena searched "The Dinner Table." An installation created in the 1970s, it features a massive triangular table laid out with thirty-nine place settings for women from history, real and mythical. Among them are Theodora, Hildegarde and Christine. The floor below it names nearly a thousand more women. When it was first shown, it was heavily condemned by critics who accused it of being all sorts of things including vulgar, preachy and racist.

That night in bed, Helena tossed and turned as she deliberated about Clare's book. It needed to be written. These letters had to be seen, and Clare's project should be finished. Helena wasn't the person to do it though. She couldn't begin to conceive how to write a book and even if she did miraculously succeed in writing it, she wasn't resilient enough to take any criticism its publication might generate. Maybe she and Cynthia could collaborate with an experienced ghost-writer who could produce it for them. Chris might be able to advise her. Would Cynthia be disappointed though? No, she'd understand.

After a couple of hours of this, Helena had tested the fitted sheet to its limits as she'd thrashed around. It was no longer fulfilling its function of being fitted, so she had to drag herself out of bed and tuck the corners back in place. If only she could smooth out her mind as easily. *Right, woman. Try to get some bloody sleep.*

The following Monday, Helena got up earlier than usual, deciding she was going to make the most of her tidy flat. She prepared a cooked breakfast for the first time since she had lived there, and ate it sitting at the little fold-down kitchen table that she hadn't used before. She could see everything she owned from this position. The studio flat was a converted loft with sloping ceilings and skylights and ever since she'd lived there, it had retained an atmosphere of being a place where forgotten things were stored out of sight. Now she'd had a tidy up, it felt more homely. The carpet was no longer covered in debris, and the shelves were no longer covered in dust. Instead, they displayed her few books and her small collection of ornaments. She'd enjoyed handling these objects again as she put them out. Nothing was of any monetary value, but each object was significant. Her grandmother's little Peter Rabbit she had taken in to all her school exams for luck. Her grandfather's cigarette lighter in the shape of a beer bottle. A couple of porcelain *Wade Whimsies* animals she had bought with birthday present money in the arcade. An olive dish brought back from a trip to Rhodes. She didn't like olives, but she had a few coins left at the airport on the way home, and bought the dish as a reminder of the sun and the sea, and the little bit of sex she'd had with one of the olive-skinned waiters in the hotel.

At lunchtime, she sat with Lily and Chris in the staff room. They ate silently for a few minutes, and Helena was very conscious of her loud crunching and chewing as she ploughed through her salad. Trying to eat more healthily was noisy.

'So, it'll be interesting to see how effective these new Cilip guidelines are. Have you seen what's going on in America?' Chris asked. 'My books wouldn't stand a chance of being published in certain States.' Lily nodded and smiled.

Hang on a minute. Helena had always been a bit in awe of Chris. Well presented, brain the size of a planet, obviously. And a Dad too. But he'd written books? *And hang on another minute. How come Lily knows about these guidelines?* Helena had never heard of them.

'You've written books?' She blurted. 'Sorry, that was a bit abrupt. Of course I'm not surprised you've written books, but I wasn't aware.'

Chris smiled as he finished a mouthful and turned towards Helena. 'Oh, I've done a few children's books, involving a group of mischievous kids who get into scraps. It started, as a lot of kids' books do, with me inventing stories for the boys. I have a little series being published by a small indie publisher. Similar books to mine are being banned in the US, so it's reassuring we've got these guidelines.'

'Banned?' said Lily. 'No way!'

'Yes way I'm afraid. I read a report saying over ten thousand books were banned last year alone in public schools. Scanning the list of banned titles in Florida, it's shocking how many literary masterpieces are there. Books that mention abuse and slavery for example. It's as though they are attempting to whitewash history. Library staff are being pressured left right and centre. Hence the new guidelines for us here.'

Helena stared blankly at him.

'Oh, sorry Helena, of course you missed the briefing last week. Hang on a sec, I put the handout in my locker.'

Chris bounced up and strolled over to the lockers which lined one side of the staff room. Half of them no longer locked. Instead, their doors hung wide open and banged into staff as they edged past them to get to the door. Staff weren't supposed to claim lockers, or store anything in them overnight, but this was one rule Carol overlooked. A few chose to personalise theirs with stickers and photos or by taping their name on the front. Chris's was plain, but everyone knew it was his. His energy was quiet but powerful.

'Ah here we go. Carol said she'd make sure you got a copy, but I expect she forgot. She's got a lot on her plate.

You take this one and I'll make myself another copy.' Chris handed her the sheet.

Helena read the title: *Managing safe and inclusive public library services.*

'Thanks Chris. I'll read it properly later,' said Helena.

'It's reassuring to see in black and white there are no plans to create lists of banned titles here. We'd only have books banned – quite rightly - if they are breaking the law, The Equality Act for example. It's plain common sense in my opinion.'

This was all incredibly scary. If, and it was a big if, a huge if. A massive ten-foot-high neon red "IF". If she did get involved with this book, would the language and the subject matter in some of the letters be unacceptable? Quite apart from being criticised, would such a book be breaking the law? Get banned? *This is what you do, you silly cow. Shut up, you're not even writing it. And even if you did…*

At times, the only way to overcome the inner monologue was to talk over it. Unfortunately, in these moments, her mouth often started before her brain could catch up and filter.

'So, if…well…let's say I've been asked to write a book…'

'Have you? That's great!' said Chris.

'Yes, a friend has suggested we work on it together. But I've got absolutely no idea where to start. I don't think I can do it, and you saying all this concerning the law and everything. It's all a bit overwhelming.'

They finished their lunches while Helena explained what she and Cynthia had been doing. Her stress levels and guilt rose as she spoke. It was as if she was stealing Clare's ideas and Cynthia's memories. She asked Chris if he knew anything about ghost-writing and how she might arrange it.

'Sounds absolutely fascinating, Helena. And a lot of hard work. But there's no rush is there? You've got all the time in the world to decide which direction to go in.'

'Well, that's the thing. Cynthia's really not in good health. She'd love to get it done but she can't do it on her own, which is why she's asked me to help. She has convinced herself I am going to write it with her input.'

'Oh I see,' said Chris. 'Yes, you're in a difficult position there.'

Again, her mouth shot off before her brain had been consulted.

'Exactly. And, the thing is, I would be doing it for her. It should be done, but I just don't believe I can do it. And even if I did, I'm terrified of being banned or being criticised for anti-male or racist writing or something. I wouldn't want to offend anybody.' *Shit woman, what are you saying? You're rambling as usual.*

'Gosh, there's quite a lot to unpack there, Helena. I hope you don't mind me saying this, but authors don't tend to work in that way unless they are actually ghost writers. You have to take ownership of your book.'

'Yes, I know. There's my problem though. I can't.'

'Hmmm. It's tricky. On the one hand you need more time, and on the other you're feeling pressured to decide.'

'You're spot on. If I had longer to think, maybe I'd be ok.' *Or maybe I'd carry on going round in circles ad infinitum.*

'And as for criticism; the world we live in can be extremely divisive. I belong to various writers' groups on social media and there are some extremely angry people out there, especially white straight men I am ashamed to say, who claim the world is against us, and we're at the bottom of the pile. I used to try and engage with them, hoping they'd listen to another white straight man.' Chris scooped up the last morsels of his reheated cottage pie while Helena tried to control the rising panic. 'For instance, I'd say we have had all the privileges to ourselves for long enough and it's only right things were more level, but people have deeply entrenched views. It's seriously concerning.' He arranged his knife and fork neatly on the plate. 'There will inevitably be those who don't like your work, it's the writer's lot. But this shouldn't stop us. Even if our books get banned in certain places. My little mantra is that we should all try to believe in our own integrity.'

Helena fell silent as she finished crunching, and ruminated on what Chris had said. Lily and Chris got up simultaneously to clear away their lunch things. Chris gestured to Lily that he would clean her bowl and spork, and took them over to the sink in the corner, which was overflowing with various people's used teaspoons and mugs. Chris washed everything without comment. He stacked the clean items on the drainer then faced Helena again as he dried his hands on a paper towel.

'Look, how's this for a suggestion? If you do decide to go ahead, which I consider a marvellous idea by the way, I'd be delighted to be to be book buddy, be a beta reader for you perhaps - read your manuscript and give you friendly feedback.'

'You'd do that?'

'I'll do anything I can to help a fellow writer. Righto, I'd best get back.'

Chris stepped forwards to shake her hand. He was such a decent man. And wise.

'You can always ask friends to read through it too,' he added as he turned to leave.

Easier said than done. At best, her smattering of friends were lucky to get a birthday message these days, and that was usually thanks to social media prompts. There was Sue, her school friend. They had once been particularly close but had lost touch since she'd moved to Yorkshire with her husband. Then there was Effia, a colleague from her old job who had helped her deal with a difficult manager, after which they'd become friends. Other than those two, her friends on social media were mostly strangers she'd met once who had subsequently sent friend requests.

Later at home, Helena's unsettled mood worsened. Could she ever write this book? Could she leave the security of a job at the library and work for Cynthia? Could she risk all the consequences and uncertainties? For all her moaning, she loved the services libraries offered and was starting to get on well with various of her colleagues and customers. She couldn't bring herself to read any more letters. Instead, she read through Clare's notes on the early ones, hoping for inspiration and insight into what Clare had intended to do with them.

Nefertari. Celebrated co-ruler alongside Ramesses II, involved at the highest level in politics, foreign affairs, diplomacy, and religious celebrations. Virtually unprecedented. Her elevated status benefitted Ramesses II who understood they could achieve more together. Monuments to her emphasise this, where he has depicted her as his equal. The Temple of Hathor at Abu Simbel was built to venerate her and the goddess Hathor. Both here and in her tomb she is equal with the gods. Studying her I'm transported.

Trung sisters. First century leaders of current-day Vietnam. United a nation while in England we were still living in tribes, waiting to be invaded by the Romans. Across Europe, patriarchal societies were emerging. Letter hints at Vietnam being a matriarchal society, or at least a society where women and men leaders were accepted equally. Compare how his-

torians from China and Vietnam tell the story…the sisters were either rebellious bandits or national heroines. Fascinating how the Vietnamese managed to hold on to sense of national identity through 1,000 years of Chinese rule, and later through French occupation. Hardly surprising that when the Americans arrived, they were simply not prepared to accept invasion again without a fight.

Mawia. Arabian Queen during First century CE when the monotheistic religions were taking off. Founding leaders of Judaism, followed by Christianity and then Islam, sought to move away from ancient religions and civilisations and their many gods of different genders, and instead created mostly patriarchal societies with the one male god at the helm. As humans evolved into a species with capacity to question, these leaders provided answers in the form of religious texts. Authenticity and meaning of religious texts are still debated, just as authenticity of Mawia is still discussed, and various versions of her history exist.

Clare's notes on Wu Zhao and Theodora and had a similar tone – Clare compared these queens with one another, and looked at how they stood out from other rulers of their era. It was exciting to begin to get an inkling of Clare's train of thoughts and intentions. Maybe, possibly, there was a way she could move forwards with this after all. If she could get inside Clare's mindset, by concentrating hard on what she was saying in the notes, and if she could work out what the women in the letters were saying, then perhaps this could give her a starting point. She wasn't promising herself though.

Take Theodora. *Come on Helena, what was she saying, in a nutshell? That it's possible to be a woman not born into privilege to achieve great things? She wasn't merely the Emperor's wife; she influenced policy changes concerning women's rights, anti-corruption and maintaining the peace. All these women effected great change during their reigns. But why did Clare select the ones she did? Are the letters annotated with red question marks ones offering less details about their lives? Did Clare intend to present letters illustrating more context? Or maybe Clare wanted to showcase lesser-known queens? And of course, not all the letters were written by queens.* Helena was going round in circles again, trying to understand a woman she'd never met who was going to write a book on other women she'd never heard of, and not understanding at all where Clare intended to go with it.

'OK, enough of this, woman. Come on, get a grip. Keep reading and things will hopefully start to become clearer.'

Amongst the rest of the medieval letters, one in particular caught Helena's eye, as it mentioned Kilkenny. Helena had been there on holiday. It had an interesting pub.

Chapter Sixteen

Alice

Petronella, my faithful servant,

I write to you from a wretched cold tower within Kilkenny Castle jail walls, where I believe you are held also, in the dungeon. This letter shall be delivered and read to you by my trusted son and associate William and shall be written evidence of my innocence and of my solemn promise to you.

You will have been told of the many outrageous and ridiculous crimes with which we are charged. I have thought on it and there is only one feasible plan. What you do next will seal Sarah's fate, so take heed.

I am accused of refuting Christ and the Church, based on observations that I do not enter Church to hear mass, nor take the bread and wine. They claim by association I must be a devil worshipper, failing to comprehend one can be worthy without worshipping a god. They say I sacrificed animals to a demon-lover who is the incubus Robert Artisson, and claim I performed a sexual union with the said incubus while he took the form of Aethiops the founder of Ethiopia, a hairy black dog. It is supposed I asked demons for advice on witchcraft, and held meetings with burning candles, imitating the power of the Church with my coven. They profess you and your daughter Sarah to be part of this coven. I am charged with making dark magic powders, ointments and potions created with the most disturbing of ingredients, such as body parts of unbaptized children, pieces of animals and human skulls. Lastly, I am accused of killing my former husbands after corrupting their spirits with those potions and with my sorcery, and of causing the decline of my current husband John.

This is not the first time I have been accused of murder. Nor is it the first time I have had to flee. But now, I have no option other than to leave forever. I appealed to the royal government, to the Church, to noblemen and to the people of the town, but my appeals have failed. I refuse to apologise for or confess to the sins concocted, and for crimes not committed. Confession would give them reason to execute me. No reform has been offered me as an option, therefore the only viable path ahead for me is to depart.

Our choice is thus: either both of us die leaving our children to their fate, or one of us dies and the other will protect the children. William will help you. You must confess Petronella, to save your child Sarah. In so doing you will become a martyr. I too am sacrificing my life, leaving my beloved Ireland and my only home, Kilkenny, leaving my successful business, sacrificing myself to be Sarah's keeper.

Here is the truth of it all, to ensure my name is cleared.

Since my father died when I was but eighteen, I toiled daily to maintain my claim to Kyteler's House, the place where I was born which is rightly mine. It will sadden me greatly to leave it for I have made it a location exceptional for the people's entertainment and employment. I had it extended and built there an Inn for the people, from where I ran my money lending business and provided entertainment for the gentlemen with a group of ladies such as you. The people flocked to my Inn, rich and poor, to be part of the most lively and successful venture in the town. Men came from far to see this place and to see me, lavishing me with gifts in return for my extraordinary services. From the many potential suitors, I chose my first three husbands wisely; men of wealth who could offer me a most comfortable life, and in the unfortunate circumstance of their deaths, a handsome dower's pension. Tis a challenge for a woman to gain her own wealth and I am a woman of merit for finding suitable husbands. I should not be punished for this.

William Outlaw, my first husband, gave me William my son, who is known to you. After William's death, a hasty second marriage was necessitated, and I chose Adam Blund. The match worked well enough until his own children began accusing us of stealing money and killing my first husband using witches' tools. Thus, our troubles began. The king himself stepped in to put the matter right. After Adam's death, rumours about me increased, as you will remember, spread by his children. Men who were jealous of my success and wealth began to say I was wicked. My third husband Richard de Valle's son, whom he named Richard also, became chief troublemaker, forcing me to fight for the money rightfully mine after his father's death. It was he who went to the evil Bishop of Ossory, one Franciscan friar named Richard de Ledrede with stories of witchcraft.

Four years ago, I was betrothed to the feeble man John Le Poer who blames his decline in health on me and makes false claims gainst me, telling Ledrede I lead a coven of witches. Ledrede is under Pope John's spell, believing false claims of heresy and witchcraft. An English man on Irish soil, Ledrede is obliged to prove himself, make a name for himself. This is his chance. These men will do anything to protect themselves and their blessed

Church, and in the name of their church will readily flog us and kill us. Ledrede's first attempts to seek my destruction failed. He wrote to the Chancellor of Ireland demanding adherence to Ut Inquisitiones, the law of the church, urging my arrest. Ha! The Chancellor is my brother-in-law, Roger, who declared the case should be dropped. Instead, the Chancellor decided I should be excommunicated and flee for my own safety. Enraged, Ledrede accused me and my son William outright of heresy and led the inquisition against us, finding me guilty of all this witchcraft and magic, heresy and demonic rituals, with William my accomplice.

Ledrede has convinced John Darcy, the Lord Chief Justice, to believe the false claims are authentic. Ledrede pronounces that my husband John suspects me to be poisoning him and adds my other husbands suffered the same. He claims my son William has confessed, but that vile monk will say anything. John now colludes with my stepson Richard de Valle. They have gone through my belongings in my bedchamber and found my most private things, including my stick and ointment. For a man to pleasure himself is a sin, but for a woman they say tis wicked. Even if our husbands do not perform, they insist we should not satisfy ourselves.

In short, I helped my husbands to increase their wealth. I deserved their money after their deaths for I had earnt it. I deserve better than this ridiculous case now brought gainst me.

So, Petronella, to your part. Find courage, for you will be dealt with severely. If there is a Heaven, then you will earn your place in it and if there is a god, he will protect you, as he will comprehend the true circumstances of your martyrdom. Here is what will happen. Roger will bring Sarah, and you will say your goodbyes. You can console yourself that you save her life by forfeiting yours. Sarah will be taken by Roger into safe hiding until we are ready to escape.

They will come to you in jail and interrogate you. Tis legal to whip a servant so be prepared for it. They reason they will beat a confession from you and thus they will have me. At first, resist and plead innocence. They will torture you. Endure this for a while, and then confess. Tell them you saw the demon Robert Artisson in different forms and watched as he and I engaged in intercourse. Agree that I perform magic spells, and I taught you to become a witch, and we fly through the air on a wooden stick covered with ointment. They concoct this idea from the pleasure stick and ointment they found in my bedchamber. They will assume they force the confession out of you and force you to betray me. They plan to humiliate me in public, to beat me, drag me through the streets of six parishes by horses, and then burn me at the stake, as a Chief Priestess. They will have to find me first! Your confession will not condemn me, it will save me! Your daughter too.

After your first confession, they will come again. They will do to you that which they plan to do to me. When the whipping and dragging has taken place, appease them and the gathered crowd, and as you are led to your execution, confess to more. Say I am the leader of the pact (tis true). Confess I possess more powers than you (tis also true). They will be delighted with your confession and will celebrate their victory and be distracted. Their guard will be down and precisely at that time, Roger will collect your daughter and come for me, and we will make our escape.

I might change Sarah's name. I favour a finer name, such as Basilia. We will go into hiding and never be found again. I have money enough from my dowries to disappear and forge a new life, probably in England where I am unrecognised. There I will care for your daughter. Maybe life will be even better in England. Perhaps I shall travel to London and find a more open society there. I hear they have a statue of a phallus in the street, and that since Roman times they have celebrated intimacy without shame. A friend talks of a one Cock Lane. Perhaps I shall venture there. It sounds liberated. A better place for me. Your daughter too.

If I was a man and proud of my wealth and status, I would be treated to the best positions in town, probably even mayor. If I was a man complaining about my wives, they would sympathise. But a woman complaining about her husband is a sinner. A woman who has her own charms and wealth is a witch and a heretic.

You have been a faithful servant to me. If you believe in God, pray to him for your salvation as you are taken to the centre of the town to be burnt. Go proudly and be strong.

Thank you for your service.

Dame Alice Kyteler, your friend

Chapter Seventeen

Alex

This was the first letter Helena had come across that mentioned a place she had visited. She'd actually sat in the pub Alice had run hundreds of years ago. Alice must have been a familiar figure in the town, but Helena didn't warm to her. She painted herself as a heroine, but she was utterly selfish, letting her servant take all the blame while she escaped. Helena wasn't sure she should be celebrated in a book. However, Clare's notes had a big green asterisk at the top, signalling that she intended to include it.

AK. Dates 1260 to sometime after 1324. First woman on record to be charged with witchcraft and sentenced to death. Possibly poisoned her husbands for personal gain but this couldn't be proven. Divorce wouldn't have been an option for her. After her disappearance Ledrede continued on his mission against so-called heresy. No records anywhere of what became of Alice. Mention the pub and what it's like, how you can feel Alice's presence.

Petronella - burned to death at the stake on 3 November 1324 after being tortured and confessing. Discuss the spread of charging women with witchcraft after this case. There were a few in the Middle Ages, but it came to a head in England during the Puritan era - Civil war. First Witchcraft Act 1541. Approx. 500 people killed, mostly women. Same in the US – Salem Witch Trials in particular. Petronella is in Judy Chicago's Dinner Party in NY but not Alice. Petronella is the hero of this story. Also, bring in the common practice of face slashings – Bernini is an example – ordered his lover's face to be slashed shortly after creating a sculpture of her Costanza Piccolomini. Slashings, acid attacks, honour killing and forced marriage are all modern equivalents of burning witches at the stake.

Alice, the same as everyone, was a product of the society in which she lived, and had to adapt to the circumstances she faced. It would have been commonplace for servants to be treated as sub-human and for women to be branded as witches if they didn't conform. Helena had never heard of face slashings. These assaults, and the others, were due to the same concept as the burning of witches– the belittling, the torture of women for being unacceptable according to a fabricated societal convention. The letters reflected that women through history were connected by this invisible thread.

Helena remembered the exposed brick on the walls inside the pub, the polished wooden ceiling, and the archways separating the rooms. It was comforting and exciting that Clare had visited there too. Alice was there, Clare was there, then she was there. Perhaps they had all sat in the same corner next to one of the blackened fireplaces. As Clare had felt Alice's presence, Helena was feeling Clare's.

The next time she had lunch with Lily, Helena decided to broach the subject of the book again. If she talked about it enough, perhaps it would begin to feel real. Lily was sweet and hopefully wouldn't snort at her with derision.

'Wow! We've got two authors at work! Isn't that cool!' said Lily.

'Oh blimey, no! I am not an author,' said Helena.

'My dad says if you are writing, then you are an author.'

'Strictly speaking, I haven't written anything yet. I am merely reading all the letters, jotting down scrambled thoughts and worrying over where on earth to start if I decide to give it a go.'

'I was meaning to say, and I don't know if it's helpful, but my dad works at The National Archives. I'm not sure exactly what he does, some kind of research I think. His colleague Alex has written articles on history. I bet Dad would introduce you. Alex is nice and likes a project my dad says. Shall I ask?'

'I love your enthusiasm, Lily,' said Helena. 'But why would anyone want to meet me?'

'Oh, sorry,' said Lily. I didn't mean to…I get a bit carried away. Too keen my mum says. I'm interested though. Mega interested, and I thought they might be able to help, that's all.'

'No. I'm sorry, Lily. I was being dismissive. If you could ask, there's no harm in that, is there?'

'My dad keeps saying he's going to bring Alex to the library one day, so I could ask them to come in one lunchtime. We'd have to ask Carol to arrange for us to get our break together, but she won't mind. Not if it's for my dad.'

'I would like that. Thank you.'

It was not always pleasant being in Helena's head. Helena's egg and tuna salad suddenly tasted of cardboard, and she had trouble swallowing each mouthful, her senses dulled while her mind raced. It began spiralling as they sat quietly, finishing their lunches. She was so quick to judge, so quick to dismiss and to negate. Lily was trying to help. Why couldn't she just be grateful?

Driven by an unidentified compulsion, Helena continued to spend her spare time reading letters and researching. She'd always struggled to make sense of her own reasoning, especially when she was stressed. Everything got jumbled, like a mixed wash stuck on an eternal cycle. She was acutely familiar with sensations of fear and inadequacy. But this was different. What on earth was it? Thoughts began whirling around in her head. Thoughts about patriarchal societies, women's roles, their invisibility, their lack of opportunity, the challenges they faced to be noted for their achievements, and their fates if they upset the status quo of male authority. She began using her nighttime awakenings to jot down these thoughts and started carrying round a notepad in the day on which to scribble. She wrote comments on what might connect this letter to that one, and why some letters resonated with her most. Her research into the author of one letter particularly piqued her interest. The letter was one of the briefest in the collection. It was from Elizabeth Cellier who lived in seventeenth century London, who wrote to Anne Errol, a Jacobite activist in Scotland.

Dear Anne,

The date is set. On Wednesday next I shall appear before Their Lordships in whom I lay my trust as I testify the truths. I wish and pray they will not find it strange a woman born to Protestant parents has changed her faith openly to another Church. As a woman with sympathies for the Catholic faith, you will be furious, as am I, at the lack of mercy shown to those Catholics incarcerated since the Popish Plot. It was my duty to offer them charity and these acts of mine came from compassion and love. I trust that my pamphlet "Malice Defeated" will be used in my defence to convince Their Lordships that my private beliefs and my public duty are one and the same thing, as guided by God. By His will I shall be released and able to visit you forthwith.

Elizabeth.

When she wrote this note, Elizabeth had already stood trial for her alleged part in a plot against the King. On this occasion, she was on trial for writing a pamphlet justifying her actions. For this, she was imprisoned. Undeterred, she later became an advocate for women's health and especially for midwifery services, and campaigned for the establishment of a Royal London Hospital. Helena jotted down a few notes on how difficult it must have been advocating for women in these circumstances. As she wrote, she pictured herself as Elizabeth writing the letter. Perhaps Elizabeth was sitting on a stool at a small wooden table with a single candle in the corner of a simply furnished darkened room, wearing a plain gown with a modest head covering.

On her day off, Helena visited Cynthia, eager to share she was feeling a shift in her thinking. She was beginning to imagine herself starting to write. It struck her as completely daft, but the seed was planted, and she couldn't ignore it. She let herself in with the key Cynthia had given her. *Damn she's been smoking again. What have I done now?* She headed for the dining room as usual, hoping to see Cynthia waiting, tea things ready. But as she passed the lounge, she saw Cynthia's little frame outlined on the sofa, head supported by several cushions and body covered with a threadbare check wool blanket. She didn't stir when Helena entered the room and approached. Helena dropped her bag and knelt down, her face close to Cynthia's. Her hair drooped towards a full ashtray perched precariously on the sofa's arm. She picked up the ashtray and placed it as far away as she could reach, then laid one hand on Cynthia's shoulder, gently so as not to break her. With the other hand, she stroked Cynthia's hair. Such intimacy would have felt inappropriate before. Suddenly, it was completely natural. Helena had been taught not to appear shocked at the appearance of a gravely ill patient, but it was impossible to control her reaction. This wasn't a patient, this was her friend.

'I'm s-sorry, dear.'

'What on earth for?'

'I must look frightful.'

'No, not at all, don't be silly. Can you try and tell me what's happened?'

With effort, Cynthia shifted her weight slightly towards Helena. Her eyes were sunken and dry, and her cheeks were the same colour as the ash in the ashtray.

'I had an exacerbation, dear… It was a bad one. I was in hospital… for a couple of nights.' Cynthia had to pause for a breath after every few words.

'Oh no, you poor thing. But you're ok now?'

'No dear. My lung function recovers… less each time…after an attack…They have let me home for now… but they have started… talking about… palliative care. I'm to see… someone tomorrow… about getting carers in… and we'll… take it from there.'

'Oh, I wish you had told me, Cynthia. I could've been there for you. Maybe you shouldn't talk for now. Do you need your oxygen?'

'It's getting… a bit late… for oxygen.'

'You mustn't say that. I'll get it now. Let me help you, please?'

Helena retrieved the oxygen from the dining room. She'd forgotten how heavy these cylinders were, even the ones that were supposed to be portable. She lifted Cynthia's head to place the oxygen mask on her face, careful not to catch her long wispy hair in the elastic as she moved it into position. After a few breaths, Cynthia stirred. Her hand appeared from under the blanket, pushed the mask off her face, then retreated again.

'Would you get me…a whisky? The bottle is…in the sideboard.' Helena recoiled slightly.

'Cynthia, I really don't think you should…'

'I'm dying, Helena. I don't have many… pleasures. If you… wouldn't mind.'

Helena realised she had no choice but to oblige. She went over to the sideboard, took out the bottle and a cut crystal glass, and poured out a small-ish measure. Then sighing as she glanced over to Cynthia, she poured out a glug more.

She placed the glass on a nest of tables next to the sofa, and surveyed the room for something to sit on, settling on a carved oak corner chair. As she dragged it across the room to sit beside Cynthia, an idea rooted inside Helena's head. This must have been how Cynthia felt when she had the idea of writing the book. With the idea, a rush of emotion caught her off guard, unaccustomed as she was to sensations of excitement and hope.

'Why don't I come and stay with you? I can care for you here. I've got nurse's training, and I can easily check out how to care for your specific, well your needs. Shall we see if they'll agree?' She reached for the whisky and offered Cynthia a sip, thinking that if she was staying, she could also try to regulate Cynthia's smoking and drinking.

Cynthia's hand appeared again from under the blanket. She lifted it towards Helen's face. The skin on her hands was transparent.

'I can't… ask you… to do that.'

'But you're not asking me. I'm asking you. Cynthia, if you agree, it could work out perfectly. I can get to work much more easily from here and be with you in the mornings and evenings and my days off. And we could work on the book together, when you're strong enough.'

'You're… going to do… the book?' Cynthia's eyes brightened a little.

'Oh God. I said that out loud didn't I? I figure, well… Oh Cynthia I'm not sure.'

'What is your… gut feeling dear? I don't wish… to pressure you.'

'Cynthia you're so understanding, even when you're ill. The thing is, one of my main problems has always been I don't trust my feelings. I've never really understood it when people say they go with their gut. My default I think is to run away. But this. It's different.'

'Helena. Dear. Don't torture yourself. What does your heart tell you to do?'

'You're so patient. Ok. What DOES my heart want?' Helena waited for her heart to tell her its desire, but it remained silent. She had to rely on her head, aware this could lead to all sorts of problems. 'Oh, dammit! How's this? I am going to try. For you and for Clare.'

'And for you?'

'Yes, and for me too. I feel I've got to. And sitting here with you now, I want to. Well, I want to give it my best shot.' Was she saying all this aloud? Yes, apparently she was. How did the conversation progress this quickly from Helena helping to care for Cynthia to Helena writing a book?

'Anyway, will you think about me staying here, please? I am so fond of you, and I'd love to help, otherwise I wouldn't be suggesting it.'

'I will…think about it. And we must… get your money sorted… for working for me.'

'Oh please don't pay me anything, Cynthia! I'll care for you because you're my friend.'

'Money to write the book, dear. If you…leave the library…and work…for me.'

'Oh.'

Was she honestly going to do this? It was a huge leap into the unknown and Helena wasn't keen on huge leaps. She wasn't even keen on little jumps. On the other hand, it would do her good to attempt a challenge for once. While she cogitated on and off, Helena persuaded Cynthia to eat half a sandwich and to drink something which wasn't forty percent proof. Cynthia perked up a little after the food and more oxygen, but it was difficult leaving her, even though a nurse was coming round later.

Helena visited again the following day as Carol gave her a day of compassionate leave. Cynthia took frequent naps, and Helena tried to concentrate on researching but only managed spurts of about an hour before her concentration lagged. She busied herself with housework, enjoying handling Cynthia's lovely objects as she lifted them to dust, and satisfied by a sense she was being of use. These breaks proved fruitful; they allowed her mind to wander. Ideas, words and phrases appeared which she would note down. *No pressure, remember*, she kept saying to herself. It was as difficult leaving Cynthia as it had been the previous evening. When she got home, she made a list.

Pros and cons of writing the book.

Pros: It would be the most significant thing I've ever done. I would definitely enjoy the research. I would possibly enjoy writing it. It might even get published. I could leave work and care for Cynthia properly. It would mean Clare's work hadn't been in vain. Cons: I'm terrified, meaning I'm stuck.

The next day, she couldn't face walking. She trudged in the rain to the bus stop, caught the condensation-filled bus, and paddled soggily into work. And as soon as she started moving books, the wrist was painful again; it wasn't thankful for this job at all. Carol seemed to sense she was feeling as bedraggled inside as she must look on the outside. She asked how Helena was getting on, and suggested they retreat to her office, so they might sit and talk privately.

'Might I suggest you take a period of sick leave?' said Carol. 'And get your wrist seen to?'

'Thank you Carol, I could do with getting it sorted. But, well, actually, I was going to talk to you. I'm not sure yet, but I'm considering handing in my notice. Can I pick your brains about it?'

Before Carol could answer, Lily popped her head round the door.

'Hi guys!'

'Oh hello sweetheart,' said Carol. 'I hope you don't mind me saying, but I don't appreciate being called a guy. Helena and I are not guys. We are women. I'm fully aware it's a term people use increasingly nowadays, but it makes me prickle. I think of it like this: imagine you walked into a room of men and said, "Hello ladies." It may seem silly, but it's how I feel.'

Helena made a mental note to remember this explanation as she didn't like being called a guy either.

'Oh sorry, my bad, Aunty Carol. It's habit I s'pose. I thought everyone said it.'

'It might be my age. I'm all for language evolving, but not that term used in that way. Some people insist it's a gender-neutral term, but for me it isn't and never will be.'

'Got it. I'll try to stop saying it to you. But what should I say instead?'

'Do you need to say anything? Why not just say Hi, or Hello?'

'I'll try, Aunty.'

'Thank you.' Carol's face softened. 'Now, you had something you wanted to say?'

'Oh yes. I was going to say, sorry to interrupt you both, but Dad and Alex are here.'

Helena had completely forgotten this meeting had been arranged. She'd started planning what she might say and how she would try and avoid making an idiot of herself in front of these academics. Then it had completely slipped her mind while it had been preoccupied with Cynthia's situation and her own deliberations. This was going to be excruciating. It would be similar to that "conversation concerning a topic of interest" she had been subjected to for her oral English O' level. How she'd got an A was beyond her.

'Go,' said Carol. 'We'll talk later. I'll swap the rota so we can catch up this afternoon.'

'Thanks Carol. Actually, would you like to join us?' said Helena. You could maybe introduce me to your brother?' Was she being too cheeky? Was she taking advantage of Carol? Or was she overthinking as usual?

'Good idea! I can find out what you're up to.' She was a bit brusque, but Helena's opinion of her was shifting. She wasn't a monster. The monster was of her own creation.

Carol led the way, waving to the two people in the corner as they entered the café. It was such a short walk there wasn't any opportunity to gather her thoughts, and in an instant they were standing beside the table. Carol pulled over an extra chair.

'Helena, meet my brother Colin. And his associate, Alex.'

Helena shook hands with the two guests and sat down beside Lily, who nestled in next to her dad. He gave his daughter a wink and a nudge, and she beamed as she nudged him back. It was such a simple and quick exchange, yet it said everything. It said family. They ordered drinks and established how everyone was and whether they could discern the first signs of Spring. Carol then offered a brief introduction, explaining that Helena had befriended a woman who came into the library, and now they were working on the idea of a book, based on letters collected by the woman's daughter, a historian. Helena was impressed at how much Carol had taken in, and at how kind she was being in her introductions. Remarkably, Colin and Alex acted as if they were genuinely interested. Colin asked pertinent, if probing questions regarding Clare's travels, and Alex smiled and nodded a lot. Helena worked hard not to feel threatened, trying to remember to look at them when she spoke and make interested noises when listening. She got the impression they weren't having to work hard at all. After several minutes, Alex spoke.

'This is exactly the kind of project we seek out, Helena. Hearing the basics from Lily had already piqued our interest, and I know I speak for us both when I say that meeting you today has cemented our enthusiasm.' Alex turned to Colin, who nodded but maintained a serious and inscrutable expression. Helena found him just as difficult to read as his sister. Alex continued. 'Colin here is the historical research buff, as I'm sure you've gathered, and I am more of a writer. I'd gladly meet with you to talk it through more, if that sounds alright to you?'

Alright? It sounded flipping amazing, and not only because she was desperate for any help she could get. There was something else. Something unexpected. As Helena listened to Alex, she felt a little sensation she hadn't felt for ages. It was a tingle, albeit a faint one, but it was definitely there. Alex's voice was deliciously smooth. It reminded Helena of an advert for expensive chocolate caramels. Alex's countenance was intriguing also; here, thought Helena, was someone supremely comfortable in their own skin. Helena forgot for a moment she was supposed to say anything.

'Oh goodness, sorry, absolutely, yes, I'd love to,' she said, meaning it in more ways than one.

'Good. Shall we go out for a drink in the week. Let's see, Wednesday is free?'

'Perfect. I'm free pretty much all the time.' *Careful, don't sound too keen.*

'Wonderful, it's a date.'

Of course it wasn't a 'date' date. Nevertheless, she whooped a little internal whoop. They finished their drinks, joking how they were unidentifiable by either appearance or taste, and then Carol left them to chat a little longer. Helena found it hard to concentrate on the academic stuff. A lot of it was over her head, but quite apart from that, she was somewhat distracted. She tried surreptitiously to study Alex in more detail, and spotted a little lapel pin of yellow, white, purple and black stripes. It vaguely reminded her of the suffragette colours. No, they were purple and green, weren't they? Anyway, the badge was quite pretty, and she made a mental note to find out if it signified anything. Alex was dressed simply in a jacket, plain tee shirt and jeans, and yet looked a million dollars. Confident, self-assured and approachable. All the things Helena felt she wasn't, but all things she admired in other people.

'How did it go?' asked Lily later on as they worked together tidying the children's picture books.

'Quite well I hope,' said Helena. 'They seem surprisingly interested, and I'm going to meet Alex to talk it through a bit more.' She was attempting to come across as nonchalant, but felt the colour rise up her neck and spill across her face. Hopefully Lily hadn't noticed.

'Brill. I wanted to say earlier, I would like to help too. I could type the letters into Word documents and save them? I love practising my typing and I would get to read the letters as well.'

'Would you be willing to do that?' said Helena. People kept surprising her today.

'Defo,' said Lily. 'I liked Cynthia when she came in and I think the book idea is so cool. I am a bit slow though.'

'Oh, anything you can do to help would be great. Honestly, thank you very much.'

Carol came out of her office mid-afternoon to find Helena, rescuing her from a couple who thought they could open their emails on a library computer by typing their email address in the search bar. When Helena had asked for their password they didn't understand what she meant. Their daughter had set up the email address for them. At home, they simply opened the emails on the tablet, but now the screen was broken. Couldn't they open them on any computer? Thankfully, Lily was at hand to take over.

'Come, take a seat,' said Carol, leading Helena to a small table and chairs in the corner opposite Carol's desk. Her office was small, but it was warm and cosy. She'd recently decorated it with a few pictures and posters of inspirational quotes. There was one by Carl Sagan that particularly caught Helena's eye. "To read is to voyage through time."

Carol leant forwards, her eyes fixed intensely on Helena, her head nodding slowly while Helena explained the situation with Cynthia and described her half-baked ideas about the book. Helena had learnt by now not to be so fazed by Carol's stare. Maybe her face had become set in stern mode over many years of practice, but its apparent ferocity didn't necessarily reflect her intention. She was just listening intently.

'Why don't you give yourself a few days to mull it over Helena. It's a big decision. Whatever you decide, I'll support you as best I can.' It was a brief response, but spot on.

At Cynthia's later, Helena mentioned again the idea of staying, although Cynthia remained reluctant. The local authority had agreed it was an appropriate interim arrangement, but Cynthia was adamant she didn't wish to be any bother. One thing she did made clear though: if Helena stayed over at all, she should use Clare's old room as it was the most comfortable, and it had a view of the garden. As she left, Helena selected a letter with a picture attached to it. It caught her eye as one of the girls in the picture had the same colour skin as Alex's. Beautiful.

Chapter Eighteen

Dido

Dearest Elizabeth,

Thank you kindly for your letter and all your news. I have read it through many times, it is most exciting. I am delighted for you, and glad you are settled at Eastwell Park. Is it much like our lovely Kenwood? I wonder if I might visit once your building programme has finished. I hear Kent is pretty. You have children now too! How sweet they must be, with you as their dear mother. You must be extremely busy with it all.

The day when I too will leave Kenwood House is almost upon us after the death of our dear guardian. I shall miss my home dreadfully, although not as much as I miss you together with Lord and Lady Mansfield, the only family I have known for many a long year. It is all changed so, now they are gone, and you are moved away.

They were most kind to us both, our great uncle and aunt, were they not? I often think on what might have become of us had they had not taken us both in. They truly kept us well, giving us an education and all manner of nice things. He never once treated me as a slave, and was generous enough to extend to me an allowance and let me join you and the other ladies after dinner. He was a true gentleman indeed.

I miss you most of all, dear Elizabeth. You are a sister to me. Growing up with you was the loveliest aspect of my life here, you always treated me kindly. I felt as if I were a lady in your gracious company. It is our walks in the gardens I cherish the most, arm in arm as we chatted while strolling on the lawns and on the terraces. I loved hearing your accounts of merriment at the dinner table, and learning of your adventures during the sumptuous parties and the many family trips you all took. You listened gladly to my tales too, of working for the Lady and the Lord, and laughed heartily as I told of my adventures caring for her person and being his secretary, of running the dairy and the poultry yard, of the hours spent rounding up the chickens, how the Lord and Lady would call for me in the middle of the night if they needed anything.

Do you remember when we posed for the painting, how much fun we had? We were gleeful and carefree. The artist captured well our likenesses, and made clear our bond. Since you left the house, it has never been the same, though your happiness matters more. I was delighted for you when you found your true love George. You were beautiful and radiant on your wedding day, when you came back here for the celebrations after the ceremony. It was sad indeed Lady Mansfield did not live to see it.

After your departure, I cared for Lord Mansfield as best I could while he became ever more frail. It was the least I could do for him, and I was glad to do it. I am told in his will, he has granted me my freedom and also left me with money, a lump sum and an annuity. It will help me greatly. It is right and proper you should have the greater share, for you are a lady, and must receive the funds needed to do all the things a lady does, especially now you are a mother and run an important house.

My thoughts turn often to my own poor mother. I wonder how she fares, specially as I am to be married and may one day become a mother myself. I am 32 and am restless at the prospect being such an age. She, my dear mother, was by contrast so young, at only 15. I never speak the man's name, and never shall. He ravished a slave girl on board a ship when there was no chance of escape. Then he abandoned the infant, leaving me with nothing as if I were nothing to him. He would not admit to my existence even in death. I used to fret on it, but you helped me comprehend the facts and temper my emotions. He is nothing to me now. From his guilt he gifted my mother land, but it was far away in America. He would surely understand we could never meet again. Apart from this gift, the only other reasonable thing he ever did was to pass me over to the Lord and Lady.

So, to the crux of it, dear Elizabeth. I am to be married to Mr John Davinier. It is my sincere hope you and George will attend the wedding which is to be in December. As you can see with this letter is a card with all the details in case you can come. Oh, do come! We are to live in Pimlico. It is a sweet home, most suitable for us, with two rooms on each floor and even a little garden. I am already excited to receive your response.

I remain always your sister and friend,
Dido.

Chapter Nineteen

Amy

Children. Helena couldn't comprehend how women carried these little creatures for nine months, expelled them from their bodies, and then instantly turned into a food factory for them. She observed with disbelief a mother's ability to balance a wriggling being on one hip whilst unfurling a buggy, hanging shopping bags on it and preventing an older child from running into the road. To watch them arrive at the library for the weekly Rhyme Time session was to observe another species. These people could tolerate clearing up poo without being able to hand over at the end of the shift, they could zone out patiently during temper tantrums, and could fathom intuitively when the little aliens needed to nap or play or feed. And then, in those precious moments when their child was asleep, when they weren't actually having to do parenting, they were discussing aspects of parenting with one another. ALL. THE. TIME. How did they stay sane?

Her only direct experience of motherhood was being on the receiving end of her own mother's parenting style. When she was a little girl, there had been a lot of shouting, quite a bit of smacking, and long periods of being left alone in disgrace, when she was supposed to consider her failings and how to apologise for them. She came to find comfort during those quiet hours in her room, which often lasted most of the day. She'd shut the world out and converse with her odd little collection of toys as she staged scenes of imagined domestic bliss. Besides, it was the only room in the house that didn't stink of booze and cigarettes.

Her father left when she was ten and her memories of him were patchy. He always voted Conservative, was seriously strict, never told her he loved her, and was emotionally and physically absent for long periods. He was intolerant of anyone who wasn't exactly the same as him, pointing them out and explaining why they were inferior. Her mental image of her dad was perfectly captured in the memory of one specific event. During their only family holiday, on the Isle of Wight for two weeks, they sat in a tiny caravan as it sank into the mud, while the rain lashed down outside. She recalled her father yelling to his wife that no, they were not going to get fish and chips, because they weren't common people, and yelling to his only daughter that no, she was not going to be bought any toys on holiday because she had toys at home. She longed for a plastic ring she'd spotted inside a vending machine outside the amusement arcade she wasn't allowed to go in. It had a large red plastic "jewel" which glittered temptingly to the eight-year-old Helena. It was housed in a plastic ball, and for the price of ten new pence, it could be hers. But she didn't have ten new pence. Pocket money had to be earned, and she evidently hadn't behaved well enough. Towards the end of this ordeal, he complained to the campsite organisers and everyone else within earshot about the "bloody foreigners" who ran the campsite store. When they were leaving a few days later and their car was stuck in the mud, a few campers stood in small groups and stared, but no-one came to help. It was excruciating.

She jolted herself awake after drifting off, and tried to recollect what had been on her mind before her unplanned afternoon nap. Oh yes, parents. Dido's letter had fallen onto the floor. She scooped it up and studied again the picture of the two young girls smiling joyfully. Slavery, especially England's role in it, wasn't taught when Helena was at school, although she had picked up a little from listening to her work friend Effia, who had told her about Ghana's long and complicated association with slavery. She'd explained that although slavery had existed across many parts of Africa going right back to the Ancient Egyptians, slaves were usually looked after reasonably well, as if they were staff, but this all changed when the Europeans arrived, and slaves became no more than chattel. Effia's parents, who'd arrived from the Caribbean in the 1950s, gave all their children English-sounding names, to fit in. Effia was her chosen name, reflecting her African heritage. 'I am proud of where I come from, not ashamed of it,' she had said.

Everything Dido's mother endured was most likely experienced by many black women. Clare's note shed more light on Dido's situation.

Dido Elizabeth Belle. Born 1861. Her biological father Sir John Lindsay raped her mother on board a slave ship when she was 15, then dumped her with his uncle William Murray, first Earl of Mansfield, who lived at Kenwood in Hampstead. Extremely unusual for a black or mixed-race girl to live with a white family. She was treated relatively kindly as far as I can make out, although she had to work hard for her keep unlike her cousin, and was never given the same status as Elizabeth – financially or socially. This is hinted at in the letter – she wasn't allowed to attend social events such as dinner parties, and her allowance was significantly lower than Elizabeth's. Her caretaker Lord Mansfield was Lord Chief Justice of England and Wales, and he ruled that slavery did not exist in common law. His ruling was used later to begin moves towards the abolition of slavery.

Helena searched for more information on slavery, and was embarrassed to learn the deep involvement of many celebrated British men in the slave trade, and to find out how much of England's grand architecture was built from their resulting fortunes. Various commentators argued enough time had elapsed for this to be forgotten. Others emphasised this history had to be remembered, and that these men should no longer be revered, for example with statues.

The research was engrossing, and kept Helena busy while she waited to see Alex again and deliberated about resigning. Perhaps Alex's ancestors were slaves. Would it be insensitive to ask? She didn't want to say the wrong thing having realised it remained an emotive subject. It was one of many matters on she was ignorant. If she were to write the book, her lack of knowledge would have to be addressed. It would be a steep learning curve, up a precipitous mountain of slippery scree. As for the other matter of resigning, it was insignificant in the grand scheme of things, but for Helena, it involved making a decision of epic proportions and inevitably her deliberations went down numerous rabbit holes of doom, all starting with the same two words. An entire evening was spent churning out "what-ifs." Cynthia's offer to employ her was typically generous but whenever she contemplated taking her money she got a knot in her stomach. The same thing happened when she contemplated being an author. Hours passed. *Oh, for fuck's sake, get a grip, woman. All you do is complain. It's about time you bloody well took a chance. What's the worst that could happen?*

When it came to it, handing in her notice was less unpleasant than she had anticipated.

'I can't quite believe I am saying this,' Helena said. 'Resigning makes it all a bit real.'

'For what it's worth, I think it's a great idea,' said Carol. 'At our age, we should do whatever we fancy with our lives. You've got me reflecting, as a matter of fact, about myself.'

'Really?' It had never occurred to Helena she could be responsible for anyone else's self-reflections.

'Absolutely. I've not told many people, but I've started on HRT. It has helped enormously if I'm honest. You have too, actually. You've spurred me into feeling I should be more pro-active and positive.'

Blimey.

'Anyway, if it would help, we can reduce your hours while you work your notice, especially if you're going to be working on the book and caring for Cynthia. Lily has asked for more shifts, and I reckon she's ready. This could work out nicely for all.'

Job done. Just like that.

Wednesday evening arrived eventually, and Helena found herself in the pub, sharing a bottle of Merlot with the striking Alex. She gabbled nervously about the weather improving slightly, Carol being nice over her resigning, her anxiety when she thought about writing, and how she marvelled at the variety of letters Clare had collected. Alex nodded but said little. Was that a frown she could see? Worried by a few seconds of silence, Helena carried on blathering, changing the subject again. She talked about Cynthia, doubting Alex would be interested. She described Cynthia's house and how lovely and homely it was, despite being a little tatty round the edges.

'Hold on, Cynthia, the piano teacher?' said Alex.

'Oh, you know her?'

'She was Amy's teacher! What are the chances? I took her there every Saturday morning and occasionally Cynthia's daughter was there too. Her name was Clare, yes, I remember now! Amy loved it there. Amy is my daughter, as you may have gathered. She is away at uni. Empty nest syndrome is taking a lot of getting used to.'

Helena supposed there weren't many piano teachers in this small-ish town. Nevertheless, it was quite a bit to take in. *I had one interesting thing in my life and Alex can trump me on it. Alex met Clare. Alex KNEW Clare, and knew the house and Cynthia before I did. And worse… Jesus! Alex has a child.*

'She's my pride and joy of course, said Alex. She's studying music now. Hopes to be a concert pianist one day.'

'That's incredible,' said Helena, forcing a smile. *Incredible. I've finally met someone I really fancy. Stupid, stupid woman, daring to believe anything might ever…*

'Oh shit, the time! Sorry Helena, I ought to be heading off. Early start in the morning.' Alex stood, and put on a black leather jacket. 'Right, phone, wallet, keys. OK I'm set. Anyway, as I said, she's at uni now, meaning I have more freedom to do things… things for me. Which brings me to what I wanted to ask you.' Helena heard keys being rattled in Alex's pocket.

'Fire away,' she said, expecting to hear more enthusiasm about Amy or pianos.

'I'm not normally so forward, but… would you like to go out for a meal? I could do with having a bit of a social life.'

Was Alex coming on to her? Surely not. Nope, not possible.

'I'd like that,' she replied, her attempt at casual lets-be-friends nonchalance failing miserably as she flustered around busily in her bag, searching for something, anything, she had no idea.

'The thing is, Helena, I have this strong sense that I would like to get to know you. Really know you. Am I being too forward?'

'I…I…would. I mean, No. I mean…Thank you.'
Thankyou? What the hell?

Alex reached for her hand under the table and looked at her. Straight at her. Into her. It was the single sexiest thing she'd ever experienced. Until five seconds later, when Alex leaned forward and kissed her. In the pub. In public.

In bed later, she couldn't stop reliving the kiss, and fantasised about exploring more of Alex. She tried to imagine a life with a proper partner doing all the mundane but precious things people with partners do, such as going for walks in the country, taking romantic breaks, choosing the paint colour for the bedroom. These were ridiculous dreams, but they were far more pleasant as a nightcap than the default self-loathing.

They met the next evening for a meal.

'Our kiss yesterday…' Alex said afterwards as they headed out. '…was the best kiss of my life. I can't stop thinking about it. I find myself yearning to do it again. And keep doing it.'

They stood against a wall round the corner from the restaurant and kissed. As the kisses became deeper, they began to hold each other more tightly and then Alex's hands began to explore.

'I really want you.'

'I want you too, Alex.'

'But there's one thing you should know.'

Here we go. Alex is married. Alex only has weeks to live. Alex is an alien. What, in the name of everything, is coming next?

'Know what, exactly?' Helena said, her voice sharp and clipped.

'Oh, it's nothing to worry about. At least I hope it isn't. It's… you may find bits and bobs under there in places you aren't expecting.'

'Oh, Alex, I don't care which bits are going on where under your clothes.'

The relief was enormous. She really didn't care what bumps Alex had, and where: top bumps strapped down, or lower bumps tucked away in tight underwear. Somewhere deep within her, a place where unselfconsciousness still lay low, stirrings were occurring, having waited years for their moment to surface. It felt bloody good. Could she trust it?

They hurried back to Alex's smart rented townhouse, holding hands and giggling. Once inside, Alex led her upstairs. They explored one another totally. It was the most natural and beautiful experience of her life.

All of a sudden, Helena was living in a charming dream, where she had a loving relationship and became an author. It was a fantasy which wouldn't last long, and she'd soon enough be back to waking alone, feeling unfulfilled and miserable, but she was damn well going to try and enjoy it while it lasted.

Alex asked to see her most evenings, but she only agreed to meet three, maybe four times a week. She told Alex this was because she needed headspace to start working on the book, but in reality she wanted to avoid getting too involved, knowing Alex would tire of her sooner or later. She began delving more into how life might have been for the women who wrote the letters, and made copious notes as she became swept up in the stories. She read one from a woman called Mary who discovered fossils in Dorset. She had an extraordinarily hard life, was almost destitute, and was barely credited in her lifetime for the incredible work she did. This one affected Helena; she found it disturbing but couldn't pinpoint why.

Chapter Twenty

Mary

Dear Sir Henry,

It is me, Mary Anning. Thank you for the parcel, you are extremely kind. I like very much the print of your picture Duria Antiquior - A More Ancient Dorset. It is hanging in my room and I look at it often. It is our only proper picture. The money you sent from selling your prints is also accepted with gratitude.

Have you heard news from the Geological Society yet on whether they are going to let me in? I think it right, as it is me who found all the creatures - the sea dragon, the flying dragon and the others. They didn't believe me at all at first. They claimed a girl couldn't find these things and said they were not real. The 16-foot fish lizard

I found with Joseph when I was a girl, they talked about it for years, saying this, that and the other. Said it was a monster, said I didn't find it, said it was a fake. How could anyone say such things? I knew it was real; I found it. But they would never let me in to the meetings to tell the truth.

It took years for them to believe it was me finding them, cleaning them, drawing them, and saying what they were. I knew all them creatures like I knew my family. It is terrible hard labour, Sir Henry, and I have fallen more than once. My poor pup Tray lost his life in one such accident, it was so bad. But I didn't stop. I found things no-one has ever found. And not only one. I found plenty. I still find them. I know my finds are special. I am good at what I do.

They believe me now. They want to learn all about my work, so I know it is important. They take away my creatures to study. In secret, they ask my opinion. They come to visit me and quiz me. When they meet me, they marvel at my knowledge and then they go away and write about the creatures in their scientific reports as if it is them that found them and understand everything. They will not say in public it is me what does all the work. They discuss with each other where my creatures came from. Mr Cuvier, he thinks my finds are of creatures from long ago. When he tells them this, they believe it. My work helps him with his work. I fully comprehend why they all do this. It's because am not educated or proper. I am from a poor family, and most of all I am a woman.

They are well aware of our position since Father died when I was a child. We need to earn money from the fossils to live. We do not care for charity. But the little we get from selling the smaller fossils isn't enough. You and Mr Birch are the kindest. He buys many of our best creatures and then auctions them. We get money from that. And you are the only one who uses my name in your research. I am ever so grateful, honest I am. But most of the men who buy from me and sell to the museums don't ever mention me. Some of them even lie and say they found them.

Can I get money if my name is added to the science reports? Can you help me with that? If they won't allow a woman, can they call me by a name that is neither man's nor woman's? Would that satisfy? The books you send me to practice my reading, some are by Currer Bell and Ellis Bell and Acton Bell. They are women, you told me. Or you could even use a man's name. I don't mind as long as I know it's me, and I might get money for my work.

You should be President of the Geological Society. I hope that happens soon. You write good books and you did that survey of the whole country, all its rocks and stones. You are a fine gentleman.

We hope to see you down here again soon in Lyme Regis. You will be most welcome. Maybe when you come, you will bring favourable news.

From Mary Anning.

Chapter Twenty-One

Constance

Cynthia was still reluctant for Helena to move in. Instead, they settled into a routine of Helena visiting most afternoons. Carol allowed her to be flexible with her hours so she could leave work early enough to prepare Cynthia's tea.

'Can I come with you to Cynthia's today?' asked Alex one morning as they sat in her studio flat and had coffee and buttered toast. 'I'd love to see her again.'

'Yes, of course,' said Helena, licking the melted butter from her fingers. 'I'm sure she'd be delighted to see you too.'

'I'll drop by for you later. The car could do with being turned over.'

'I honestly can't think of the last time I was given a lift anywhere,' said Helena.

'I'm hoping it's one of the many things you might start getting used to,' said Alex, getting up to clear the plates.

'I can try,' said Helena.' I can't guarantee it'll be easy though.' *You're having breakfast with this beautiful human, who's offered to collect you and drive you to see a mutual friend, and who is currently doing your dishes. This is really happening to you.*

It had been a few years since Amy's last lesson with Cynthia, but it had become such a regular fixture in their diary that Alex remembered precisely how to get there, and pulled up exactly outside Cynthia's gate.

'Oh, it hasn't changed a bit!' said Alex as Helena opened the door. 'Even the smell of, what is it? Soap and wood and…'

'Dust and cigarettes?' whispered Helena.

'The scent of a bygone era, I was going to say.'

Alex took Helena's hand and they both smiled as they entered the house. Helena called out but there was no reply, so they began checking all the downstairs rooms. Cynthia wasn't in the lounge, or the dining room. Nor was she in the kitchen or the downstairs loo. Helena called up the stairs. No answer.

'Maybe she's in hospital again,' said Helena. 'I should've insisted that I stay here. She said it was too much bother. It wouldn't have been a bother and now maybe…'

Alex took her hand again.

'We don't know yet what's happened. She might be having a nap in bed. Shall we go upstairs to check? 'I'll come with you.'

Helena led the way, tiptoeing up the gently creaking stairs.

'Oh no.' Helena hesitated for a moment in the doorway of Cynthia's bedroom. The curtains were open and the street lamp outside shed a dim light across half of the room. It was impossible to make out any sign of movement from the figure under the bedcovers in the shadowy corner. Helena crept forwards. When floorboards creaked under the Persian rug, the tiny body didn't stir. Helena signalled to Alex to turn on the light.

'Cynthia? It's only me,' she whispered. 'Can you hear me?' A muffled wheeze emitted from deep under the bedclothes. Thank God for that. Gently, slowly, she peeled back the pink candlewick bedspread, the green woollen blanket and the white cotton sheet shrouding her friend. Cynthia's lips were blue, and her eyes were closed.

'Alex, can you call an ambulance please?'

The next day, Helena tried to keep herself occupied by researching Mary Anning as she waited for visiting hours. Helena had naively supposed that by the nineteenth century, things were getting easier for women in terms of earning a living. But Mary, like many others, basically had to beg for any kind of recognition let alone remuneration for her exceptional work. Mary was never properly credited with her achievements in her own lifetime. She lived in poverty while men in the scientific community benefitted academically and financially from her knowledge and her finds. She never knew her work would eventually be celebrated. Rooms would be named after her in the Natural History Museum, a portrait of her and her dog Tray would hang there, her finds would be displayed in the most prestigious museums, an ichthyosaur would be named after her, she would be recognized as one of the most influential women scientists in British history. No, she never knew any of this. Instead, she died of breast cancer aged forty-seven. Women wouldn't be allowed into the Geological Society for another eighty-seven years.

Helena stepped away from her laptop to make a hot drink. She banged around in her kitchenette finding a clean mug, and spilled a fair bit of coffee as she tossed it in. She tapped her fingers on the worktop waiting for the kettle. She scalded herself with boiling water as she poured it into the mug, then whirled the teaspoon round at breakneck speed. Suddenly, it dawned on her.

Of course. This one feels so personal because Clare never lived to see her own work published, and it's increasingly likely Cynthia won't either.

That evening, Helena arrived to find that Cynthia's condition had improved enough to have brief conversations.

Cynthia explained that she had been chatting with her nurse Constance. Throughout the day, during Constance's regular checks on her breathing, oxygen levels and blood pressure, Cynthia learnt her family were part of the Windrush generation, coming over from the Caribbean after World War Two to help rebuild the British economy. Her mother was a nurse too, whose services had been specifically called for. They uprooted from everything they knew to come to the cold and damp of England and make a new life for themselves, only for her father to be caught up in the Windrush scandal because he had lost some of his paperwork and the Home Office had threatened to deport him.

'I said to Constance that I'd read the review which concluded The Home Office were ignorant and thoughtless and how I thought it was awful, after all her parents' generation did for this country. And after the way their ancestors were treated, how it makes me ashamed to be British when I think about it. She was so generous, saying she tried not to brood on it too much, and added that most people have a good heart, especially if you are good to them.

'I'm not entirely sure I'd be as generous in her position,' said Helena.

'I said much the same thing,' replied Cynthia. 'She said she thought I would as she could tell I was a kind person too. It was a bit embarrassing.'

'Well, she's right. Hopefully I'll meet her soon,' said Helena.

'I hope so too dear. I've told her about Clare and the letters. When I mentioned there had been one from a young woman whose mother was a slave, she remembered Dido and said her son studied the story in school. She said he loves his history and how good it is nowadays that children get taught history from various angles.'

She sounds like a lovely person,' said Helena.

'Oh, yes, dear, she is. She's even been kind enough to help me with some of my arrangements, finding phone numbers and such. There's not a lot I can do from this bed, and she's been so kind.'

Helena shifted in her chair. She wasn't ready to have a conversation about Cynthia's situation.

'I'll look forward to seeing her. In the meantime, I've brought you these.'

Helena lifted a small bag of toiletries and nightclothes she'd brought from Cynthia's house.

'I hope they are ok,' she said. 'It felt odd being there without you.'

'I am sure they're fine,' said Cynthia. 'It feels odd for me too, leaving the house empty. In fact, I have a favour to ask, if I may?'

'Anything.'

'Would you mind staying in the house while I am in here? It would be a comfort to know you are there. And of course, invite friends over if you wish. As I said, please take Clare's room. The bed will need making though.'

Without hesitation, Helena agreed. She went to her flat to pack an overnight bag for the second time in one day, and headed back to Cynthia's. When she went to bed, she perused Clare's room properly for the first time. It was decorated in a tasteful off-white, and generous cream linen curtains cascaded to the floor, delicately framing the window which looked out over the tall trees and shrubbery of the garden. Her furniture was whitewashed wood. Not fussy, but full of understated elegance. Helena loved it. Various pictures and items must have been collected on Clare's travels, and presumably many were connected with the letters. On one wall hung Nefertari in all her jewelled splendour. Beside her, Mary Anning couldn't be more plain. Opposite them was a highly decorated circular picture by Hildegard that reminded Helena of an Indian mandala, and rather a sexy drawing by an artist called Patricia Preece; perhaps she would find a letter from her soon. Helena snuggled down under the duvet she'd found in the warm airing cupboard and read several letters, before having the best night's sleep in months.

'I can't believe it's your last day!' said Lily, as Helena battled with her locker for the final time. 'It must be mega exciting, leaving here and going off to be a writer.'

'Actually, I am petrified,' said Helena. 'It's all happened incredibly quickly, as if I'm hurtling along on a train without a driver; I have no sense at all of being in control. Part of me loves the idea of writing and working for Cynthia, but part of me is scared shitless. Ooops, sorry for swearing…'

'Ha ha, good job you didn't do it on the shop floor near Aunty Carol!' Lily glanced behind Helena's shoulder briefly, perhaps checking for Carol in the passageway. 'Anyway, I meant to say, I've started typing the letters. Some of them are a bit hard to understand when you don't know the people who wrote them. Did you find that?'

'Absolutely, yes. I am trying to research each one, and I'm also relying heavily on the notes Cynthia's daughter Clare made. I am hoping it'll all magically start to make sense if and when I ever get round to writing it properly.'

'I'm sure you'll slay it, Helena. You're, like… you'll be brilliant.' Lily appeared to be distracted as she looked over Helena's shoulder again, apparently straining to see something.

'Nice of you to say, Lily. But I'm struggling, not sure what the main themes will be. There are women from so many walks of life and from so many times and places. I'm trying to work out why Clare collected these in particular. Anyway, huge thanks for helping me out. Erm, hadn't we better get out there?'

Lily glanced over Helena's shoulder for a third time, then nodded. 'You'll work it out,' she said, apparently far more confident in Helena's abilities than she was herself. They walked out of the staff room and into the library, where, instead of being at their allocated stations for the ceremonial opening of the doors, all the staff were gathered in the back corner, near History.

'I understand you don't want any fuss,' said Carol. But we felt it important to mark the occasion and wish you all the best, so here's a card and a little present for you.'

Carol stepped forwards and gave Helena a little gift bag, and a little kiss on the cheek. Inside the bag was a card, a black pen with a gold trim, and a leather-bound note pad. She opened the card to see an array of hand-written messages from her colleagues. "All the best, Helena, we'll miss you" … "Come back and see us when you're a famous author!" … "Thank you for all your hard work."

'Chris mentioned you write notes on scraps of paper, so we thought this might come in handy,' said Carol.

'It's wonderful,' said Helena, her eyes rheumy. 'A lovely surprise.'

After work, Helena was surprised again when most of the team joined her at the pub across the precinct for a farewell drink. It was an old boozer, the kind where the seats are slightly stained and sticky and the tables are scratched, but it served a decent pint and there was a homely atmosphere. Alex had promised to come along, and every few minutes, Helena glanced towards the door. Soon enough, a familiar face came in from the cold, accompanied by an unfamiliar one.

'Amy asked to join us, I hope that's ok,' said Alex.

'Oh, no, of course not. I mean of course it's not a problem. It's ok, it's fine. Oh god, sorry Amy. Hello. Lovely to meet you.' A petite young woman with brown curly hair emerged from behind Alex's shoulder, her hands clasped in front of her.

'Hello,' said Amy quietly. 'I've heard a lot about you. Sorry to surprise you. Hope it's alright.' She didn't seem to have inherited Alex's confidence. But then it wasn't every day this kind of introduction happened. Helena tried to find vaguely appropriate words.

'No, it's great, honestly. Come, sit down.'

Once everyone had a drink, Alex turned to Helena.

'I hope you don't mind. I thought it best to make this introduction low key and casual as you were both a bit nervous.'

'No, I don't mind, really, it's fine.' She was desperate to believe it was fine, but a bubble was burst. After only a few days of getting to know Alex, she was now supposed to get to know this young girl. Perhaps she was soon going to wake from the dream.

Late afternoon turned into evening and slightly awkward chatter turned into more relaxed and free-flowing conversation, fuelled by several rounds of drinks. By seven-thirty, people were starting to say their goodbyes.

'Some of us have got to get up for work in the morning,' joked Carol.

Helena ordered burgers for the stragglers. Veggie for Alex and Amy, chicken for herself, and beef for Chris.

'So,' said Chris. 'How are you getting on with the book?'

'Not very well,' said Helena.

'You are doing research, making notes and chewing it over constantly. It's a great start,' said Alex.

'Yes, maybe. But I'm so confused about how it could come together as a book. How was Clare going to tie all these letters together? I'm clueless.'

'So was I when I started mine,' said Chris. 'My books evolve as I write. They are always very different when they're finished from how they began. That's part of the joy of writing. But you don't seem to be feeling that joy. You seem instead weighed down by a responsibility towards Clare and Cynthia because you're trying to write the book Clare didn't write without understanding fully what she was going to write.'

'That's exactly it! I don't want to let everyone down.'

'How could you possibly be letting anyone down? Who else is going to write it, if you don't?'

'You?' said Helena.

'Nice try! I am happy to help with structure and as I said, I will beta read it for you. But this is yours Helena.'

'You're right. I am hoping inspiration will miraculously appear.'

'I'm sure it will come.'

Chris hesitated. Helena shifted in her seat, waiting for the "but." Chris continued. 'Erm, while we're on the subject, there's one thing that intrigues me. It's not a concern exactly, although I think it's worth mentioning.' This wasn't exactly a "but", but it wasn't exactly reassuring either.

'Oh gawd, what have I done?' said Helena.

'Nothing, Helena, nothing at all. It's… all the letters were typed by Clare, am I correct?'

'Yes, that's what Cynthia said.'

'Well, I've been speculating, and as I say, it's merely inquisitiveness. But, where are the original letters? The hand-written ones? In their original languages?'

'Oh. I hadn't thought about that,' said Helena. The "but" when it came, was worse than she could possibly have imagined. It was a "but" of mammoth proportions. A little knot of anxiety formed in her stomach. She began to rub her tummy gently and inhaled deeply, letting out an audible breath through rounded lips. From experience, Helena knew this wasn't going to be good.

Alex nodded towards Chris, then said, 'Honestly, it had crossed my mind too. I was going to mention it later, but Colin at the Archive wouldn't consider collaboration unless we can prove some provenance, by which I mean evidence to indicate the letters are genuine. When we came to meet you at the library, we hadn't realised the letters were all typed out. And we weren't aware some of them were from such acclaimed figures. Sorry if this is bad news, Helena, but...'

'It's ok,' she said. But I have to go now.'

Before anyone could answer, Helena jumped up and charged out of the pub. The knot of anxiety in her stomach had begun to grow into a ball, threatening to spill out messily from within. A ball of anger had started to grow alongside it. A rapid exit was necessary to avoid anyone witnessing the moment the two spheres collided and exploded. She sped past the bus stop and into the dark streets beyond, towards the sanctuary of Cynthia's house. Why hadn't she considered this? She had been so immersed in reading the letters and deliberating with herself as to how she was going to attempt to organise them, she hadn't considered the bigger picture. She had allowed herself to start believing in this project, Moreover, she had allowed herself to let people in again. Surprise, surprise, look what had happened. *When are you going to learn, you silly cow?*

You can't be trusted with yourself. You throw yourself in and every time you try to do something, every time you get close to someone, every time you kid yourself it's going to be ok, it goes tits up. You're useless.

Early next morning, Alex called. Helena didn't answer. Alex messaged.

I'm so sorry about last night. I was clumsy. I realise this means a lot to you and I should have been more sensitive. I was going to suggest I discuss the letters further with Colin, now I am more familiar with them. We can ask around, put feelers out, see what we can dig up. It's a long shot, but there might be references to help us determine provenance for at least a few of them.

Please can we talk?

Helena read the message but couldn't reply, unable to trust herself or fully understand her emotions. She decided to stay in bed where she was safe from the outside world and distract herself by reading Dorothea's letter.

Chapter Twenty-Two

Dorothea

My dears William and Lucretia,

I write to you my friends, for the purpose of requesting you might extend your kindness to me once again, and should you see fit, that you might offer and provide much needed comfort with regards to my current sorry predicament. I trust I can speak with great plainness to you. I will endeavour to express myself clearly, though as you may recall, I am prone to elaborating my sentiments with many words. Please forgive me therefore if I say too much, it is a sign of my passion. I feel bound to explain everything for the purpose of your understanding and appreciation of my circumstance. Since I last saw you, substantial successes have been won across several of the United States, but progress has recently been stalled at the highest level, and my health has been adversely affected, as I find myself back in the throes of melancholy and despair. I desperately require respite, reassurance and hospitality, so much so I am obliged to appeal to you once more, such is the wretched being I am become.

When you are finished reading this account of my most recent misfortunes, I have every confidence your generosity will be of the utmost benefit to me, and that your excellent moral standing will prevail, should you have the desired possession of good health and be in such a financial position that you may to consider extending your generosity to me as you did in the past. If you can help on this occasion, it will ultimately and in no small way help the most feeble people of the United States, as I will explain. My body is weak, and my mind is fragile, yet I cannot lose heart. Once recovered, I remain compelled to continue with my endeavours as soon as I am able, in the face of an increasingly desperate situation here. Should I receive the desired invitation from you, my plan is to recuperate with you in England for a while, to rest and delight in your company and warm hospitality and then, upon my recovery, continue forth on my travels, rejuvenated and ready to resume my research across Europe, where I will enhance my findings through further enquiry, bringing back information regarding new European laws to my homeland. It is my intent to gather the necessary evidence so as to seek further support from our Congress and ultimately our President, who has failed to take up the reigns of responsibility, concerning the national crisis unfolding in front of him in his very own country.

You may recall I began as a teacher to a handful of the local poor children, but this became an insufficient vocation once my eyes were opened to the harshness of the world in which many of our Indigent citizens are barely surviving, and the true nature of their suffering was exposed to me. When I first set foot on English soil and met you all those long years ago in 1836, it was at the recommendation of my physician a change of scene was in order for my health. By then, at thirty-four years of age, I had already been working some twenty years towards my object, in my endeavours to improve the lives of the unfortunate.

Over the years following my last visit to you and your friends, my mission has been to understand the extent and methods of incarceration used in various parts of the United States, and to research how conditions could be improved. I presumed provision to be inadequate, but the size of the problem unveiled to me was shocking beyond my imagination. In the Jails and Asylums for the poor, I found Criminals, Insane persons and Idiots, Paupers and a general mass of the most unfortunates dwelling in circumstances overwhelmingly adverse to their own physical and moral improvement. In Almshouses, I found conditions as dreadful. One man I met was a former respected legislator and jurist who had suffered from a most severe mental decline and fallen into hard times in old age. I found him lying on a small bed in a basement room of the county Almshouse, bereft of the most basic and necessary comforts. Reduced thus to a wretched soul and a helpless pauper, he evidently still remembered who he once was. He knew of his downfall, and it agonised him to think on what he had become and on the wretched place where his life was reaching its conclusion, forgotten by the society he once served. I presented his case to the local State legislature, as many members there knew him, to offer them insight into how this can and does happen to anyone, even most successful and respected of people in society. As I made clear to those assembled, it could happen to them.

His story was but one of thousands. In cages, closets, cellars, stalls, and pens, I found people chained naked or half-naked. They were beaten with rods, and lashed with ropes or whatever weapons were available until they succumbed into obedience. These helpless beings were incarcerated for such a length of time, they were entirely forgotten by family, friends, colleagues and society. Men and women sunk to a condition which would startle and horrify even those who are usually unconcerned with anyone but themselves.

As I travelled, I made detailed notes from my observations. Thus, with a high degree of accuracy, I could report the conditions. I visited buildings ill-contrived, ill-built and ill-suited for their inhabitants and their purpose. Spaces were crowded, unsanitary, damp, and, on more than one occasion, flooded. One hospital was housed in a basement with damp walls and no circulation, water constantly on the floor from the rain and goodness knows what else. Workshops were uncomfortable and unsafe, with no seating provided for the men and women who labored all day until darkness. I saw walls completely collapsed or yielding ready to collapse. I met inmates confined in one small space for decades. I measured cells three feet three inches wide by seven feet long, with the number of convicts constantly exceeding the number of cells, resulting in these souls having to share two to a cell. Where there was no cell space, the most unfortunate were detained in cellars or chained to the walls.

No attempt to remedy the conditions was made. The object of the penitentiary is reform, and yet I saw nothing attempting to achieve such. Many institutions had no arrangements at all for bathing or any sufficient means for inmates to maintain a tolerable level of personal cleanliness. These inhumane conditions directly affected the health of the prisoners and produced an effect of extreme disadvantage to themselves and to all other persons around them.

When their sentences expired, inmates were discharged onto the street without money and almost naked, their clothes falling apart. Having received no moral support or reform of any kind, the likelihood of criminals reoffending was high and the likelihood of insane people deteriorating further was almost guaranteed, for none of them were in a condition fit to survive in the world. They had no friends or family, they had forgotten how to care for themselves, and they were oblivious to any form of decency. The probability of repetition or continued outrageous behaviour was immensely high.

The wardens, keepers and other staff I interviewed were mostly honest and candid. Not unkind or cruel by nature, they were untrained, unskilled, and lacking in consideration for their wards. They never behaved towards the inmates with pity or kindness, and had become so familiar with witnessing immense suffering that they were immune to it. Staff either had not the means or the knowledge to conduct rightly that which would normally have been done out of sheer human decency to provide for those whose care was their responsibility. They had stopped caring, hardened to sufferings they could not remedy, and which consequently they would strive to forget. In one Almshouse the patients pleaded for companionship, and for help to find employment, but those in charge said they had no time to assist.

Across the country, I witnessed the same; every State I visited had abandoned their convicts and their lunatics. In each State I compiled the evidence and delivered it in detailed reports which were presented on my behalf, pressing the State legislators to recognise their obligation to correct such abuse of humanity. I made sure to be noticed at the highest level. I urged them to appreciate that lunacy can affect any person, not one human being is invulnerable, whether rich or poor, of high or low pedigree, whether unlearned or learned, with small or huge intellect, old or young, with full vigor or feeble with weakness of the body. I asked them to place themselves in the situation of these poor wretches, and consider how they too could be inflicted by this insane malady.

Measurable success was eventually achieved in New Jersey, New Hampshire, Illinois, North Carolina and Pennsylvania. I learned how to articulate effectively so as to formulate and win my case, and thus I moved on to Maryland. By now, the scale of the task ahead weighed mighty heavily, as the more I researched, the more evidence I amassed. I surmised that the problem was one of National significance. Increasingly, I felt as though work ahead was becoming insurmountable. I came to understand State officials would most likely follow a National lead. Only a National change in law would be enough to ensure an end to this national suffering.

When my 1852 Memorial paper was presented to State legislators in Maryland, I paid particular attention to the detail in this report in the hope it might be used as reference for a national case. I presented my evidence respectfully but plainly and earnestly to bring to their knowledge a summary of the records gathered through cautious enquiry and meticulous investigation. I informed them most clearly, no eye could be blind to the significance of these records.

I focussed attention on the Insane and Idiots, reporting there were but two institutions in Maryland, both insufficient in providing suitable treatment and offering cure. I explained that the miserable alternatives were either the Almshouses, which accommodated hundreds of insane persons with no proper means of treatment or cure, or else the County Jail or penitentiary, with its dungeons, cells, chains and manacles. I wrote in the strongest terms against the perpetration of this great abuse and pleaded for the urgency of the objectives, though language, however strong, was insufficient to describe the terrible conditions and the abject sufferings of the insane I witnessed.

My report recommended the establishment of a State Hospital, putting an end to these scenes. Such atrocities, I said, should not be suffered for a day, let alone decades. A Hospital would offer dignity, appropriate interventions and hope. Allowing the current situation to continue was blemishing the reputation not only of the local community, or the State, but the whole of our civilized nation.

The provision of a State Hospital would be an opportunity to commence rectification. Medical men of sound minds and rare skill could be called upon, I argued, to support patients in preventing further deterioration. They could treat the young before the disease attached itself to them for life. The facts and figures I presented demonstrated this was better for the individual and cheaper than providing lifelong care, cheaper too than cure at a later stage.

Prevention and cure should not be the only concern, I said. Of vast importance also would be the secure and comfortable provision for those poor individuals who are incurably insane. It is perfectly possible to ameliorate any condition and to elevate even the most severely affected by malady to some degree, however small, that they might be offered relief and be of usefulness in society. Useful employment contributes so profoundly to the restoration of the patient.

A full economic breakdown was offered through charts and tables to illustrate and provide evidence for all my claims. Thus, it was shown, while the interests of humanity would be satisfied by the establishment of well-regulated hospitals for the insane, the political economy and the public safety were no less guaranteed.

My final plea was to seek their decision, reassuring them they had the means to exercise justice, through moral and civil obligation, and urging them to consider a future day when they would look back on their lives, recalling with consolation their part in the accomplishment of a great work of humanitarian reform and social justice. I went so far as to place an exclamation point at the very last for emphasis, in my concluding proclamations on the advancement of knowledge towards perfection!

Through facts and statistics, I documented and demonstrated the rapid and fearful increase in this terrible malady across the whole country. I made a point to show this was not due to immigration, as claimed without any substantial evidence. I sought out persons to corroborate my work and further the cause, and am indebted to Senator Solomon Foot of Vermont for his unwavering support in Congress, who has argued there for the passage of the National Bill. I have concentrated much effort on this Land-Grant Bill For Indigent Insane Persons for years, and my ally Senator Foot has presented several amendments and proposals, thus far to no avail. He is armed with the facts and argues frequently and eloquently, explaining the amelioration of the condition of this suffering by a large and increasing number of our impoverished citizens, is of primary interest and of national concern. He uses my words but makes them his own in putting the case. We are seeking for ten million acres of

American land to be sold, and ask that the proceeds from these sales to be distributed to ALL the States to build and maintain asylums across the Nation. Senator Foot uses my argument that it is the duty and proper business of all the States to provide adequately for their indigent insane, and explains this National Bill will encourage and aid them in the discharge of this duty. With my memorial reports as refences, the economic case was included in the Bill and all the benefits listed, inclusive of the benefits to those suffering with insanity, to those around them, and to society. The Bill was passed in BOTH Houses of Congress, and we were assured, and allowed ourselves to believe, it would succeed.

But alas! Our own President Pierce has argued against it and has vetoed the Bill at the eleventh Hour! He declares social reform is the responsibility of each State. What, I questioned myself, am I to do? I simply do not possess the strength to visit every State, research every institute, report to every State legislature.

I am exhausted. But I remain determined, and can imagine no better place to be to gather myself again, than back in England with you. There, I can seek the restorative company of splendid friends, and assimilate more knowledge from you and your countrymen and women. When we last met, I troubled you to offer me insights into the English lunacy reforms. You did this willingly and without hesitation, such is your generosity and your eagerness to advocate for those who are helpless and forgotten. I have often spoken in my correspondences, but I do not hesitate in mentioning again, that the labors of your group and the way you conduct your affairs enlighten and inspire me, and it is this inspiration I seek again.

I wish to become acquainted with your Acts of Parliament, in particular the Lunacy Act and The County Asylum Act championed by Lord Ashley, and to witness with my own eyes how these are implemented across your isle. I understand the Acts provide for the compulsory creation of asylums across your counties, and that each asylum has written regulations and a resident physician. Conditions and treatments are monitored and inspected by the Lunacy Commission. I wish, if possible, to meet members of your Alleged Lunatics Friend Society who campaign for the protection of the British subject from unjust confinement, which we must address here in the States.

I require reassurance it is possible to provide for the desolate, the outcast, the forgotten idiotic men and women of a Nation, beings reduced to such a condition even those previously unconcerned would shrink back in horror at their most inhumane treatment. I wish to see with my own eyes facilities where accommodation is sanitary, where people are occupied and adequately fed, and where staff are knowledgeable and compassionate towards their inmates.

I know of no better place to start than by connecting with your honorable selves once again. I am unsure whether I will possess the mental or physical strength to conduct much, at least to begin with, especially as the journey itself will be challenging. I suspect I may become a permanent resident in one of the hospitals we have managed to establish, such is my frailty on occasion. But with your help, my challenges, at least for the present, will not be impossible.

Your dear friend,

Dorothea Dix

Chapter Twenty-Three

Jean

'Bloody hell,' she said to Mary Anning on the wall, as she put aside the letter and hauled her reluctant body out of the perfectly warm, perfectly comfortable bed. 'I'm worrying about my own irrelevant life, and this woman was worrying about the mental well-being of the entire population of America. Why does her name sound familiar? "My dears William and Lucretia…" Oh, blimey! This was the first letter I saw when Cynthia showed me the letters. God, that seems so long ago.'

She read Alex's message again. Maybe it was genuine. Maybe she could trust this person. She decided to reply, and aimed at keeping it polite and unemotional.

Hi Alex, I'm sorry too. I shouldn't have run off. Yes, let's talk. Later today maybe? We could visit Cynthia if you want, and ask if she can shed any light on the letters.

She spent the morning at Cynthia's dining room table delving into Dorothea's world and investigating whether it would be acceptable to include verbatim the words she used. Words such as "lunatic" and "idiot". In Dorothea's time, a lunatic was broadly speaking a person with mental health problems and an idiot was someone with a learning disability. An asylum was a place of refuge, retreat or safety for people with mental health problems. "Indigent" meant needy, destitute and impoverished. Helena recalled Chris talking about integrity, and concluded the language used by Dorothea was appropriate for the time. She made a note of the suggestion online that any book referencing language from a particular period could include a caveat explaining this.

Dorothea couldn't vote, couldn't attend many of the meetings she prepared reports for, and was herself blighted by mental illness, and yet she was a pioneer, one of the first people dedicated to reducing the stigmatisation of people with mental health issues, who were popularly viewed as inferior and deserving of the atrocious conditions in which they were kept because of perceived sin, poor intellect or weak morals. She sought out like-minded compassionate people, such as her supporters in the States who represented her at the highest levels, and

William and Lucretia Rathbone, who supported her on her visits to the United Kingdom. Helena found it hard to get her head around how much she achieved, given her mental health problems and the society in which she lived. It was heartbreaking to read that after everything she did, poor Dorothea did indeed find herself in one of the thirty-two hospitals she was instrumental in founding.

The more she researched mental health, the more Helena suspected she had unresolved issues, as stuff she tried to bury kept resurfacing at the first sign of stress or conflict. She remembered Carol explaining how depression affected her. Helena considered her own tendencies to become extremely anxious, and to feel intensely low and inadequate. She used to assume everyone felt the same. Now she believed perhaps they didn't. Inevitably, her thoughts began to centre on her mum. She had read somewhere that writing letters that would never be sent was a useful therapeutic tool. The recommendation was to let it all out, no holds barred. Using her new pen and notepad, Helena began to write.

Dear Jean,

I don't know where to begin.

You were so cruel to me. Why? Why did you always have to put me down? How did you think your being nasty was going to work out for me? I guess you probably didn't ever stop to think about what it would do to me. You were too wrapped up in yourself.

Here is a selection of the things you said to me.

- You'll never get a boyfriend looking like that.

- Sometimes I really am ashamed to be seen with you.

- Your dress sense is so drab.

- You're getting fat.

- Why don't you do something useful with your life?

- You should try nursing, they are so desperate, they'll take anyone.

- Don't you dare think about being a lezzer. I've seen the way you look at girls.

- Don't you dare be late home. I'll need my tea, if you can be bothered to get me anything.

- My life could have been so different.

- Ooh don't you look lovely. Not.

- Ooh isn't this coffee nice. Not.

- Oh, don't put yourself out for me.

- After all I've done for you.

All this would be in the mornings when you weren't completely bladdered yet. You had wine and soda for breakfast, saying it was fizzy apple juice. Did you honestly think I was so stupid?

When I came in from school, you were often more or less unconscious, you were so drunk. There was no money as you'd squandered it all on booze and fags. I had to rummage in the kitchen for scraps to eat.

Your only friends were the cigarettes, the wine and the gin bottles. No-one ever came to visit you, to pop in for a cuppa and a natter.

Not once did I have a friend over for tea or a sleepover.

You'd send me out on errands when you were too pissed to go out of the house. It was ok for me to see you in a state, but god forbid the neighbours or the man in the corner shop saw you. He would have known though. Every morning you must have walked down there for the day's supply, once I was packed off to school.

No wonder Dad left you. I expect he couldn't stand you any longer. But I had no choice. I was stuck with you.

Why do you think I never did very well at school? Actually, I was good at English, no thanks to you. I could escape into my stories and pretend I was anywhere but with you.

When you weren't pissed you'd tell me how different your life could have been. What you would have done, how clever you were, and how it was everyone else's fault you ended up as you did. But it wasn't anyone else's fault. It was your own stupid fucking fault.

You have never been a proper mother to me. You have been a burden. I am glad I am out of your life. Maybe in your old age, you wonder why you are alone.

In some ways, I feel sorry for you. Perhaps you had a tough upbringing I don't know, you never mentioned it. But that's no excuse. Not everyone who has a tough upbringing ends up like you.

When I picture you, all I see is this pathetic figure slumped on the sofa, surrounded by the unwashed cups and plates of the day, commanding me to wash up, put the laundry on, get your food, take you to the loo.

I hate you. I will never forgive you for taking away my childhood, for ruining my life.

Helena stopped. She released the pen from her grip, suddenly aware that her fingers were aching. The pen was wet from her sweaty palms. Her heart was pounding. These were things she had never uttered to anyone, including herself. She questioned if this was a therapeutic thing to do after all, unconvinced it was doing her good to feel this bad. It was obvious she should deal with her pent-up emotions. But for now, she needed to try and focus elsewhere. She spent the day working on letters from other nineteenth and early twentieth century women, all the while trying to quell billowing sensations of inadequacy at everything these women achieved.

One was from New Zealand, mountaineer Constance Barnicoat, who had a mountain named after her. Another was from Lucy Parsons, the daughter of a slave, and an American activist. She highlighted in her letter the plight of starving children in Chicago and was in favour of violence in political campaigns. Several letters were from women whose lives had been marred by lack of recognition or by great despair. Helena jotted in her notebook these could be themes. Emily Hobhouse was a British anti-war campaigner who reported on the terrible conditions in which inmates were held at concentration camps in South Africa during the Boer War. She was never acknowledged for this work, but instead was criticized by the British government and deported from South Africa. Edith Ellis was a lesbian author who had an open marriage and a nervous breakdown. The artist Mabel Nicholson was overshadowed by her famous husband William. Clare's note explained how many of Mabel's poignant paintings were of her children and the quiet interiors of the house, presumably where she spent most of her days being the dutiful wife and mother. A brief letter from an actress called Peg Entwistle stopped Helena in her tracks.

Dear Uncle,

Thank you for taking care of me and my brothers after Father died. It was only in his will I found out my mother had not died when I was an infant, as I had always been told. This revelation affected me tremendously. My attempt at marriage was a complete failure; you were right, he wasn't to be trusted. I should have listened to you. I tried to become successful as a serious actress, and labored in vain to find suitable roles to convey heart and depth. Finally, the opportunity came with "Thirteen women" but I fear it will fail miserably. I am sorry for everything. Sorry for the burden I have been and for the pain I am causing.

Peg.

Peg killed herself by throwing herself off the "H" of the "Hollywood" sign not long before the film was released. She was twenty-four years old. The suicide note found in her purse at the scene implied she had sought the finality of death for a while. She divorced after only two years, saying her husband was cruel and hadn't told her he had been previously married and had a child. Bette Davis and others had greatly admired her gifts as an actress. Clare's note included one sentence that particularly struck Helena: *"This is what happens when a vulnerable young girl has no proper support, having lived a life of loss and suffering. She was beautiful and talented, but this wasn't enough."*

Being beautiful and talented hadn't been enough to heal gaping internal wounds. If Peg had received proper treatment, she might have been successful and lived a fulfilling life. Instead, her life, her future, her gift, were all wiped out in an instant. Helena couldn't help but reflect on her own situation. *Peg had no-one to help her, and yet here I am, pushing people away who might genuinely want to help.*

Later, Helena and Alex met outside the hospital. Alex seemed awkward too, judging by the amount of hand-in-pocket key shuffling. Helena decided it was best to avoid mentioning the previous night. They walked down the corridor and turned to enter Cynthia's ward, discussing how they could broach the subject of where the original letters might be, but as they entered and saw her, they glanced at one another and shook their heads. Alex mouthed silently, 'Not now.'

Cynthia was propped up in bed with an oxygen mask, her eyes closed and her mouth slightly open. Various tubes emanated from the bed, leading to machines which beeped and hummed. Without batting an eyelid, Alex bent down and gave her a little kiss on the forehead. Helena marvelled at this natural ability for affection and intimacy. Cynthia slowly opened her eyes, and blinked repeatedly as she came to.

'How are you feeling?' Helena asked.

'They are so good to me,' Cynthia replied. Her voice was small and quiet. 'There is a shortage of pillows, but they managed to find me extra ones.' Helena bent down towards her.

'I'm really glad you're being well looked after, Cynthia. I'm sorry I didn't come to you sooner the other day. But you're in the right place now. How are you feeling today?'

'You have done nothing to be sorry for. You have your own life to live,' said Cynthia, glancing at Alex.

Cynthia obviously wasn't going to tell her how she was feeling.

As if hearing her thoughts, Cynthia said,

'They need to move me into a hospice.'

Chapter Twenty-Four

Susan

Dear Sara,

I trust all is well with you and your family, and sincerely hope your work at the Connecticut Indian Association continues to bring you much satisfaction.

It is with an extremely heavy heart I write. Unfortunately, I must resign from my position as government physician after only four years in the post. It was my intention to continue for much longer than I have managed, and I am obliged to write to you with my decision as I wish you to hear this news directly from me. I could not bear it were you to question my dedication and question your wisdom in supporting me.

I am writing to explain why this situation has arisen and aim to reassure you that your faith in me has not been in vain. If my life is spared, my mission will continue. But in case anything should happen to me, I am writing to offer you my most honest and plain account of my experience.

I longed to be a physician for my people since being a little girl. I recall as a small child sitting at the bedside of an elder as she died waiting for the reservation doctor to arrive. Four times a message was sent out and four times we were reassured the doctor was coming. But the doctor never came. I always felt it was because she was "only" an Indian, and if she had been white, the doctor would surely have attended. It was most unjust. From that very day, a seed was planted. This seed was able to grow into reality, thanks in large part to you.

It was clear to me I was a person ideally suited for the job – not due to any misguided arrogance on my part but because of my unique position. I knew the language of my people and I understood their customs, but I appreciated also that the white man's advancements in medicine went beyond the knowledge of my own people who lacked the expertise to treat the modern diseases encountered in recent years. Further, my parents brought us up to understand the essentials for the survival of our people. You have heard me speak of my parents. They raised their daughters to believe we could achieve, and should not settle for the impression we were merely

Indians. But they knew we had to adapt and fast. "It is either civilization or extermination," my father used to say to us. Many criticized him for sacrificing much of our land and say he is not true Omaha because of his mixed background. He had no choice – if he didn't agree to selling a portion of the land, we could lose all of it by force. He believed he was saving us. He did not brand me with tattoos as he knew I would need to fit in with white people if I was going to succeed in their education system. He did not wish for me to be branded as any one thing over another. I remain loyal to this is idea even now. Although I dress in the American style now, in my heart I remain Omaha. Having parents of mixed heritage means I see things from every angle, can see where the problems are, and am in a position to fix them. I must admit though, I often feel I am not American enough to fit in with the other scholars, and not Omaha enough to fit in with my people. Being of mixed heritage has its advantages and disadvantages!

I am forever in your debt, dear Sara and will never forget your appeals on my behalf and your kind words of recommendation. I blush at your statements of my refinement, gentleness and sweetness, and without you supporting my case and your financial and moral backing through the Connecticut Indian Association, I might not have succeeded in qualifying. I have much respect for your branch of the Women's National Indian Association. However, as I am sure you appreciate I do not much care for all of their values and claims. The idea of a woman being submissive is not a concept I was brought up to believe. I realize, knowing both societies, that Omaha women enjoy more freedoms and rights in our society than white women. We are not owned by our husbands, we are not obliged to do as they tell us. We have rights to our property, our possessions, our children, and our bodies. The American idea of a woman being the housekeeper of one household does not sit right for me. I desire nothing less than to be the keeper of my people. It is not true they live degraded lives, as the WNIA claims. I openly acknowledge we can learn from the Americans on such affairs as business, medicine and money, but our way of life has much to offer too. There are many things the Women's movement in America could learn from us! Indeed, I believe there have already been meetings between Omaha woman and American ladies; hopefully both sides are open to sharing with and benefitting from one another's wisdom and experience.

Some 1300 miles away from the plains of home, I was exhausted and nervous when I arrived in Philadelphia as the first Indian female medical student. I decided to dress as a white woman. I had no desire to draw attention to my heritage lest it got in the way of my studies – people would be more interested in me being Indian than being a student, and might not take me seriously in traditional dress. That being said, I wasn't always serious, and once held a knife during cadaver dissections, playfully announcing it was not a scalping knife! However, beneath the joking and my American appearance, loyalty to my tribe never wavered and my mission was to return home to them as soon as I was able.

My three years at the Women's Medical College was invaluable. I came to appreciate my people lacked vital knowledge regarding cleanliness and avoiding disease. Additionally, I became versed in matters of business, land and money, the American way of doing official things. I loved the city life in Philadelphia, especially the music and theatre. Despite this, I never faltered in my resolve that I had to leave there. As you will remember, I visited the Omaha reservation in my second year of training because my nursing skills were needed by my parents and by those afflicted with the measles epidemic. I had acquired a fair amount of knowledge by then, and could see clearly how much my people were desperate for a skilled physician.

My graduation was an especially joyous occasion, and I was honored to receive high praise for my results, and to be the first Omaha woman to qualify, though I would never boast to anyone but my dearest friends. Many of my tutors advised me to stay and work with white people rather than "waste all that education on the Indians." How little they knew me. I was not going to be dissuaded by anyone. Besides, if I had assimilated into American culture, I would enjoy less freedom, and I could not sacrifice my freedom. I politely refused their offers and suggestions. I have learned to be such a diplomat!

On returning to Nebraska, I found it daunting to imagine myself the sole physician and medical missionary to all the Omaha. I was so anxious after treating my first patient, I felt obliged to visit his family the following day, only to find the child outside playing as if nothing had been wrong. This gave me a degree of confidence, and I hoped too, my people would begin to come to me and trust me after seeing him recover.

I savored the opportunity to live at the government school with my dear sister Marguerite, who is still the principal. She sends you her sincere and best wishes. Being employed directly by the government's Office of Indian Affairs, I had access to funds enabling me to furnish my clinic with all the latest medical treatments and a smart desk, and I tried to make it welcoming with games and books for the children, and magazines for the adults. I intended my little clinic to be a haven in the community. At first, I thrived on the work, tending to all the ailments as they were presented to me. Had I been able to remain in the clinic and receive my all patients there, perhaps I could have continued with this job. Unfortunately, not all of the people could get to me, and required home visits. I gladly dedicated myself to travelling across the land to wherever I was needed. I began to teach the people about general health, especially modern hygiene, the preparation of nutritious meals, and the dangers of alcohol. I was happy to spend extra hours advising them too on money and business matters, and on protecting their land. They all came to know me as Dr Susan. I was fond of being called such, I felt gratified by it and was proud of it.

The more I went out to visit my patients across the tribal lands of Omaha, the more I realized how desperate the situation was becoming. The spread of white people's diseases and a lack of basic knowledge on matters of health and hygiene has led to catastrophe. In four short years, I have seen a lifetime of desperation and disease, including consumption, influenza, dysentery, malaria, cholera, and the most awful conjunctivitis epidemic, all of these diseases spreading easily due to the poor sanitation. The way Indians are forced onto designated reservations packed tightly together has aggravated the spread of disease amongst us, and the demon drinks, especially rum and whiskey brought in by the white fur traders and now peddled among our people, has only made things worse. It was the same for other tribes. I saw this when I began visiting the Winnebago people as their plight too was perilous.

I stretched myself beyond capacity, rising at five in the morning, and going out in all weathers, with a buffalo hide for a coat in the worst of the blizzards. Despite working fourteen hours every day, it was impossible to keep up. In the space of a few months, during one bitter winter, I saw over half of my people for one reason or another. Temperatures were almost unbearable. The buggy and horse helped enormously, but travelling across the Omaha reservation which measures thirty by forty-five miles, and which I can only traverse slowly as the roads are poor and still consist of uneven mud and rocks, has become too arduous.

Now, I must concede. I cannot care for the people properly. The first Indian woman doctor in America has been defeated by the enormity of her task and it is not right for me to carry on, not fair on my people. It has all taken its toll on this poor little maid's body. I am extremely frail compared to how I was. My health has never been robust, but in recent months it has worsened considerably. The pains in my neck, back and ears are worse, and I must resort to my bed with them when they become hard to bear. My body demands me to slow down, and I have no choice but to oblige. I hope I can recover enough with rest, that I may carry on in whatever form I am capable. The conditions to be remedied remain many and severe.

There is much to do: people to tend and minds to persuade. They still need to be convinced to accept the American medical methods. Rest assured, my spirit is not defeated, and my will is strong. I am comforted by the prospect that I might continue to help the poor souls of my community in whatever way I am capable. If I ever become too frail to practice medicine, I may become a missionary. Speaking several languages will be an advantage and there is much to be done there too. Marguerite and I already assist at Church and my religious work sits well alongside my medical. The Christian faith is rejected by many Omaha, but I believe it to be part of our salvation. I am told I was the first Indian girl to be educated by Quaker missionaries. They saw my potential and had me help out with teaching the other children, allowing me to learn much more than the usual domestic duties expected of girls. The Quaker Policy has had a huge influence on me, and without the gentle but strong Quakers, I fear our people might been exterminated altogether – through disease and alcohol, or through annihilation by force. We have much to thank them for.

Even with the Peace Commission and the Grant Peace Policy our people continue to suffer greatly. Many simply were not inclined to live as the white man lives, to become "civilized" and "christianized." Not all my people feel the way as I do, and fear at times I belong nowhere, but I have faith that God will continue to guide me as He sees fit.

For now, I will remain here. I hope to continue in private practice. My dream is to open a hospital on our land, a place where people can come and stay, where they can expect and receive the best treatments with doctors and nurses to attend them, in a clean environment, to help them recover and thrive. I will strive also to ensure we install at least one Field Matron to take on a proportion of the home visits, a person the Indians can respect and begin to trust. Many remain hesitant to accepting services from white men and women however well-intentioned they might be. The building of trust will take time, many years perhaps, and the medical and missionary people must have patience and understanding.

I continue to learn from and greatly admire many white people. I assimilate their culture into my own and try to use the best parts of both in my work. I believe this is how we must go on. We can preserve our Omaha traditions and incorporate American ideas. In return, the Americans may learn from all we can offer them. We should respect one another's cultures and appreciate both have merit, both have their place, we can co-exist. The financial cost will be tiny compared with the benefits it will offer. We can make amends for the suffering of our people as a result of poor education, poverty and discrimination in provision, especially health services. White people became civilized over a period of years, so it will take us a period of years to catch up. Rather than put us down, they could help us. As long as we can retain our culture, this blend has to be the right way forwards. I believe we are owed this much. I believe we are on the cusp of great progress in our country. My dream is to run a service where I can treat Indians and white people alongside each other. I shall always carry on advocating for this, even if I must do it alone.

Some may say that my father and I are responsible for weakening our people's position. I say we made it stronger. At least we are still here! As a woman I cannot vote, and as an Indian, I am unable to gain American citizenship, but as an Omaha woman and doctor I can have a degree of influence across both cultures. I will continue to make the most of my life. Your investment in me has not been wasted.

I remain your friend and grateful servant,

With sincere best wishes to you Sara and your husband,

Susan LaFleche

Chapter Twenty-Five

Rachel

Each day stretched out in front of Helena as an amorphous entity through which she had to navigate and with which she had to try and achieve something. She had moaned about having to get up early for work, but now she didn't need to, there was a void where structure had once existed. Into this void inevitably crept unhelpful thought patterns that churned around incessantly.

She was concerned for Cynthia, whose health was failing fast. And selfishly, she was concerned for herself. Losing Cynthia was like losing the only proper mother she'd ever known. She desperately wanted to make Cynthia proud, but she had no clue how to manage such a big house and garden, and all she had to show for her creative efforts were a bunch of scrappy notes and a whole lot of muddled thinking.

Then, there was Alex, who genuinely seemed to be a remarkable, kind, and loving person. Helena convinced herself she was going to ruin this relationship before it had even had a chance because she was so difficult to love. Why would anyone desire her? She was an overweight, inadequate, plain-looking ball of angst, with little to show for her five plus decades on the planet. Not exactly a great catch.

Trying to occupy herself by reading more letters and contemplating the book didn't help, because the more she read concerning the remarkable things other women had done, the more she felt inferior. Women such as Susan La Fleche. Like Cynthia, her spirit remained strong even when her body was failing. She was a woman who defied all the odds, assimilating into white society to ensure her people could benefit from what it could offer, and tending to her people with grace, enduring immense hardship in the process. She was criticized by white people for treating Omaha people, and criticized by Omaha people for selling out. But she didn't give up. She carried on bridging two cultures and working, despite being in pain, being criticised, being unable to vote and being marginalised. She succeeded in opening a mixed hospital, for treating white and native American patients together. She died at only forty-nine; the pain she had endured for years turned out to be bone cancer. Sara Kinney, to whom the letter was written, was quite a woman herself. She was President of the Connecticut Indian Association and with her husband carried out vital fundraising on Susan's behalf, raising the required funds for her to attend medical school.

Helena could choose any letter and feel shitty. Ruth Homan, for example. She was a progressive thinker and activist who, amongst other things, was on the London School Board, was a founding member of what would become the Humanist movement, was President of a Nursing Association, was active in the Children's Boot and Clothing Help Society and the London Schools Dinners Association, was on the council of the Women's Industrial Council, was a vice-president of the Pupil-Teachers Association, was in the Club of Working Girls, was president of the Cornish Union of Women's Liberal Associations and of the Hammersmith Women's Liberal Association, and was a member of the Women's Local Government Society. All this, on top of being a wife and mother.

Helena wasn't any of those things. Helena was lost. After wasting the morning inside her spinning head and drinking endless cups of tea, she remembered over lunch that Carol had mentioned the name of a counsellor. She stared at her phone for twenty minutes, imagining how she'd be criticised for admitting to her weaknesses. Eventually she concluded that whatever Carol said, it couldn't be worse than everything she was already thinking. She scrolled to Carol's number and clicked "Call." The phone went straight to voicemail. No, no, and no, this wasn't happening. She hung up. Ten minutes later, Carol rang back.

'Hi Helena. Sorry, I was in a meeting. I saw I had a missed call from you. Everything ok?'

Carol listened while Helena talked through her tears. Not once did she criticise.

A week later, Helena waited for five seconds after ringing the doorbell, and was turning to flee when she heard footsteps approach from within the house. She was already regretting this, having walked up the perfectly swept pathway past the perfectly mown lawn bordered by the perfect rows of white cyclamen to reach the perfectly painted glossy black door. How would a person with such a perfect life be able to help her?

The door swung open and a neat woman approximately her age offered her a smile and a hand to shake.

'You must be Helena. Hello, I'm Rachel,' said Rachel. During the handshake, Helena inadvertently crossed the threshold into the perfectly beige hallway. Literally, everything in it was beige, from the carpet and walls to the triptych of leaf pictures in their beige wooden frames.

Since ringing Carol, Helena had embarked on a mini-mission in an attempt to care for herself a bit better. She'd signed up to an online CBT course and was trying to work on couple of the exercises. One of them was to be non-judgemental and keep an open mind. That was her mantra for the week. Even so, this was the blandest place she'd ever seen. She'd also been to her GP for the first time in years, and he had prescribed a mild anti-depressant to get her over this hump, as he put it. Nothing to worry about, lots of people took them nowadays, he had said. Finally, she'd invested in a pair of supermarket reading glasses. She figured it was wise to accept she needed them, as the typed letters had begun straining her eyes.

Rachel took her coat, and led her into a lounge room where the beige theme continued save for a large soft green armchair, towards which she was ushered. Beside it was a small table set with a glass of water and a box of tissues.

'Thank you for sending in your form,' said Rachel, settling into an upright chair a few feet from Helena. Everything about her seemed considered, down to where she placed herself in relation to her client. 'It's always helpful to get the housekeeping out of the way before we start. That way, the whole fifty minutes is devoted to talking. I'll begin by asking where you wish to start.' Helena hesitated slightly, and then began. Fifteen minutes later, she stopped for air and said,

'God, I am so sorry. I don't know where all that came from.'

'You've been bottling up a lot, and for a long time, Helena. It's an important first step, to let it all out. My job is to give you the space to do it.' She was being very pleasant, measured and reasonable. A small part of Helena wanted to find fault. If anything, her only fault was that she appeared to be faultless. She wore a perfectly fitting cream jumper dress over her slim figure and skin tone tights, her feet positioned neatly on the floor in brown pumps. Her trim figure and her pose suggested she was self-assured, and went to the gym often. The kind of person Helena usually avoided, to be frank.

'Would you be ok if I made a couple of observations from what you have said?'

'Oh, please do,' said Helena. As you can probably tell, I need all the help I can get. Can you tell me where I am going wrong?'

'I don't have the answers, Helena. And there is no right or wrong. Your feelings are all valid. My role will be to support you in finding ways to manage them. I do this by reflecting on everything you say as you work on making sense of your thoughts, and talking through ideas and strategies which aim to help you manage better. It may take a while, but you've already taken the first huge leap by coming here. Does that make sense?'

'Yes, it does. There's no magic pill, right?'

'Exactly. My initial observation, Helena, is that you are tremendously hard on yourself. You carry a lot of self-doubt, and perhaps you feel unworthy – not worthy to be staying in a lovely house, not worthy of writing a book, not worthy of having a loving partner. It's as if a barrier is stopping you from embracing these things and enjoying them, even though I sense you desire them.'

'You have…wow, you've worked all this out after me blathering on for a few minutes?'

'What I said rings true?'

'Absolutely. I had never been able to put it into words, but yes, you're right.'

'It would be helpful to identify the root cause of these feelings, and explore how you might challenge them, if this sounds reasonable to you?' Helena nodded. 'This may involve facing issues that make you uncomfortable, but it will be beneficial in the longer term.'

'Yes, I understand. No pain, no gain.'

'Precisely. Bear in mind though Helena, there are no right or wrong answers or feelings, ok? Perhaps we could start by recalling a recent event which made you uneasy.'

Helena turned away slightly, face down, and hid behind her hair as the knot of angst in her stomach tightened and she fought the urge to get up and walk away.

There were so many recent events to choose from, she couldn't fathom where to start.

'It doesn't have to be anything huge, Helena, just the first thing that comes into your head.' *OK, maybe Rachel understands. Maybe Rachel has seen people like me before. Come on, deep breath.*

'Well, one thing happened recently when I encountered a Chinese Empress called Wu Zhao. She was incredibly horrible to her son, and completely full of herself. It upset me deeply, and it took me right back to how my mum was with me.'

'Thank you Helena, this is a great start. So, reading about this Empress triggered traumatic memories?'

'Absolutely, yes. It happens a lot. Something apparently insignificant will happen and suddenly I am a young girl again being told off.'

'This is certainly an area we can work on, Helena. Don't worry, we'll go at your own pace and see where it leads us. I can see you are nervous. That's fine, it's completely natural. You've made an important connection already, and I believe you're absolutely ready to do more, if you agree.'

Helena agreed.

For the remainder of the session, they touched briefly on other potential triggers, including relationships, emotional and physical absence, slim people, high-achievers, and a fear of letting herself and others down. These were all things they could explore further, assured Rachel.

'Other people sail through life, dealing with whatever is thrown at them, much more than I've had to deal with, and yet I always struggle,' said Helena. Then she remembered Cynthia's words, as she studied the plush green velvet chair.

'You are reflecting?' said Rachel. 'We should start wrapping up soon, but I would be interested to hear your thoughts, if you are comfortable to share.' Rachel glanced at the pale wooden clock on the wall.

'Yes, I was pondering that each of us is on our own journey, and perhaps this is a theme for the book, maybe?'

'That's a book I would definitely read,' said Rachel. I'd also be interested to read how you came to this project and how you are dealing with writing it.'

'Are you suggesting I should include myself in the book?' Helena scoffed. 'It would be rather messy!' Rachel remained neutral, her expression unchanged.

'It's your decision, of course, but in my opinion it's a fascinating facet. It connects with the concept of us all being on our own journey. Now, if it's ok with you, may I finish by making one more observation?'

'Yes, anything.'

'I have an idea you are not as judgemental as you may believe.'

I daren't tell you what I thought when I entered this beige palace. 'Yes please.'

'You mentioned that you researched the meaning behind Alex's badge, discovering it represented the non-binary colours. You commented also that you didn't mind Alex's lumps and bumps as you called them. You accepted Alex without question. Not everyone can do this. You also became close with Cynthia, who, from your description, might be judged by other people on appearances. As I said, I believe you are rather hard on yourself.'

'I'm sure you're right. I guess I've always compared myself unfavourably to everyone else. I must try to stop doing it as much.'

'The key is to give yourself time and space, not seek to find all the answers overnight. You are exposing yourself emotionally and it's not easy. Before our next session, I'd be grateful if you would consider ways in which you could be a little kinder to yourself.' Helena's eyes began to sting, then a single tear ran down her cheek. She reached for a tissue and blew her nose.

'I'm very grateful to have found you. Thank you.'

Rachel nodded and smiled. It was a professional smile but a kind one. Then, in a seamless movement, she reached for the arms of her chair and stood, signalling the session was over, and Helena followed her into the hallway. They neared the front door, and as Rachel handed Helena her coat, Helena said,

'There's one thing I've recently realised about myself, actually. Alex lent me a book on LGBT+ lives and history. It's got lots of interesting information and I was especially interested in the section on people who are pansexual, attracted to others for who they are, regardless of their sex or identity. I think this might be who I am.'

Helena returned to Cynthia's. She practised positive positioning as Rachel had advised. This involved taking a negative thought and attempting to turn it around into a positive one. The negative: she had an issue with trust. The positive: she had good people around her. She needed to start trusting them, and herself. Maybe this was a turning point. Maybe now her head might start settling down and allow her to concentrate on writing. She selected the next letter from the box and rummaged in her bag for her new reading glasses, then wandered down to the summer house. Being in it might inspire her as it had Clare. The air was still crisp as she crossed the lawns, but there was a hint of warmth, indicating Spring was coming.

Once inside the summer house, she closed the door and sat on the small wooden chair at the small wooden table. Both still had remnants of pink paint on them. Helena traced her fingers across the indentations on table's surface, created over years of use, and imagined Clare scribbling notes in here. Helena touched the round metal keys of the old black metal typewriter Clare had used to type all the letters. Every key had a raised outer edge and proudly displayed its white letter on a black enamelled background. She pressed the 'h' key, and a satisfying click resulted as its other end flew up to hit the empty roll where a piece of paper should be. Typing on this must have connected Clare in a physical and literal way to each letter as it appeared in front of her on the paper. Helena cast her mind back to Cynthia's tea pouring ceremony during her first visit, and how she did things with purpose. Clare probably inherited the same trait.

Helena cautiously lifted the typewriter off the table to give her space to place the letter there, and bent down to place it on the floor. A sharp pain shot along her arm. When she sat upright and removed the hair from in front of her face, she saw a note on the table in Clare's handwriting which must have been hidden underneath the typewriter. That was odd, she had found all the notes for the letters. Squinting, she read the first line: "What to do with the letters." Helena stared wide-eyed, her mind in excited overdrive. This was it. It was all coming together. In a moment, Clare would reveal to her how she was planning to write the book. She would explain how she was going to write a history of women. How appropriate, how brilliant! A gift from Clare, in the summer house, would be the serendipitous catalyst she had been hoping for!! Helena grabbed her glasses and began to devour its contents.

What to do with the letters.

I have over a hundred now. So, what's next? Write a non-fiction on the lives of women through history and include the letters to add flavour and give depth to their stories? Or write a fiction and formulate a story to blend them together? Either way, I should use them...I spent long enough researching each one. It all started as a fun aside to my studies but has evolved into something else. Creating these letters helped me get inside their heads, find each woman's voice. Would it be an interesting way to present history, through a series of imagined letters? I'd need to consider the target audience – any discerning historian would immediately ascertain they're not genuine, and any discerning linguist would probably work out they were written by the same hand. Might talk to mum.

The note started shaking as Helena re-read its revelation. She threw her glasses on the floor and slammed the note down on the table, covering the words with her hand to try and make them disappear while she attempted to process what the actual fuck was going on. Clare had fabricated all the letters. It was a hoax. Helena had felt protective towards her when Alex and Chris had gently quizzed her regarding the whereabouts of the original letters. They were questioning their authenticity. Of course they were right. She was annoyed with Alex and Chris for not being more candid with her, for letting her believe in this rubbish, letting her dream. She was upset with Cynthia for getting her involved in the first place. She was fucking livid with Clare. How dare she put her through all this for nothing. Helena wanted to rip up all the letters there and then to spite her. Most of all, she was furious with herself for being such a fucking idiot. Again.

What the hell was she going to do now?

She had barely left her job to try and write a book but now there was no book to write. This meant there was no money either. She was fucked. She didn't even try to suppress the ball of anger. She let it out in loud, harsh, guttural screams, stamping the wooden floor of the summer house, not caring if the neighbours heard or whether they might judge her.

Once her outburst subsided, she grabbed the letter she'd brought down to the summer house before the dream was shattered. She ought to shred it to pieces. What was the point of reading it now? What was the point of anything? But she had nothing else to do.

Chapter Twenty-Six

Edith

Dear Nina,

We have not always agreed in our approach, but I respect you. I admire your resilience and dedication. You take being arrested and imprisoned in your stride. I admire the way you broke from the Pankhurst group. It was becoming too violent, and your approach of civil disobedience and astute political campaigns is the by far the most effective and superior way to proceed. I recall you made the news in 1914 when you chained yourself to the Marlborough Street Police Court before the War. Your commitment to the cause goes far beyond getting the vote. I appreciate your key role with the Women's Freedom League in initialising the campaign for women to become special constables, and I read with interest an issue of your magazine "The Vote," outlining your central idea that the best people to deal with problem women are women. I disagree with your claim that the women in trouble are not to blame, and are forced into prostitution. No doubt you consider me most old-fashioned. But I was brought up to understand the difference between right and wrong.

The outbreak of War offered women opportunity; we couldn't be denied involvement in important services any longer once the men were gone to fight. Women were essential in filling the roles. You and Miss Dawson were instrumental in ensuring we were organised enough to do it, to get the Women's Police Volunteers started. It was astute of you to begin by recruiting women as volunteers. The National Union of Women Workers had succeeded in drawing attention to the drunkenness and disorder around the military camps, but were too amateurish. Your volunteer scheme paved the way for paid women police officers, with military uniforms and more rigorous training. For this I am most grateful. In my own way, I contribute to the women's movement. I am living proof women are blessed with the stamina and aptitude to do work previously deemed suitable only for men.

I am going to be frank with you. I am in a most unfortunate situation, and seek your counsel. I have long suffered with my nerves. I do not disclose this information freely because it is not polite conversation, and because it is extremely hard to explain to those who do not suffer. My mind is often overrun with darkness and dread for reasons I cannot explain, and not only since the death of my dear husband. On occasion, I am almost consumed by the blackness within my heart. My work has in many ways been my salvation. My job as a sub-postmistress working alongside William, when he was still alive, gave me a degree of assurance that I was capable of holding down a responsible job whilst continuing with my duties as a wife and mother. Having Lillian, our servant, was a great help and allowed me to work the unsavoury hours required for the role. Then it all fell apart when William died, and I lost everything. I was forced to move away to seek alternative opportunities, and went to London, a place familiar as it was my mother's birthplace. Still, it was terribly hard to uproot and leave, to be separated from my children while I found the means to earn enough money. I happened upon the idea of studying to become a nurse midwife. Seeing lots of babies while I rarely got to see my own, it was extremely tough, Nina. My poor little lad James was in an orphanage for a while. Can you imagine the heartache for me as a mother? And the girls were scattered, cared for and schooled separately from one another. It was a challenge finding the strength to keep going.

The War changed everything once more. I am glad I stayed in London as I got to hear of the Women's Police Service. I joined immediately and did my training. I was considered extremely well suited to this position, and a colleague noted I was a woman of outstanding personality, fearless, motherly and adaptable. The first two women who had been stationed in Grantham pioneered a new and vigorous service. When they were moved to Hull I seized the opportunity and applied to replace them. They had been greeted with a degree of hostility initially but had managed to achieve a degree of success and paved the way for us to follow.

Such a disturbing place I found. The arrival of thousands of Kitchener's Army men stationed at Belton Park outside the town had a massive impact on Grantham and there was much fear concerning the spread of disease and the moral danger of local young girls. I got straight down to sorting it. My curfew was the subject of controversy, but it worked, and we got hundreds of girls off the streets at night when the men were drunk and roaming around. Even so, there was more than one occasion when I happened upon a couple in the bushes and had to physically part them, explaining they had a duty to themselves and the country to refrain from getting into trouble or spreading disease. Many of them thanked me for my efforts.

I heard you fell out with the WPS and your original co-founder Miss Dawson, as you disagreed with their methods. You are all for the rights of women, but in Grantham I'm afraid we were faced with a dire situation that necessitated setting aside such notions. We simply had to get on with the job of clearing the streets of disorderliness. The work I did with Miss Teed was quickly recognised and a letter sent to Miss Dawson by Major General F Hammersley himself, commander of the 11th Division at Belton Park Camp, praising our work. It was acknowledged we achieved what the military police could not.

In December 1915 the Council organised direct salaries for us, the same way the men were paid, though at first our income was woefully less than theirs. In the same month, my warrant card was signed by Grantham's Chief Constable Casburn after approval by the Watch Committee. I didn't then appreciate that I was the first woman in the country to have the power of arrest. This status elevated my position, and the work could be carried out more effectively. So it was that I embarked upon the arduous task of rescuing the girls of Grantham. You believe we should perform the same work as the male officers, taking on other duties. One day such a time may come, but what was needed then were women officers specifically dealing with the problem girls and women. Believe me, I was there, it worked.

It soon became apparent who were the girls from our own town, and who were the fallen women flooding in from nearby areas hoping for an opportunity with the men and to earn a few pennies. The risk of venereal disease or pregnancy did nothing to deter them, and many were ignorant of the potential harm, or else they cared not. There was a party atmosphere between the young men stationed near us and the girls, as if they cared nothing for their futures. The young men were desperate to lose their virginity before possibly losing their lives on the field, and many of the girls more than happy to oblige.

My appointment wasn't popular with everyone. The Chief Inspector of Constabulary, Mr Dunning, wrote a Home Office memo complaining that Chief Constable Casburn had fallen into the hands of strong ladies and proffering I was perhaps more of a man than the Chief Constable. The Home Office went as far as advising that women could not be sworn in because they did not count legally as "proper persons" having not yet the vote. But my Chief Constable stood by his decision, and I became directly answerable to him. He recognised my suitability to the role as a woman of maturity and ability. Although of working-class background (my father was a nurseryman and seedman and I was one of six mouths to feed), and although beset by tragedy and the prospect of destitution when my husband died leaving me with four mouths to feed, I made my way in the world.

The following year, we had 411 cases in Grantham, most of them dealt with by me, as Miss Teed left the service. I dealt with no less than a hundred wayward young girls. When cautioning them, I made them realise that prostitution does not pay and is not worth the risk to their bodies and wellbeing. I had much success with the prostitutes: no less than fifty were cautioned, ten were convicted, eight were institutionalised, and ten were returned to their parents. Many left the town willingly due to my persistent presence, rather than get caught. Sixteen drunk women were cautioned, and unsuitable houses were dealt with, including ten dirty houses reported.

In 1917 my salary was raised in recognition of my service and my fine work. Much to their annoyance, I was earning more than the old male Constables. I was praised by Alderman Lee for being the healer of many breaches, a rescuer of girls, a saviour of homes, and the provider of wise counsel and I prevented many cases from reaching court – I was able to deal with them so effectively. Merely my uniformed presence on the streets became enough of a deterrent. This military approach with the girls was necessary in wartime. The Black List of frivolous and wayward girls I developed was an important part of my effective approach. Once this was instituted, even the worst of the girls came into line, for being on the List would deny them access to their favourite places, such as the cinema and the theatre.

I seldom rested. When I wasn't out patrolling, women and girls would come to me at my home for advice on everything – with my nursing background and police training combined with my local knowledge and harsh life experience, I was the only local person equipped to offer this invaluable service. In addition, I went beyond the call of duty in several ways, such as my reporting to the men in service how their women were behaving. I wanted to assure the men their women were being watched carefully. There were those who called me a nuisance, but everything I did was for the common good.

Working those long hours in the most difficult of circumstances gave me purpose and kept my mind occupied. I carried out my duties seven days a week, never taking a holiday, often working well into the night, and seldom seeing my own dear children. I could have stayed in London as a nurse, and sent for the children there, but I sacrificed my family life. It was my war effort, and singlehandedly, I achieved more than was imagined possible. I remain the only woman to be attested, given the power to arrest. Such was the respect I commanded I didn't once need to use it – the threat of it was enough deterrent, as was my presence and personality. The public appreciated my efforts and even most of the male officers eventually grew to acknowledge me. I was, however, becoming immensely weary, and my health started to suffer – to the point where in January 1918 I was forced to resign, due to a combination of mental and physical exhaustion and chest trouble, made worse by the winter weather there.

I moved to Runcorn to take up a nursing position here, and carry out my duties with diligence and care. Since being in Cheshire, I have not only worked for the Halton District Nursing Association, but also gone out of my way to raise much needed funds for them, doing a variety of good deeds including holding whist drives, giving talks, knitting, and running classes. As a direct result of my efforts, the finances of the Association are now healthy. I have made numerous friends here and am a popular person around the town. Many admire me for my straight talking. I have been invited to give talks and am respected not only for my work but also for my musical abilities and sporting prowess. At house parties in the town, I am a popular entertainer and take part in all the indoor games with gusto. To everyone, I always appear to be in high spirits.

Here's the awful truth, Nina, and the reason for this letter. A complaint has been received by the Cheshire Nursing Association. It concerns my methods I believe, and the complaint is from a patient. As a result, Mr Hooker and the rest of the Halton Association are casting aspersions regarding the way I conduct my business.

Instead of coming to me, they invited the County Superintendent of the Cheshire Nursing Association to a Committee meeting. I have not been shown any details of the complaint and was told most bluntly I am not to attend the meeting. If I were allowed to attend at least part of the meeting, I could plead my case, reassure them that the concerns are unfounded. I am in no doubt my methods are sound, and I have done nothing wrong. If they do not let me say my piece and protect my honour, then I fear I will not be able to take it. To suppose decisions surrounding my character and my future are being made without me is simply too much to bear.

I have already handed in my notice and am due to leave next January, as I am to be married again, but apparently that is not enough. I gather I am called matronly. I think it's not only my physicality they refer to but also my ways. I expect I am deemed unfashionable now, and dispensable.

I am waiting to hear the outcome of the meeting. Despite my outward demeanour, I suffer when I am unjustly criticised. It has taken all my strength to find the ways and means to support my family, and it is most unreasonable all my efforts will have come to this. I live for my patients and do not wrong anyone. The Association are treating me terribly cruelly.

I am sure you are extremely busy. With the men returned, and despite the Vote, women have all but disappeared from many key roles we held during the War. I expect you are still immersed in campaigns. I imagine you might be involved, for instance, with Lady Astor's work. I am sure you're delighted with the Vote and with the Sex Disqualification Act, ensuring a woman cannot be disqualified by sex or marriage from the exercise of any public function. I sincerely hope this Act might help me.

I would appreciate a response at your earliest convenience. Can you offer me any advice? Perhaps you have links through your journalism or campaigns and could suggest a person who would support me to fight my case against this discriminatory situation. I am completely alone. I am criticised by those who oppose women's rights, and I am criticised by the women's movements who declare that my methods are too harsh. It is apparent my ways of working are not wanted anymore, but this official involvement excluding my input is completely unreasonable. I am simply at my wits end.

Yours sincerely,
Edith Smith.

Chapter Twenty-Seven

Nina

It was quite uncanny how Rachel could get inside her head and unpack everything that was churning around in there, and how she knew exactly what to say to help Helena make sense of it herself. Maybe she was simply a natural empath. Maybe she'd been well trained. Or maybe having a beige palace was the answer – no distractions. Whatever it was Rachel had, Helena was extremely glad to be on the receiving end of it.

Rachel was the first person to see the note Helena had found under the typewriter. She helped Helena accept that Clare was not deliberately trying to annoy her, Cynthia was not trying to upset her, and Alex and Chris were perhaps in a difficult position. She asked Helena to consider who she could genuinely trust for advice and support. She reminded Helena of the risks in making rash decisions when experiencing intense emotions. She taught Helena how to practice relaxation through deep breathing. She offered to see Helena more often if it would help. It did. After three sessions over the next week, Helena was beginning to understand why she felt the way she did, and how she might address it. She tended to launch herself into things without weighing up the wisdom or otherwise of her decisions, then get completely tangled like a fly in a web; paralysed, and unable to leave or cope. The more this pattern had repeated, the more convinced she had become it was unavoidable. It was a self-fulfilling prophecy of failure. Rachel suggested she should practise trying to appreciate being in the present moment, and observing examples of empathy, either towards her, or by her.

Seeing Alex face to face again the following Saturday, Helena summoned from somewhere the confidence to talk about what she and Rachel had discussed, and to apologise for her outburst. This, she told herself, would be a good test of Alex's character. She would gauge from this conversation whether she could go forwards with this relationship. Alex's response was to hold her, stroke her hair and reassure her she had nothing to apologise about.

'Any one of these letters, had they been genuine, would have been the discovery of a lifetime. It's perfectly understandable that you became swept up in the excitement of the prospect they were genuine.'

Helena had to admit, this was a really good answer. She decided to try again, to build on what they had started. And if things went wrong again, she could always turn to Rachel. They talked for the rest of the day about everything from trust to cooking, and from music to women's suffrage. By the time they went to bed, Helena had put thoughts of betrayal and anger aside. At least for now.

Sunday morning and what would normally be Sunday lunchtime were spent mainly in bed, mainly rediscovering what love-making could be like. Afterwards, Alex offered to prepare some food and scuttled off into the kitchen. Soon, smells of spices and sounds of baking emanated from downstairs as Helena showered and dressed. Her hair still damp, she hurried downstairs and waited, eager to see what had been produced.

'Here you go, a Sunday afternoon treat,' said Alex, entering the dining room carrying a tray of tea and slices of Jamaican spiced cake. 'You look gorgeous there, staring out into the garden with your thoughts. You know, I'm incredibly lucky to have found you.'

As Alex laid the table, Helena managed to catch the words and prevent her mouth saying them out loud. *What have I done to deserve this? What have I done to deserve you?* Instead, she said,

'Thank you. I feel lucky too. I was thinking you've done an amazing job clearing the back garden. Cynthia will be so pleased.'

'Thank you, love.'

'And I was practicing my breathing, noting the sensations of the air on my skin. I love this time of year, when the cold bite yields to a kind of mellow softness, with the promise of warmth to come.'

'Beautifully expressed.' Alex handed her a plate of cake and cheese, and a cup of tea. The cake was still warm, and smelt of spices and fruits. 'Here you go.'

'It looks and smells absolutely delicious. I've never had cake and cheese together.'

'You're welcome. I like doing things for you. It was my grandmother's recipe, a traditional Easter treat. Alex sat down at the table. 'Listen I've been meaning to say, and there's no pressure, but to tide you over, I can help out financially, if you need it. I earn enough.' Helena glanced up and opened her mouth. Alex raised a hand slightly. 'And before you say no, promise me you'll think about it?'

'I promise you I'll think about it.'

They both savoured a few bites. The sweet cake was crumbly yet moist and the salty cheese proved the ideal accompaniment.

How are you getting on with the letters?' asked Alex, wiping a crumb.

'Honestly? I'm still confused and conflicted. I have just about forgiven Clare. After all, she wasn't even aware I existed. I just can't envision what to do next. I am still interested in the letters…well, I'm interested in the women and their stories, but…' Helena's voice drifted off and she turned to face the garden again.

'Perhaps you should take a break. Remove yourself temporarily from it all and come back to it with fresh eyes?'

'That's good advice. Rachel said something similar, but equally, I need to be occupied.'

'I see. Staying busy is important to you.'

'Yes.' Little did Alex know how close she was to unravelling entirely.

'As we were saying yesterday, coming across any one of these letters would have been remarkable. It would be extremely unlikely, even for the most fortunate and hard-working historian, to come across as many. And a find as remarkable as a letter from Nefertari? It would be the discovery of the century. I can't imagine any historian would keep such a find secret for long.'

'I know. I've been so stupid.'

'No, you haven't. I do wish you could stop beating yourself up. You're not a historian, you weren't trained to think like one.'

'You're right. I suppose at least I could finish reading them. Then I can try to fathom out where I go from there. I've been looking again at one from the first woman police officer.'

'Oh, interesting. Go on.' Alex handed Helena another slice of cake.

'Thank you, God, this is really moreish. Hmm, yes, the policewoman, Edith was her name. I'm sure she meant well, but I'm struggling to relate to her. Her views on the women she policed appear really old fashioned, even for her era. My image of the 1920s is all flapper girls and women's liberation. Her tone is unnerving me. I am trying and failing to understand her.'

'Have you read Clare's note on this one? Might it shed any light?'

Helena hadn't yet. She hadn't read any of Clare's notes since the one she'd found in the summer house, afraid of any more revelations. With Alex there, she felt safe to read it out loud.

Edith lost her husband and had to find ways to avoid destitution for her and her children. She put everything into her work and was then criticised, which she believed was completely unjust. She was deeply sensitive and probably had severe depression. Perhaps she continued to treat girls in the same way she had during wartime when it had been accepted, and her methods weren't appreciated in the more liberated twenties. Nevertheless, she contributed to the war effort, doing her duty in the way she thought best. She killed herself by overdosing, left a suicide note saying she'd done nothing wrong and that she'd been treated terribly despite all her hard work. Teresa May issued an apology 100 years after her death for the way women police officers were treated.

It was hard to finish reading the note as her eyes were welling and her voice faltering.

'How did I not see? Why couldn't I read between the lines and understand what she was going through?'

Alex went over to her and held her, rocking her gently as her snivelling quickly accelerated into bawling.

'Try not to torture yourself any more lovey,' Alex said. 'Clare spent months, possibly years researching all this and composing the letters. You are only now starting to catch up. Oh, love, it's ok, I've got you, darling. Let it out. Let it all out.'

Helena began heaving and sobbing big fat ugly sobs she had been storing for decades. Until this moment, she had never felt safe to let it all out in front of anyone, assuming she'd be judged or the world would fall apart. But here she was, letting it all out with Alex, and the world was not falling apart. After several minutes of messy crying, the sobs eventually started to subside, and her breathing began to settle. Through the tears emerged a smile.

'Thank you. I must have needed that.'

Alex offered her a tissue and she wiped away the residue from her eyes and nose. Only once she had put the tissue in the bin and was fully composed did Alex speak again.

'There's writing on the back of this one, love. It says, "See Nina."'

'Oh really? Ok, shall we come back to it later? We'll be late for Amy if we're not careful. I should try and get my face looking less like it's been in a car crash.'

'Hey, hey hey, come here.' Alex cupped her face and kissed her swollen red eyelids. 'Your face is beautiful.'

Helena had dreaded visiting the hospice, expecting a depressing clinical environment where maudlin staff attended to people who lay around in pain waiting to die. But St. Jude's was light, airy, and homely, with plants and pictures and comfy chairs. The kind and helpful staff created a calm, warm and welcoming atmosphere. There were extra services such as massage and reflexology, there were social activities, there was psychological support, and there were practical sessions on things such as finances. Not at all a place obsessed with death, it was bursting with life. Helena looked forward to her visits there, and was determined to cherish every minute with Cynthia, never sure if each visit would be the last. Amy was coming, and was due to meet them there in half an hour.

'We must remember to take in Cynthia's post,' said Helena as they walked down the hall towards the front door.

'Oh I nearly forgot,' said Alex, picking up a pile of books from the hall table along with the letters. 'I found these beside the piano. They are the same books Amy used when she was learning. I haven't seen them for ages. I'd never noticed before, but look at the name on all of them.'

Alex fanned out the books for Helena to read the covers as she wrestled to get her arm in her coat. On every single one was the name "Ms. C. Partridge."

'Cynthia wrote them all. She is quite a remarkable lady.'

An hour later, Helena, Alex and Amy were all at Cynthia's bedside. She was wearing a pink nightie Helena had brought in which swamped her diminishing frame. There were hardly any monitors or tubes now, as Cynthia was receiving palliative care rather than active treatment. They were at the stage of keeping her as comfortable as possible. Even though her skin was deathly pale, and her hands were freezing cold, she did seem comfortable, surrounded by fluffed up pillows and friends.

'You were my favourite teacher,' said Amy after they had embraced. 'I'll never forget all you did for me.'

'Come, sit here on the bed,' said Cynthia, patting her bruised little hand onto the bedcover. Her voice was weak, but her presence remained strong.

Amy sat down and Alex handed her the music books. Together they flicked through them, reminiscing about their Saturday lessons.

'Oh, do you remember, I always got stuck on this allegro piece?' said Amy.

'I do dear, yes. You would stop and announce, "No!"'

'I still do sometimes! I've brought in a recording for you, in case you'd like to listen. It's of me performing in the end of term concert. I can leave it here?'

'I would be honoured to listen to it,' said Cynthia.

Later, while Amy made supper, Alex and Helena placed the letters in a set of lever arch files Alex had snaffled from work.

'Even if you don't do anything with them, they're worth preserving,' Alex had said.

Meanwhile, Amy was clattering away in the kitchen making supper for them all, and the smells of garlic bread and homemade pasta sauce wafted through into the dining room. These, Helena surmised, these demonstrations of affection that come so naturally to Alex and Amy, these acts of kindness with no strings, these must resemble the meaning of family.

'Ah, here she is,' announced Alex. 'It's "Nina." This must be the letter Clare was referring to. Here, have a wine top-up.'

Alex sat down in the opposite chair and began to read aloud while Helena sipped her chardonnay.

Dear Edith,

Thank you for your letter. I was quite surprised to receive it. I appreciate your kind words concerning my work and recent progress. I am genuinely sorry to hear you are in a predicament, but I am afraid I am not in a position to help you.

As you observed, I am never afraid of breaking the law, particularly when the law is an ass. Our protests were banned but we did them anyway, and I have been arrested and imprisoned enough that I understand much in connection with the legal system in this country. One of my campaigns has been against the male dominated legal system at all levels, from the law-makers to the law-enforcers. Being in prison, I witnessed how poorly women prisoners are treated. Regretfully, the approach favoured in Grantham would result in more women being exposed to these dreadful conditions. My experience of being in prison inspired me to campaign for women police officers. My goal was to take care of the women, not penalise them as the service in Grantham set out to do.

You are aware, I am sure, of the reasons I left The Women's Police Service in 1915, the same year you were appointed. I was happy to see women promoted from volunteers into paid work, but your remit was specifically to punish so-called "loose women" rather than to support and protect women and girls. You mention the need to set aside women's rights in Grantham. This, I am afraid, goes against everything I stand for. I do not blame you personally; you were fulfilling the role you were appointed to do. However, for me to do anything to support you at this crucial stage of the women's rights movement, would be grossly inappropriate in the circumstances. I will never compromise my principles, you see.

Removing barriers for girls that they might gain a decent education, removing barriers for women that they may gain employment, and promoting welfare for women – these are the ways to get women and girls out of prostitution. Perhaps you are unaware of the exploitation of our young girls, the sex slavery and the trafficking of women occurring in the depths of our society, forcing many of the most vulnerable to become prostitutes? I witnessed this practice first hand. It is this we must stop, rather than punish the poor wretched women who wind up on the streets.

Getting the vote in 1918 was only the start. The work won't be over until women achieve equality in all aspects of society, and it will take decades, no doubt continuing long after I have gone. But all the while I am alive, I will fight on. When I was nominated to stand at the Keighley by-election, I was the first woman to have a nomination accepted, although much to my annoyance it was deemed invalid on a technicality. But it did achieve something. It paved the way for the law to be changed. At 27 words long, the new law is the shortest piece of legislation in history, but they are just about the best 27 words ever written, because they finally enable women to be MPs.

My work always has been, is now, and always will be, to promote women's and children's welfare and rights. It began way back before the War when I lived in South Africa, and my work here and overseas must not be compromised in any way. In my novels, the women are strong. They need to be. In a world where men are tiring of women's rights and hostility is rising, everything I write, everything I do, is scrutinised. If I were in any way seen to be endorsing your attitude to women by offering you any support, my integrity would quite rightly be in question.

Certain individuals complain we should be quiet now we have the vote. But we don't all have the vote. Only women over thirty with property have the vote. The anti-suffrage movement is thriving, full of misled women and men who are old fossils. They are encouraged by things they hear in Parliament spouted by the likes of Sir Charles Henry MP who said, "One of the greatest features in connection with this country is the responsibility of men towards women, and I would view with the greatest apprehension any step which would tend to relieve men of that responsibility." Sir John Rees MP was as bad. He said, "Women are tremendously accessible, extraordinarily impressionable, noted for the adoption of any new thing, and for the easy acceptance of other people's views. Are those qualities which fit women to rule over the home and foreign affairs of a mighty empire?" I keep these quotes on my desk, along with more statements of a similar sentiment, to remind me of the challenges we continue to face against such prejudice and ignorance. The women who join the anti-suffrage movement are sadly influenced by the misinformed words of these politicians and of Lord Curzon, who claimed in his ridiculous pamphlet that women's suffrage would damage the Empire, would be subversive to peace at home, and would fly in the face of nature. The likes of Gertrude Bell and her Women's Anti-Suffrage League were taken in by this rhetoric. She too believed that women who had the vote would be a threat to the Empire. Her actions oppressed women. She displayed all the Imperialistic traits of the men she worked with. This despite being Oxford University educated. She lives a similar lifestyle to many suffragists, unmarried and devoted to her work. It defies logic.

Others complain we are taking the men's jobs from them, contributing to the economic difficulties we have faced recently in this country. Many of these women are war widows, endeavouring to make ends meet with mouths to feed. Why should they be denied the right to work? Meanwhile, things that would actually benefit women, such as education on birth control, are being banned, such as Marie Stopes' book and film "Married Love." Even middle-class women seeking university degrees at the older universities face a battle to secure a place.

Despite all this, our place in society is gradually changing. Many, yourself included, have become wage earners, refusing to go back to housekeeping. Skirts are shorter, sanitary wear is widely available, and a social life is now possible with new technology making it easier to run the home. Women are gaining more freedoms, gradually. Freedoms men take for granted.

I will not, cannot, do anything to jeopardise this progress, or my part of it.

I understand this is not what you want to hear, Edith. I hope I explain myself adequately. I do wish you good luck with the Committee.

Yours,

Nina Boyle

Alex went on to read Clare's note, which consisted of one simple sentence.

This letter from Nina would have been found unopened in Edith's home after she had killed herself.

'Oh my God,' said Helena. This was all she could manage to say as a ball of angst bounced around in her stomach and her mind began racing. The letters may have been fake, and the situations imagined, but the lives of these women and their experiences were all too real. She hadn't told Alex or anyone, that in her darkest moments, she had more than once contemplated taking her own life. Of all the things she loathed about herself, this was the one she loathed the most, believing suicidal ideation made her weak. It was at night when the inner monologue was hardest to control. She often resorted to shouting at the self-deprecation to shut the fuck up. Once or twice, suicide had seemed the only option, to get away from the demons and finally have some peace. She suspected Edith experienced the same.

'Are you alright?' said Alex.

'Yes. Well, I will be. Can you give me a couple of minutes? I fancy a wander in the garden for a bit.'

'Of course. I'll call you when supper is ready.'

With her glass of chardonnay in hand, Helena walked out into the garden. Its freshly mown spongey lawn was vibrant in the late afternoon sunshine. She practised her deep breathing as she stepped along the path towards the summer house. She was getting better at it, and it was definitely helping. She had been accustomed all her life to thoughts that bulldozed and escalated, leaving a path of destruction. At last, her default state of mind seemed to be changing. The bulldozer effect was fading. Thoughts still bobbed around, but they were flitting gently rather than thrashing violently. A butterfly maybe. Helena hoped this quieter mind was a place where creativity might finally find the space to grow.

She entered the summer house. It retained a degree of warmth from the sun earlier in the day. Was it here as she typed that Clare decided once and for all on the themes and purpose of her book? Was it about loss, strength, sacrifice, identity, defying the odds? Helena closed her eyes. She relaxed her shoulders and tried to be in the moment, taking in the woody smell, the cosiness of this little room. She was convinced she felt a whisp of warm air pass by her face.

It's all going to be ok, Helena. You're overthinking this, desperately searching for something that doesn't exist. Step back and look at the bigger picture.

'Helena!' called Alex.

Over Amy's delicious supper, Helena was animated in describing her emerging ideas.

'Each of these women had her own stuff going on, which she dealt with in her own way. We all do, whatever century we are born in, whatever privileges we have or don't have, whatever we achieve. All these women had interesting or important things to say. And our experience of finding the letters, maybe that's the thread pulling them all together?'

'You've hit on a great idea there,' said Alex. 'Women are not a homogenous group. Take Edith and Nina – two women from the same era but with completely opposite outlooks. And I love the notion you might include yourself in the book. Ok, hang on a sec.'

Alex popped into the hallway. Helena turned to Amy while she waited to see what was going on.

'This is lovely, Amy. Thank you for going to all this effort.' Amy blushed.

Alex returned with an envelope and stood next to her.

'I hope now is a good moment to give you this.'

Helena took the envelope, and gazed at Alex. The tingle she'd felt when they first met had evolved into so much more. It had enveloped her. She ripped open the envelope and pulled out a leaflet entitled "Creative writing retreats in Ireland."

'I haven't booked it yet because I needed to check with you first, and because of all the upset over Clare having written the letters. But I'd love to treat you to this. It's not far from Kilkenny; you'd be able to visit Alice Kyteler's pub again. And before you say anything, Cynthia is fine about me staying in the house to keep things ticking over here while you're away.'

'Oh Alex, I couldn't…'

'Yes, Helena. Yes, you could. You deserve a special treat.'

'I already have one,' said Helena winking at Alex, who snorted. 'Too cheesy?' Helena asked.

'No. Lovely. Like you.'

Chapter Twenty-Eight

Gertrude

Dear Jabez,

It's years since we met, but I bet you remember one thing about me above anything - I am one for tying up loose ends and getting the job finished. It's in my Yankee blood. I'm nearly 40 now, so you must be into your sixties. How did THAT happen? Over the years, my feelings have mellowed, and I'm writing in the hope we can make our peace, sending this in good faith you will receive it as intended, with no malice.

Can you believe it was over 20 years ago you were training me? No woman had ever swum the Channel, and only a handful of men. Lots of people said it was impossible, but you took me on anyway. You appreciated

I had already won a heap of medals and broken all those records. I was disappointed I only won Gold in Paris for the relay and not for my single events, and that my other two medals were only bronze. Still, we sure had a lot of fun driving around Paris in taxis, standing up and screaming through the streets!

When we started training, I was convinced you understood I had the willpower and drive to do it even though I was only a teenager. Truth be told, I see now my will to succeed came from a desire to please my family, in particular my father and my dear sister Meg. Father believed I could do anything, especially after I recovered from near-death with the measles. The local pool didn't want me in case I was still contagious, so Father found another way and taught me to swim in the ocean hooking a rope round my waist. He was a great support, but Meg was my biggest fan. It was she who pushed me to imagine I could one day be a champion. I hadn't been ambitious at all to start with. I loved the water, don't get me wrong, but what I enjoyed most was splashing around on holiday, I wasn't really interested in competition. Meg would fill in all the entry forms for me!

The Women's Swimming Association had been training sweet Helen Wainwright for the Channel swim, but her illness went in my favor, and they gave me the sponsorship instead. I doubt I would have gotten the finances together otherwise. Training with Charlotte Epstein was the break I needed. When we met, I was prepared for anything as long as it worked, and I'd make my family proud. In '25, when we started, you'd already tried 22 times. You sure were no stranger to the endurance and perseverance required. I was attracted to your determination. You became a second father to me, and I trusted you as I trusted him and the rest of my family.

I kept the photo of us on the tug boat La Morinie, taken moments before our attempt. You are applying grease to my legs, and I am all smiles and anticipation. The jazz band was a neat touch. I can't remember who arranged them, but they were fun. Then we failed after only swimming for 8 hours 50 mins and I took it mighty bad.

Back then, I thought you deliberately sabotaged my attempt. I couldn't get out of my mind all the things that went wrong unnecessarily. I believed you deliberately got the tides wrong to wear me out and lower my chances. I thought you were only too aware of the ebb and flow tide in the Channel, you'd swum in it often enough before! You had me swimming against the tide, something I never understood. You slowed me down at the beginning, telling me I was going too fast and wouldn't be able to maintain such a speed. I knew I had the speed right. You had me swim in a one-piece costume, saying it would be immoral and shocking for me to wear the two-piece I was eager to try. The darned heavy one-piece filled with water and weighed me down, and it chafed against my skin. You had me swim breast stroke when the eight beat crawl would have been much faster. You knew I loved that eight beat crawl, it had already helped me win titles all over the world. You told Ishak to touch me, which instantly disqualified me. Anyways, then you had him drag me out of the water. As far as I was concerned, I was resting, I wasn't in trouble. I thought you did all these things to disrupt my attempt, and I even toyed with the notion you had poisoned me, or had arranged such. I hung on to this belief for many years. A mighty long list of things isn't it? I was real mad at you, because I had trusted you. I knew I could make it, however much water I'd taken in, however far I had to swim to do it, even wearing that damn costume.

I searched in my heart for a reason. Why would you commit these atrocities? I guessed you didn't care for me, didn't want me to succeed, and were plain jealous. Jealous of me as an American? Maybe. Jealous of me as a woman? Quite possibly. Jealous I might succeed where you had failed? Perhaps. With Bill Burgess training me, we did things differently. The rivalry between you two sparked Bill's determination, and he wanted to triumph with me to get to you. He trained me to swim with the tides, not against them. I wore the two-piece I designed, and Meg made for me, and had goggles stuck to my face with candle wax. The costume was effective, proving I was right to favor it over the old woollen affairs. More skin exposed meant more of me could be covered in sheep grease, reducing friction and horrible chafing, in addition to adding buoyancy and aiding temperature control.

Despite the continued doubt a woman could do it, off I went almost a year to the day since our failure. The waters were mighty choppy, and they kept asking me in the tug boat if I wanted to get out. "What for?" I kept yelling back! "What For" became my nickname for a while after that. There were so many darned jellyfish! And the swim caused my poor hearing to worsen. But it was all worth it. I can imagine how you felt when you read the news I did it. I swam 35 miles, not the 21 miles as the gull flies, because of the turbulent water and the tides, and I got to Dover, England in 14 hours 31 minutes, a new record. They said I looked like a boxer when I finished, because the water had clobbered my face, and I was all bruised and swollen from the salt and the jellyfish stings.

On my way back to the States, they had planes flying over dropping bouquets of beautiful flowers for me. It was gorgeous. I was mighty proud then. I was on all the front pages, even though it was the same day as Rudolph Valentino's funeral! They called me "America's Best Girl" after the President used this most affectionate term for me, and I was honoured with a parade through New York. I was a national hero, and someone wrote a song about me, "Trudy." I imagine all this caused you a degree of pain.

Here's the rub: you saw it was possible for a woman to do what you had failed to do. And you saw she could do it without you.

The next four people to swim the channel after me were all women, which I think is real neat. Thankfully, I still hold the record for the fastest. I'm told I inspired women in sports and that my success helped change how women were perceived by the sporting bodies, who started to accept women deserved their place at the highest levels. I didn't feel like an inspiration, I was just glad I did it. I hope nowadays my success in part led you to help more girls after me. Back then, when I heard you were training other girls, I was plain angry. I thought you favored them above me.

I'm not writing all this to hurt you, Jappy. It was all long ago and things have changed. I am not angry with you anymore. I realise now I learned a lot from our failure, and it probably helped me to succeed. Our countries are allies in war, and I wish us to be allies too, set aside what went wrong between us in the past. Our Yankee troops are arriving on your British soil. I hear rumours your Jewish people are suffering something terrible under the Nazis. It makes me awfully uncomfortable about my German roots.

I've been imagining how it must have been for you, to be in your position. Your swimming career was interrupted by the Great War when you served as Army lieutenant. You had many, many attempts where you nearly made it. The war was such unfortunate timing as opportunity was taken away from you when you were at your peak. I understand now what war does to a fellow, even one as proud as you. My Channel attempts were snuck in between the wars – it was wonderful timing for me. I had luck on my side as well as my talent. You had the talent to make the crossing but never the luck when you needed it. They called you called the most unlucky swimmer in the world - despite all those attempts, you never made it across.

In many ways, we are from very different backgrounds. As I was becoming an adult, women were gaining more freedoms and independence. Votes for women in the US and the UK! Although of German background, I see myself as wholly Yankee. You are a Jew raised in Glasgow, Scotland. We were born in different eras too, although only 20 years or so separates us in age. I appreciate now it wasn't always easy dealing with this brash young American, all smiles but also as strong in nature as you. We have more in common than ever separated us, I get it now. Both our families were uprooted from their original homelands. Perhaps this is why we are both competitive and can't stand failure. We are both ambitious, would do whatever it took. We have both achieved much to be proud of. I had a degree of success on stage and screen, which was great fun, especially when they made me a pool for me to show off my swimming stroke on stage. Since my back injury, and now I am now almost completely deaf, I find solace in other pursuits. I have been teaching swimming to deaf children which I love. I still hold various records for swimming, but I don't mention them much now. You have done much with your life too. You've written two successful books. The Foulsham's swimming manual has become the go-to guide on long and short distance swimming. You coached many women to success, including Hilda Sharp, Peggy Duncan and Sunny Lowry, and you won a load of medals too. I adore the photo of you with all your medals! Such a proud fellow.

I see now you probably were trying to help me. You almost made it across the Channel – I seem to remember in four of your attempts you were within a mile of getting there, and for one of them, you were only a few yards away. Gee, that must have stung hard. I was too full of my own success back then, I had little understanding from your point of view. It took Bill Burgess 16 attempts after all! And he did it breast stroke back in 1911, as you wanted me to. I hope he's doing ok, I haven't heard from him in a while. I guess he is involved in the war effort.

Once this darned war is over, I wish you a pleasant retirement in Hove, with Florence. You can still look out at your beloved English Channel whenever you wish. It's such a pretty part of the world there with the cliffs and the hills. Do give Florence my best regards.

   Yours,

   Trudy

Chapter Twenty-Nine

Lilly

With Rachel's help, Helena had been working more deeply on trusting herself and others, and had started to discuss secrets from her past that lay lurking in her head, hoping this could become her new normal. However, when she read Gerturde's letter, Trudy as she called herself, Helena was reminded of a relationship she'd not yet discussed with anyone. She'd have to eventually, as it was still causing anxiety. Putting Trudy's letter down, Helena could feel her heart pounding and the knot in her stomach intensifying. These were responses she'd experienced often when she was with Martin. Even long after she had stopped seeing him, the smell of his aftershave would take her straight back to how on edge she increasingly became around him.

Helena had met the charming and charismatic Martin when she was in her mid-forties. He was one of those people everyone notices when they walk into a room, who commands attention by merely existing. The sex was mind-blowing and the attention he gave her was irresistible. "I wish I'd met you years ago," he said in their first week. After two weeks, he was saying he wanted them to live together. After three weeks, he was saying he was surprised how she ever managed without him. After a month, he was correcting her when she made a mistake or said anything he disagreed with. After six weeks, he was telling her what to wear. After two months, he was checking her phone regularly, for spam he said. After three months, it was her birthday and by lunchtime, she hadn't heard anything from him. Worried something had happened to him, she messaged.

Is everything ok? I haven't heard from you today, and I'm a bit surprised as it's my birthday. Helena xx

Mea Culpa. Happy Birthday.

Thank you x

Happy Birthday.

Yes, thank you. Will I see you later? We could go out for a birthday meal, my treat.

Happy birthday. Happy birthday, happy birthday, happy birthday, happy birthday.

Are you ok?

Happy birthday. Happy birthday. Happy birthday. Happy birthday.

Helena stopped answering and put the phone in her bag, which carried on pinging for the rest of her lunch break. Luckily there was no one around to hear. She switched it off for the afternoon. When she switched it on again, there were over 200 messages, all saying the same thing. What should be simple felicitation had become menacing.

She rang him as soon as she got home.

'Martin, what's going on? I am sorry, but this has really upset me. In fact, it's spoilt my birthday.'

'You should be careful what you wish for,' he said.

She attempted to end the relationship there and then, but wasn't able to shake him off. Out came his Mr Charming persona, and she took him back, believing she didn't deserve any better. Then, the pattern would repeat. On each occasion it would be a different issue, but always at the heart of it, was an accusation about an apparent wrongdoing on her part. He would appear unexpectedly during lunchbreaks at work, accusing her of having an affair because her phone had been engaged. He would follow her if she went out alone for a walk, telling her it was what she wanted, what she needed for her own good. He would tell her she was damaged goods and no-one else would tolerate her so there was no point in leaving him. Only he fully understood her. When he pushed her around, it was to help her, to knock some sense into her. And it was her fault anyway as she'd pushed him metaphorically to do it. He told her she liked him being authoritative. He told her she loved him for it. She would get to the point of saying she would rather be alone. Then Mr Charming appeared again. He would say she was right, he was sorry, he would change. She would cave, and take him back. This yo-yoing went on for another eighteen months, as she walked on shifting sands, never knowing where or when she would find solid ground. The final straw came when he had a fight with his brother at their father's funeral.

Sitting in the dining room at her laptop one morning after Alex had gone to work, Helena stared blankly at the empty screen, fingers hovering over the keyboard as she contemplated this mess of a relationship. If she was damaged goods, then he was broken beyond repair. Rachel was going to have a field day with this. No, Rachel wouldn't have a field day. Rachel would be empathic and help Helena to reflect on the impact of the relationship, and ask her if she could see any similarities between this experience and her relationship with her mother. She would gently prompt Helena to consider the differences between Martin and Alex, and Helena would say how Alex's way of supporting her was genuine and from a place of love and care, whereas Martin's was from a place of self-aggrandisement and a need for control, possibly as a result of his own insecurities. Rachel would tell her it was coercive control, a form of abuse, and would say it took courage to leave, and it was not her fault. She would reassure her that talking was part of healing. Helena snapped herself out of melancholic musing and looked online for information on Gertrude. She found a photo of her as a young woman brimming with self-assurance, about to do something no woman had done before, and apparently convinced she would succeed. She didn't appear to be the kind of person who would tolerate any nonsense. In Clare's letter, the same woman, now older and wiser, displayed magnanimous forgiveness and understanding to a man who didn't succeed in helping her.

It was difficult to tell what Cynthia was thinking these days. A light had switched off and in the remaining grey shadows was a flatness where there had been depth, a dullness where there had been spark. The next time Helena visited, she took in one of Cynthia's photo albums. Her intention was to give Cynthia a pleasant experience with them, and if it felt right, she hoped to try and steer the conversation towards Clare having invented the letters, in the hope Cynthia could offer some insight. Cynthia confirmed she would like to see a few pictures, so Helena lifted the album to her face. She showed Cynthia photos of her younger self with a young man on a beach, clad in their swimwear. Cynthia was holding an inflatable stripey ball against her stomach and he had his arm around her waist as they gazed at one another with glee.

'Ah, my dear Harry,' said Cynthia, lifting her hand and stroking his face. 'I had just found out I was pregnant. It was before we told anyone. We had a few days away to celebrate and plan our future, staying with a friend of his who had a cottage in Dorset. It was such a lovely holiday, the happiest I had ever been. My mother didn't approve. After Clare was born, Harry would visit regularly but she made it rather awkward for him, and by default, for me too. We had planned to move in together and were saving for a mortgage. My mother wouldn't have been comfortable helping an unmarried couple. It went against her faith.'

'Ironic isn't it? Not exactly Christian charity.' said Helena. 'So, do you mind me asking, what happened to Harry?'

'He died, dear. Car accident. It was instant, thankfully for him. Clare was about a year old.'

'Oh I am so sorry Cynthia. You were obviously very much in love.'

'We were. It was a long time ago, but I still miss him dreadfully.'

'Did you ever meet anyone else?' asked Helena.

'No desire to, dear. I had Clare and I had his memory, which was enough. I moved into a little flat briefly when Clare was small, but I couldn't manage, couldn't afford childcare. So, I had to move us back in with my mother. She loved Clare in her own way. It's a shame Clare didn't grow up in a healthier environment, perhaps she might have found the right person too.'

'Maybe,' said Helena. 'Families, eh?'

'Anyway, dear, how are you getting on?'

'Slowly, I'm afraid.' She couldn't face admitting she had yet to write a single word, other than her scrappy notes. Was this the moment to mention that she knew Clare had invented the letters? How would Cynthia react? What if she believed that her daughter was an amazing historian who had discovered all these letters? Helena had no desire to crush her friend when she was already desperately ill. It was important to stay positive.

Cynthia spoke while she was still deliberating.

I have confidence in you, Helena.'

'I wish I had confidence in me, Helena replied. 'Oh listen to me moaning.'

'It will come, dear. Meanwhile, if you're looking to occupy yourself, you might like to make a start on clearing the house, now it's obvious I won't be able to do it. I don't mind what you do with any of it. Get rid of anything you and Alex don't wish to keep. There's a small collection of original watercolours and oils, some old vases and ornaments, and a few rare books which might fetch a bit for you at auction.'

'But Cynthia…'

'Please. It would mean a lot to me. It would be a weight off my mind.'

In an instant, Helena decided not to mention that the letters weren't genuine. Cynthia had enough going on without any additional stress. If she knew, Cynthia had chosen not to say. This was how it should stay.

Over the next few days, Helena forced herself to begin going through Cynthia's possessions. It was too macabre to deal with any clothes while Cynthia was still alive, so she started packing various books and ornaments, sorting things into charity shop and auction possibilities.

She shifted all the packed boxes into the dining room. As she lifted them, a familiar pain resurfaced and caught her off guard, a sharp reminder she still hadn't had her wrist assessed. She sat down at the table massaging it and flicking it aimlessly, which achieved nothing other than making it click. In the corner of the room, a box caught her eye. What should she do with it? Against her better judgement she lifted it onto the table, and lay her hand on the lid. She began idly tracing over the writing, following the lines Clare's hand had created. Down, round, down, diagonal down, diagonal down, across…until she had traced it all.

D…I…A…R…I…E…S……E…T…C.

The first time she had visited the house, Cynthia had specifically asked her not to go into this box. But Cynthia need never find out. Her hand moved to the corner of the lid, and cautiously, she began to lift it.

Alex came back after work, and they made love on the lounge floor having barely said hello. Afterwards, they lay naked on the sofa, their bodies partially covered with Cynthia's old check blanket. Before Alex, sex had always been followed by a fumble for her clothes and an embarrassed dash to the shower. Now it was followed by blissful peace and a sense of completion.

'I feel so naughty,' she said. 'It's kind of exciting.'

'Excitement… is one of… the best things… in life,' said Alex, kissing the top of her head in between words. 'I'm… so glad… you're feeling it... with me.'

They kissed deeply. Eventually, Helena pulled away gently and took Alex's hand.

'I've decided, she said. 'I am going to try and write the book. Cynthia thinks I'm already doing it, and I didn't have the heart to tell her I am still completely stumped. But I am going to give it a go.'

'I'm glad, darling, if it's what you want to do,' said Alex, stroking her hair.

'It is. The thing is, and this will come as no surprise to you… I can't get started. It's deeply annoying for me and it must be getting deeply boring for you. Now I know Clare wrote the letters, I'm even more confused than I was before.'

'Why not look at it another way. Think about what you HAVE done, said Alex. 'You have sorted and read nearly all the letters and the accompanying notes. You have researched the women behind the letters. You've been making notes in that extremely tasteful notebook the library gave you. And importantly, you've started considering how it all comes together. What else would help you now, apart from going on a writers' retreat of course?'

Helena sat up, allowing the blanket to fall away from her. She pushed back her hair and swung round to face Alex. 'Hmmm. I need to stop procrastinating and prevaricating, I realise that. Chris told me he's a pantser – writing everything without any real plan. I'm inclined to try and be more of a planner. For once in my life, I want to do something properly.'

'There's no empirical right or wrong way, love. It's a matter of what's right for you.' Alex reached up and fondled her curls.

'Can I please bottle everything you say and keep it?' Helena took Alex's hand in hers and kissed it. 'OK, how about this? I'll finish reading all the letters, then could choose a shortlist, as a starting point. Actually, don't laugh, but a weird thing happened the other day.'

Alex ran a warm finger down her back. 'Oh, do tell!'

'Well, when I was in the summer house, I imagined Clare supporting and encouraging me. I got a real sense she was in there. What if I imagine she wrote the notes for me, and she'll help me write the book? Is that ridiculous?'

'Darling, whatever you need is fine. It doesn't matter where you get the inspiration from. If it seems to be Clare, then who better to guide you?'

'Thank you, you're very patient with me.'

'I simply hope for you to be happy,' said Alex. 'I get the impression you're torturing yourself, and I would love to see you getting more pleasure from it.'

'See, there you are, being very, very patient. You and Cynthia both.' Helena stood, taking the blanket with her and wrapping it toga-like around herself. 'Right, let's read the next letter. Who do we have?' Alex put on a pair of jeans and reached for the folder of letters, flicking through to the end.

'Someone called Lilly.'

'My turn to read out loud,' said Helena.

Dear Tessa,

I am sure you recall being on the last train to leave Prague in March '39. How could you forget? I was one of the girls you rescued that day. You may remember me, and possibly my younger sister, as you admired my drawings when we met in Prague. I was extremely keen on drawing animals, and had a degree of success when one of my drawings was published in the paper. I was helping out my father by earning a little bit from sales, and I was receiving tuition from a sculptor. My poor father – he was a wonderful man – a talented musician – was struggling to make ends meet as a private tutor. We were in an exceedingly sorry state when you met us.

Things had started to go wrong for us when it became impossible for my father to survive in Berlin as a Jew. The incidents all round us of German solders attacking and killing Jewish people remain vivid in my memory to this day. It was entertainment for them, showing off to each other with all this bravado. My mother's brother got involved, he thought it was fun. Father went to Prague first, leaving Mother and us children in Berlin. We had so little to live on, life was very meagre.

We knew it was only a matter of time before the Nazis would arrive. When we eventually joined Father in Prague, it was only to discover things were no better there, and life became extremely difficult. My mother was antisemitic, which didn't help at all.

Father was trying desperately to get us to Canada. He managed to secure a job there, but couldn't raise the funds to pay for a guarantor. While he was attempting to sort this, we met you quite by chance. You were kind-hearted and caring, and started trying to help us immediately. You tried first to help Father because if he could be guaranteed work and safe passage, perhaps the family could follow. Then you saw my pictures. You said I had potential as an artist. You took a small selection of my pictures with you and showed them to a few of your artist friends in England. They knew the Mott family, who agreed to take me and my younger sister, if we could make the journey.

Everything was rapidly descending into a state of chaos. The Germans were starting to occupy the whole country and the results were unimaginable. It was all such a rush, as there was only a small window of opportunity in which to escape. You got together false papers for us and met us at the station. We only had a few minutes to say goodbye and as we had our brief and final hugs, I knew I would never see my parents again. With nothing except a little suitcase, my sister and I were bustled onto the train and told to say quiet. She was eleven and I was fifteen. I knew you were on the train, but we were given strict instructions not to acknowledge you, or our cover might be blown. I was terrified, I don't mind admitting. We sat near the sculptor who had offered me tuition. He was Karel Vogel. You may have heard of him as he went on to achieve great success in London.

It was a terrible journey, a nightmare, especially getting through Germany. We were two children on this train with a document that was not a proper passport, and nothing else. If anyone suspected us, you would not be able to help. A German official came through the train. He looked at us very sternly and then took our papers. I recalled the last thing my parents had said – "Don't say anything, just keep quiet and let them do what they have to do." So that's what I did. Eventually, this German came back with the papers and gave me another very stern look, as if to say, "I don't trust this girl, she is up to something."

For reasons I never understood, we were allowed to stay on the train. Our carriage was disconnected, and we were stranded on the track for hours. The Germans came and emptied out everyone's suitcases all-over the place. I was terrified this would happen to us. I had a few pence left which I gave to a porter, asking him to look after our case. Remarkably, he did. We had no idea what was going to happen, or where we were going. Eventually, as I am sure you haven't forgotten, our carriage was reconnected and we continued on our journey, first to Holland and then finally arriving at Harwich on the boat. We had no food with us, and we hadn't eaten for the whole journey, and so we were extremely thankful to be given sandwiches. I assume these were provided by you or one of your friends.

As soon as we reached England, it got a lot easier. We felt safe at last having travelled all night being fearful. We got to London later that day and there to meet us were Mr and Mrs Mott.

You may have seen he has recently died. I read his obituary in the Independent. I knew he had received the Nobel Prize for Physics as I followed his career with interest. I can't say I fully understand all he did, but I knew his work was important. Reading the obituary, I realised that while caring for us, he was working on his book "Electronic Processes in Ionic Crystals", published with R.W. Gurney in 1940, and was then involved in sensitive war work. What mattered to me more was his kindness. I was a little surprised to see no mention in the obituary of everything he and his dear wife Ruth did for us in the war.

After all the upheaval, I am pleased to say life has been really rather lovely. I settled in the village of Bushey, not far north of London. My first job was teaching at St Hilda's, but it was the art community there I really loved. Bushey had been home to an art school, quite famous in its day, run by Hubert von Herkomer. He created and lived in a wonderful gothic house built of Bavarian stone, but it was destroyed the year I arrived. I don't think it was because he was Bavarian. There was so much destruction, so much lost. Lives, millions of them. And books, all those burnings. The Nazis did it all, didn't they? One of Herkomer's most famous pupils Lucy Kemp-Welch took over the school from him, and I was lucky enough to speak with her before she died. I was such an admirer of hers. She specialised in painting magnificent horses.

I married Michael in 1949, and we had three sons. We lived first in a little bungalow near Herkomer's studios, and then in a pretty Arts and Crafts house, where I still reside today. My husband was from an artistic family too – you may have heard of his famous uncle Eric Gill. He was a bit of an unconventional man. I always thought his brother McDonald was the more talented artist. He used to do the most marvellous maps. I studied pottery and sculpture and had two kilns in the garden shed to do my own firing. I was lucky to be included in a few exhibitions and I had an entry in the dictionary of artists, which I keep as a memento for my sons. Most of my work is animals. I paint quite a lot now too. I find oil a most fascinating medium and I earn a living mostly from my paintings nowadays, portraits of people's pets and horses. So my house is rather full of oils.

Dear Tessa, one of my sons has shown me an article about you. It says you helped transport 66 children that day, on what became known as the Kindertransport train. It explains you went on to do more wonderful work, helping evacuate women from the east End of London, and establishing an ambulance service, before marrying into the Cadbury family and moving to America.

I used to believe that it was my pictures that saved me and my sister. But the older I get, and the more I read about yours and your family's contributions to the war effort, I realise it was you. The day you rescued me was the very day the Germans marched into Prague.

Thank you, with all my heart.

Lilly Gill.

Chapter Thirty

Dorothy

Alex passed Helena a tissue.

'There's more', said Helena, blowing her nose and removing her glasses to wipe her eyes. 'There's a hand-written note here, but it's not Clare's handwriting.' She showed the note to Alex.

'Oh I recognise that handwriting from Amy's piano lesson days. That's Cynthia's distinctive style. I always loved how rounded her letters are. What does she say?'

Dear, sweet Lilly Gill. Clare and I knew her. Such a lovely woman, and extremely talented. Not a hint of bitterness concerning her early life. Clare met her while she was volunteering at Bushey Museum, when they were collecting audio recordings of local people for the museum's archive. Lilly wasn't famous and little has ever been written of her life and works. She was overlooked because she never pushed herself into the limelight. It was Tessa Rowntree, from the Rowntree family who make sweets, who rescued her during the war. Very fitting, a sweet lady is rescued by a sweet lady whose family are in the sweet trade. You can see a couple of Lilly's pieces at Bushey Museum. It's a dear little place. There's a collection of Kemp-Welch paintings there too, and lots of Herkomer's work. His was one of the first art schools to accept women, along with Slade. Please, Helena, even though hardly anyone knows of her, I would love her to be included in the book.

'Cynthia must have written this recently,' said Helena.

'Indeed. It strikes me Cynthia is similar in temperament to how she describes Lilly. No bitterness. Instead, a quiet, strong acceptance.'

'I am going to really miss her,' said Helena. 'I'm so disappointed I couldn't get the book written in time for her to see it.'

'She's aware you're working on it, and that is enough,' said Alex.

They hadn't visited Cynthia for a couple of days, and it was a shock to see how much she had declined. She was shrinking into the bedclothes which now lay more or less flat across the bed as if no-one was in there. She was asleep when they arrived, so they waited for her to stir.

'Oh, hello dears, lovely to see you,' she said once she had come to. 'Could you kindly pass me a cup of water?'

Helena walked across the room to a cabinet. On it sat a jug and a clean cup alongside a few ornaments and the picture of Clare's graduation, all neatly arranged on one of Cynthia's lace tablecloths. Helena had brought them from Cynthia's house after seeing a notice encouraging people to personalise their rooms. Helena poured the water and took it back to Cynthia, wishing there was more she could do, wishing the cup contained some kind of miracle cure.

'Here you go.' Helena placed the cup on the overbed table.

'Thank you dear.' And I am so sorry, could you prop me up a bit?'

Helena and Alex went to either side of the bed and lifted Cynthia, before arranging the pillows behind her, and setting her back again. She weighed virtually nothing. Helena could feel every rib through the nightclothes, and see every blood vessel through her thin transparent skin.

'Is that better? Are you more comfortable?' asked Helena.

'I am fine, dear. Honestly. You are so kind. Everyone is so kind. Yesterday, they all sat down with me and went through my options. They were all here, the nurses and the doctors. I am on what they call an advanced palliative care plan now.'

'Oh Cynthia, no.'

'It's alright. It's my time. I've managed to make all my arrangements, and I am ready. Now, you tell me what you're up to, please. What's happening out in the world of Helena and Alex?'

'Are you sure?' asked Helena as she sat down next to Alex beside the bed.

'Absolutely.'

'Ok, well then, we've been reading Lilly Gill's letter.' Cynthia spluttered a little, and Helena paused to make sure she wasn't choking. 'And the note you attached to it. Yes, of course, Lilly and Tessa should be in the book. It's such a remarkable story. It makes me feel lucky to live in a place that isn't an unstable warzone, a place where education is encouraged, where women can wear what they want, and books aren't banned or burnt. When people get angry, claiming that refugees in boats are stealing their jobs and ruining the economy, it makes my heart sink. What would they do if they were in a similar position?'

Alex gently took her hand. It was all Helena needed.

'I'm sorry Cynthia, I shouldn't go on. But Lilly's letter really got to me, made me reflect on everything that's still happening around the world.'

'It's quite alright, dear. I'm glad you have passion.'

'Thank you. Reading the letters has really brought it home to me. Many issues are universal, as relevant today as they've always been.' Helena picked up her bag. 'Anyway, we were wondering. Were there any other letters you'd particularly like included, any we haven't discussed already?'

'Let me think, yes, there is one other... Oh gosh, who was it now?' Cynthia frowned. Helena sensed she was finding the effort of breathing, of being, a monumental battle.

'I can't recollect the name of the person I'm afraid, but it was a letter mentioning Bletchley Park, where my mother worked during the war.'

'Ah, the codebreakers,' said Alex. Helena smiled. Previously, she would once have felt intimidated or threatened by a partner who was as well-informed, but now Helena felt proud.

'You know about such a lot,' she said.

'I am lucky, I get paid to learn. It could be worse,' grinned Alex. 'I know about Bletchley because we store a dossier and shared it with them for their exhibition.'

'My mother worked on the Typex machine,' said Cynthia. She was recruited because... she was a whizz at crosswords... and they wanted people... with that kind of brain. I would have been hopeless. She kept it a secret... for fifty years... they all had to.'

'How fascinating,' said Alex.' Those cypher machines were crucial to the war effort.'

'If you could find it... I am so sorry, I am a little tired.'

'Please, please don't apologise,' said Helena. She reached into her bag and pulled out a selection of well-thumbed plastic wallets. 'We've brought a bunch of letters along. These are ones I haven't decided whether to include, as they're not as detailed as some of the others. We can read them to you. You don't need to talk.'

'That would be nice dear.'

'OK, let's see,' Helena said, flicking through the letters. 'Oh, this one was interesting. It's from the Ladies of Llangollen. They were a couple called Eleanor and Sarah who lived in the eighteenth century and met not far from Kilkenny. They eloped to Wales and became quite the entertainers, hosting many notable people of the day, including Wordsworth, Shelley and Sir Walter Scott. Anne Lister, the woman they call "Gentleman Jack" visited them, and their letter is to her, encouraging her to marry her lover Anne. Here it is.'

Alex and Cynthia listened, occasionally glancing towards one another and smiling as Helena read with enthusiasm. Encouraged by their interest, Helena offered to read more. Over the next hour, she read six letters spanning four centuries. Esther Inglis produced exquisitely illustrated and hand-written manuscripts in the sixteenth century. Her letter accompanied a manuscript to be presented to a dignitary, and in it she described her techniques and explained her use of different scripts and decorations. According to Clare's note, Esther was the first woman on record to produce a self-portrait in Britain. Next, Helena read a letter from Atlanta Bradshaw, wife of a man stationed at Alice Springs in Australia at the end of the nineteenth century. She was attempting to educate her Arrernte women servants and the indigenous Arrernte people in general on her "civilized" ways of working and etiquette. The letter to a friend expressed her frustration with the Arrernte, who to her surprise, weren't desperate to be taught her ways. English parachutist Dolly Shepherd wrote to an equally adventurous woman: a Bavarian weightlifter whose stage name was The Great Sandwina. This was followed by a letter from Constance Lytton, who exposed the practice of force-feeding British suffragettes during their hunger strikes. Hannah Arendt's letter was to her secret lover, the philosopher Martin Heidegger. Theirs was a complex affair; he had Nazi sympathies, and she was Jewish. Also, he was married with children. Like Lilly Gill, she had fled Nazi Germany, settling in America. She would go on to become a leading historian and philosopher. Finally, Helena read a letter from Lucille Bogan, one of the first American singer-songwriters, who wrote and performed blues songs with explicit bisexual content in the 1930s.

Helena's voice was strong and animated, her tone slightly changing with each letter as she immersed herself into the characters, as Clare must have done when she wrote them. When Helena finished reading, Cynthia was fast asleep, so they gathered their things to leave.

'I felt ridiculously proud of you there,' said Alex. 'I'm sure you made the right decision not to discuss the authenticity of the letters.'

'Thank you. I hope so.'

Helena closed the thin floral patterned curtains and tip-toed back across the room past Cynthia. She paused to watch the bedclothes gently rise and fall, rise and fall. Most of the machinery had been taken away and the room had the feel of a pleasant hotel, with its tasteful pictures and matching furniture. A gentle light from the sunset outside turned everything a pinky-orange hue. Helena walked to the door and gently closed it behind her, before telling the duty staff Cynthia was sleeping peacefully.

Back at Cynthia's house that evening as they ate supper, Helena's enthusiasm was palpable.

'I've made up my mind. I'm going to include the letters that have had the greatest impact on me. I'll focus on ones that offer detailed insights into the women's lives, achievements, or ambitions, within the context of their era and where they lived, and I'll aim to include a diverse range of women from different backgrounds. I felt overwhelmed before by the idea of trying to write a comprehensive history of women. Now I realise that by highlighting the contributions of specific women, I can hopefully capture a sense of women's experiences throughout history. I also want to emphasize that we're all on our own path, and that many of the themes remain relevant today.' Helena paused for breath. 'Do you think that's an ok approach?'

'I think you're talking like an author.'

'Hmmm, I don't know about that.' Helena finished the last mouthful of her fish pie, then collected Alex's plate and cutlery to take them through to the kitchen.

'But I do know I have to start. Finally, I'm working out what I think the main themes are going to be. I've been lurking on social media to see the kinds of things people post in writing groups. You ask a question, and you'll get thirty different opinions. The approach of the first draft being exactly that – a draft – makes sense to me. I can write out a framework, then fill in the details, and then go back over it to fancy it up, polish the turd as it were, 'specially when I've done the course.'

'I'm glad to hear there are helpful folk on the socials. It's how social media should be, isn't it? People connecting.'

Helena leant against the doorframe. 'Quite. Talking of helpful… I've read Clare's note again, saying she invented the letters. Now I've calmed down about it, Clare has helped me consider who my target audience might be. I've decided. It wouldn't be aimed at historians or academics, but would be for people the same as me, interested in social history.'

She dumped the dirty dishes in the kitchen, then returned to the dining room to file the letters she'd read that day, careful to sort them back into date order. As she stood doing this at the table, her long curly hair dangled down in front of her.

'I love how your hair does that,' said Alex. 'How it's a bit messy but free-flowing.'

'I think you're giving me a compliment?' said Helena.

'I most certainly am.'

'I like it. I don't like, however, that I can't find anything to do with Bletchley Park,' Helena said, lifting her hair away from her face. 'And we've read through nearly all of them now.'

'It's getting late my love. I suggest we get some sleep and try looking again in the morning?' said Alex.

'Good idea. But I have one more thing to do before we head up.'

'Ok love, I'll do the washing up.'

Helena retrieved a piece of paper from the mantelpiece and took it over to her laptop, where she began typing.

'Writing retreat…information…dates…ah, booking form.'

In bed, she read another artist's letter, aware she needed to start deciding soon which of these notable women she would select for her book, the book she was going to write. Eek.

My darling Peggy,

My only comfort in this dreary life comes from hoping you have been able to save a place for me. My one consolation is that soon I will see you, feel your touch, and be whole with you once more. I imagine you putting to valuable use your charm and persuasion in order to find me a suitable spot. If you've secured one, I am sure you will have adorned it with things I love to welcome me. How sweet and precious you are. There will be pink flowers in a pot beside a white ceramic vase, a Benin head statue, a bowl of appetising apples, a green covering on the table and a simple small wooden chair, suitable for my little self. You will have found me a position by a little window, hung with plain blue curtains and offering a pretty view of the village and the hills beyond. You will have taken care to request a quiet area for us to reside, a corner where we can sit in the shadows, observing the comings and goings of everyone else, and engaging with other people only when we need to. The thought I must wait any longer is becoming unbearable. I am prone to my mad fits more than ever and I sleep hardly at all without you beside me. You were all I had and all I wanted.

I have not so much as picked up a brush in years. I cannot see to paint and my hand is unsteady, but mostly the will has gone. My last pictures were self-portraits, showing my steady decline since you left. I have become a shell without you. I see the world around me now as dreary and dull, and my paintings reflect the lack of colour in my existence. I often consider how it might end, how I might perhaps take strength from Virginia or Sylvia Plath and follow their path. But the truth is, I don't have the courage or the wherewithal to see it through. No-one would miss me or mourn me, yet I cannot bring myself to slip silently away by my own hand, even though it would mean being reunited with you.

While I retain a degree of eyesight, and with my wits still about me, I am trying to get everything in order. It is painful for me to go through all of our most personal and private belongings, as it reminds me of everything lost, but needs must. I came across our box of photos and singled out the ones you took of me in the garden, sitting with all the paintings. I am dismal, ugly and plain in most of them, although the paintings come out sweetly, as tiny representations of themselves. They remind me of our early miniatures, they are so reduced in proportion. You took the photos as a record of the truth and wanted them found, so I will leave them to their fate. I would happily burn them, and keep our secret together forever, but you wish for them to be discovered, and I will do anything for you.

You are as much of an artist as me, instrumental in choosing my subjects and arranging everything. For the still life paintings, you skilfully and carefully selected the objects, placing them to form a pleasing vignette. You booked all the sitters from around the village to come and be painted, and through your selfless efforts, found ways to secure our finances and look after me in every way you could. You nurtured me, encouraged me and believed in me, even in our darkest days when we hardly left the cottage. You were always the inspiration, the reason for me to carry on. Without you, none of the paintings would exist. Or, if they did, they would be but poor imitations of themselves. Your creativity brought them to life through your choice of colours and bright things to illuminate the canvas. To this day, I often think about old Roger Fry's assumption all those years ago, when you showed him a few of my pictures in London and he encouraged you to continue painting. Unbeknownst to him, his false assumption helped us devise our exquisite solution. Without such serendipity, I might never have painted again. I certainly wouldn't have been able to tolerate the limelight as you had to you, darling. It was hard for you, but you took on the responsibility allowing me to simply paint.

Stanley's work is doing quite well since The Tate acquired much of his archive. Remember how you called him Mad Stanley? Shirin, the daughter, continues to take particular issue with you, and to blame you for everything at any given opportunity. She attempts to elevate him and simultaneously to destroy your reputation, as if it is impossible for a world to exist where you are both appreciated. People are saying such wicked things about you. They claim you bewitched Stanley, manipulated him into divorcing Hilda, cheated him out of his home and his money, and flirted with him and everyone else, motivated by personal gain. I can't bear it and consequently I mostly hide away lest I bump into anyone.

Sometimes, darling, I long to tell the world of the abuse you endured at his hand. You did all you could to protect me and give me a decent life, especially after poor Father lost everything in that dreadful financial crash, then died only a year later. I begged you to step in and help, and you did. You found a way for us to survive without his financial assistance. Your steadfast motivation was always the same: pure, constant and true devotion to me, and you did what was necessary. Stanley was pursuing you like a man possessed and you allowed him to get close. I hated it, sneered at you and told you not to do it, but because I needed you to find a way for me to paint, at whatever cost to us both, I pushed you together. This paradox is a source of profound grief to me now. I forced you into finding a solution, and although it proved financially beneficial, it was at such a high cost to you, and marked the start of a terrible time.

It was not your fault he was still married to Hilda, not your fault he was besotted with you, not your fault he was so cruel. You were a saint to endure him as long as you did. I cannot bear to see those hideous pictures he did of you during the years you tolerated him as his muse and then his wife, painting you at first as a grotesque trophy, then later as if you were a dead slab of meat. His garish colours and the symbolic placement of his own self beside the heart of your womanhood as if he was the innocent victim of your evil charms is nothing short of repulsive. By his hand, your curves were rendered as monstrous, your strength as ugly, and your personality as base. He completely failed to capture your spirit, your charisma and your singular beauty, for the simple reason he failed to bring out those qualities in you. He knew the love we had could never be matched by him, or indeed any man, but still he tried. When he couldn't succeed is when the trouble for us really began.

You entirely earned the title of Lady Spencer after the way he treated you. Ignorant of the facts, people were unjust in their hatred for you. Men thought Stanley was emasculated by your strength of character and they sympathised with him for it. They were not aware of his scheming mind, how he wanted to have his cake and eat it with you and Hilda. It was quite extraordinary he should entertain the possibility he could succeed to bed you both together. Women hated you because you went against the mould. You refused to be the subservient little housewife they were all conditioned to be. They found you intimidating, even if secretly they envied you. But none of them knew the extent of his depravity, how he damaged you on honeymoon. I was inclined to kill him, or at least have him pay for his abuse, but you wouldn't ever speak of it again. I regret we didn't expose him, but it was your lifelong wish, even when you were ill. You were an angel.

I regret we didn't ever confide in Vanessa and the others. On reflection, I believe they would have understood our situation both as artists and as companions. Theirs was a complex and unconventional lifestyle too with its fair share of secrets, and they had more experience of how to navigate in the world than us. But you were loyal to me in every way and respected my need for privacy, whatever the cost to yourself. Even during those years we lived in Paris, I could not entertain the idea of going to one of Barney's famous Friday nights, let alone setting foot in Le Monocle as your lover, which I regret now. It was silly of me to insist we were sisters, when the truth was plain to everyone and nothing to be ashamed of. It was partly my insecurity and ridiculous shyness, but partly as I could not bear for you to risk your reputation.

However much I tried to protect you, the Spencers made sure your reputation was sullied anyway. Stanley spreading gossip about you around the village to anyone who would listen was almost more than I could bear. He spoke as if our relationship was perverse when it was he who was the ruinous one. When he finally gave up pleading for a menage a trois relationship with you and Hilda, he wrote her long love letters after their divorce and for all those years you were married. While he was busy cavorting, doing as he pleased, you were the one being blamed. Do you recall him boasting how he bedded Hilda on your wedding night, while you and I went down to St Ives to begin the honeymoon? You probably don't wish to call him to mind at all, but I have had to live with it all for so long without you. Now I watch in horror as, in death, he becomes ever more famous, his paintings inspiring others while no-one cares for the truth. Finding and seeing again your wedding photos, I am appalled by them. You are glowing as always, but everyone else looks utterly miserable. In one picture, you are standing nearer to me than to him, and leaning towards me, your hip almost touching me. I appear as disgusted by the whole affair as I felt, but it's my favourite picture from that dark day, as it speaks the most truth. And Stanley so ridiculous in the silly felt hat he insisted on wearing. You tower over him like an Amazonian; how little he really was by contrast! He tried to tame you, and he nearly broke you, but he could never touch us.

For all your sacrifices, I willingly gave what I could, in the form of public recognition. My only power was my ability to paint, and all I could give you was to sign your name on the paintings. It is completely insignificant to me, such a small offering to you after you gave everything for me. I was proud to sign the paintings Patricia Preece. The world believes you to be a good artist. I alone appreciate you to be so much more. In my heart, I wish to go to my grave with our secret, but I made you a promise and I must keep it. So, the photos will be left in the cottage to be found, along with the diaries, paperwork and letters we agreed upon.

If ever I longed for one thing, it was for us to share old age. When you left me, women were beginning to succeed. You were one of the pioneers my darling with your brave affiliation to the Suffragettes. You would be pleased with the progress made. The Sex Discrimination Act is now in place, to protect women from being victimised. Liberation has spread its wings. Women can have their hair as short as they wish and wear trousers without anyone caring. Mine is shorter than ever. We were born in the wrong age, my darling. Women everywhere are succeeding on their own merit rather than being forced to go to the lengths we did.

I continued signing myself as PP after you left me eleven years ago, because you remained the inspiration, the genius and the reason any of the paintings were put on canvas. I was never asked for my opinion on our art, for which I was thankful. As you appreciate, it was my desire to sit quietly in the corner and watch as you went about the business side of our life and went about the business of being utterly wonderful. I remain infuriated that your spirit was driven from you by Stanley. But we managed, didn't we darling, hiding ourselves away and making it work the only way we knew. Those last years were tinged with your illness, but we had the blessing of being together. We were one soul.

I love you with the same passion I did when we met at Slade all those years ago, when we fell so quickly and so completely in love. You remain the most irresistible, beautiful creature I ever laid eyes on, and I was blessed to have you. I was prone to be an egotist and wasted precious time with my nerves and my demands, but your loyalty never wavered.

Arrangements have been made for us to lie together forever in our beloved Cookham near our blessed home as per our wishes. Stanley and Hilda share a single memorial stone there, and so will we. Theirs is for show, but our stone will reflect the truth: we led a singular life, we formed a unique whole. In the future, people may discover how we chose to live. I do not care anymore what anyone thinks. One day, there might be an exhibition about us, my love. Can you imagine other people snooping amongst our private possessions? The thought would have abhorred me years ago, but now, whatever happens, my only care is to be with you again.

My battle to live without you is nearly over. I will see you soon my love.

Yours always,
Dorothy

Chapter Thirty-One

Paula

The next morning while Alex showered, Helena studied the picture in Clare's bedroom which had captivated her since she noticed it the first night she stayed. It was a pencil sketch study of a woman, drawn in simple lines that clearly conveyed the artist's adoration for the subject, and deftly displayed the artist's talent at capturing it. The slightly flushed figure was reclining on a chair, her expression and position indicating that moments before, she had made love with the artist. She wore a loose-fitting slip or dress that followed the shape of her breasts and partially revealed her pubic area. It was a picture OF Patricia Preece, not BY her. Dorothy Hepworth was the artist. What a secret to keep their entire lives! Clare's note gave more detail of how they lived, keeping their relationship hidden even to their bohemian friends Vita Sackville-West, Virginia Woolf and Vanessa Bell of the Bloomsbury Group of artists, who had a very liberated approach to sex and sexuality. Patricia's marriage to the artist Stanley Spencer sounded grim; he came across as quite unpleasant. Helena searched for pictures he painted of Patricia. She could see exactly why Dorothy would be disgusted by them.

Helena was bursting to tell Cynthia about this discovery. She shoved the letter in her bag and dashed out, hopping along the hallway as she put on her shoes, collecting her keys and phone from the hall table as she went. When she signed in at St. Jude's, she was so eager to go through to Cynthia's room, she didn't want to stop as usual for a chat with the receptionist, and didn't notice the expression on her face. It was only when the receptionist asked if she wouldn't mind taking a seat that Helena gathered something was not right. This wasn't normal protocol. Normal protocol was for Helena to make her own way down to Cynthia's room. Instead, she was told a manager would be with her shortly. She sat in one of the chairs lining the sides of the room and gazed at the well-tended pot plants framing the welcome area, softening the hard edges of the desk.

The duty manager appeared from an office to the side of the reception area and walked slowly towards her with arms folded, studying the clean salmon-coloured carpet as he approached. It seemed to take half an hour. Long enough anyway for panic to set in.

'I'm really sorry, Helena. You are minutes too late. We were going to ring you.' He sat down beside her. 'It was very peaceful. She was listening to Amy's recording. Only an hour ago, she was telling our nurse that the pieces by Clara Schumann were her favourites, and that Clara was a piano teacher too. Then she simply fell asleep and quietly slipped away. Here, let me get you a tissue and a glass of water. Take all the time you need.'

The next few days were a blur. Periods of intense activity concerning practicalities were interspersed with moments of severe inertia, when Helena ceased to function and could be found staring at a wall or out into the garden. She needed a big walloping cry, but only sniffles emerged while her mind refused to accept this was real. Cynthia's loss left a gaping hole in every room in the house. Helena understood she'd never come home again once she was in the hospice, but while she was alive, there was a still glimmer of false hope.

As if losing Cynthia wasn't bad enough, she was going to lose her home of recent weeks and would have to return to her grotty flat. She'd have to find another job now Cynthia couldn't pay her anymore, meaning there would be no time or headspace to write the book, just as she was starting to look forward to doing it. Whenever things started going well, whenever she allowed herself to believe life was on the up, another shit thing happened. When was it going to end? It was all too much.

Lily popped round one day in the midst of this to return the latest batch of letters that she had typed out in Word and saved.

'Ooh, what's the smell?' she asked as she followed Helena into the kitchen.

'Oh that's Alex. Well, not Alex. That's Alex having a bonfire. We decided to burn Cynthia and Clare's most private things. Had a kind of little ceremony as we put Clare's box of diaries on the pile. It was immensely emotional, even though neither of us knew her. It resembled a funerary pyre.'

There was a pause as Helena and Lily watched Alex forking over the last of the embers in the back garden.

'We'll never know now what secrets they held,' said Helena, remembering she had very nearly opened the lid. She'd stopped herself when the covers of a few diaries came into view. It would have been a betrayal of Cynthia's trust, and it didn't seem to matter now anyway.

Lily took a wad of letters from her rucksack. 'Here's the latest batch. I wasn't sure what to do with them after everything.'

'Thank you, you've been so helpful,' said Helena as she took the letters. 'I'm not sure myself right now.' She glanced down and noticed that on top was a letter she didn't recognise. She scanned it and saw the words "Bletchley Park" and "Official Secrets Act."

'Oh thank God, I thought I'd lost one of the letters Cynthia particularly wanted to include, and it's here,' she said.

'Oh sorry, I guess I picked it up by mistake', said Lily.

'No, it's not your fault at all. I must've given it to you before I'd read it. Honestly, you've been a godsend. I can't thank you enough for doing this.' Helena touched Lily on the arm. 'It's good to have them all as a memento.'

Lily stayed for a cup of tea and a chat. As she was walking towards the front door to leave, a letter popped through the letter box and plopped onto the hall floor. Lily leant on the wall to steady herself as she stooped to pick it up, then handed it to Helena. It was from a local solicitor. Cynthia had mentioned she had got all her affairs in order. But Cynthia hadn't explained what she this meant by this, hadn't elaborated on any arrangements, and Helena hadn't liked to pry. So, it was a relief to receive this letter. It would explain Cynthia's wishes for her funeral, a simple humanist ceremony Helena guessed. Maybe Cynthia might leave her a little keepsake, such as the tea service she admired. Helena helped Lily with her rucksack, and saw her out into the warm Spring day before opening the letter.

Two minutes later, she was speeding around the house calling for Alex, who had come in from the garden.

'I'm here, darling, whatever is it?' Alex called from upstairs.

'I haven't the foggiest,' yelled Helena as she dashed up. She stopped for a moment to catch her breath. 'But listen to this.'

> Dear Helena,
> I am writing with regards to Ms Cynthia Partridge, deceased. Could you please contact our office at your earliest convenience, and arrange an appointment. You may wish to bring a friend.
> Yours sincerely,
> *Matthew Blanchard*
> Senior Partner
> Blanchard and Henshaw
> Solicitors you can trust.

'I'm shitting myself. What do you suppose it says?' said Helena, waving the letter in Alex's face. 'Are they going to tell me I owe them lots of money or something? Or that Cynthia was in trouble? Why else would they be writing? And why the hell am I supposed to take a friend?'

'I'm sure there's a rational explanation love. But there's only one way to find out.'

'I admire how calm you stay, Alex, but I'm feeling really stressed.'

'Let's ring them now, and put you out of your misery.'

Two days later, Alex managed to get a half day, and they went to the solicitors together. Their meeting with Matthew Blanchard was brief; he was evidently a man of few words in general.

'All that worry,' said Helena when they came out, taking Alex's arm.

'Indeed. This is an awful lot to take in. Shall we go for a coffee and a cake? You look as if you could do with it. There's a new place in the High Street on the precinct with outside tables, near the little fountain? It's warm enough, do you agree?'

'That would be nice, yes. You always know the right thing to say. Cynthia did too. Oh, Cynthia.'

Helena shook her head and let out a gaping sigh. With it started to come the stored sobs that had been waiting for their moment. Alex held her as they walked towards the café, then sped inside to order, while Helena sat on a fittingly wobbly metal garden chair. She tried to compose herself, watching people pass in front of the fountain, briefly silhouetted by its watery backdrop. Mothers with young children on their way to playgroup, an older couple with sticks, a young man in a suit striding to his next appointment; all with their own lives going on at their own paces, all with their own concerns, all oblivious to her life-changing day.

'I simply can't believe it,' she said when Alex returned and handed her a frothy cappuccino and a huge piece of chocolate fudge cake, placing them on the wobbly metal garden table.

'It's going to take a while to sink in, love. Quite apart from anything, I didn't know Cynthia was my landlady. She mentioned one Saturday that she knew of a property for rent; that's how I found the house for Amy and me. It was all done through an agency though; I had no idea "CP Properties" was her.'

'She was always so modest,' said Helena.

Over the coming days, Helena undertook a deep clean of the house. Alex came in from work one day to find her in the lounge.

'Look what I found down the back of the sofa,' said Helena. She handed Alex a tattered postcard. On the front was a picture of Kenwood House in London. Alex turned over the card to see Clare's familiar handwriting.

> Dear Mum,
> A keepsake from our lovely day out together. I shall cherish the memory of our visit to the setting of one of the letters. I just wish you could have shared more of these

places with me. You're there in my heart wherever I go, and always will be. Thank you for everything. You inspire me every day.

All my love, Clare xxx

'How lovely. Now both Clare and Cynthia will live on in your heart, darling,' said Alex.

'Very true,' replied Helena. 'It's amazing to see a personal note from her. I'll treasure it.' Helena placed the card on the mantelpiece.

'By the way, Amy is delighted about the piano,' said Alex. 'I talked to her about your suggestion; as you said, it can stay here until she's settled into a place of her own.'

'Good. Although, I'll miss her playing it here.'

'We'll have to make do with her recordings,' said Alex smiling. 'Are you ok if I go and do a bit more in the garden?'

'Flippin' 'eck. I've got a garden. And all this.' Helena swooped her hand around the lounge. 'I'm still trying to get my head around it. I just can't believe it's mine. It's so different from where I used to live. Oh, talking of which, I need to pop over to the flat to collect the last few bits and see if there's any post. I'll go now, while you potter outside.'

'Where you lived is great, but in another way. It's a bit rough round the edges, but it's interesting and cosmopolitan round there. All those shops with their intriguing objects and cafes with foods from around the world...'

'Now you mention it, there is a certainly a lot of life round there.'

'I'd be happy to live there. In fact, I'd be happy anywhere with you in it.'

'Oh you!' Helena nudged Alex sideways as she walked out of the lounge.

'Anyway, I'll shoot off now. See you later.'

Helena hadn't been back to her old flat for a while. Past the grubbiness, she could see there was a charm to the area, with its variety of life and constant activity. Alex was right. Of course.

She entered the cold, stark building for the last time. Pinned to the grubby wall above the shelf where letters were left was a handwritten notice demanding people should stop slamming the front door. She closed the door carefully. As anticipated a backlog of leaflets advertising stairlifts, seniors' holidays and orthopaedic footwear had arrived since her last visit. She picked them up to be binned, then noticed one hand-written letter. She climbed the stairs and entered the studio flat before opening it.

Dear Helena,
You don't know me, but I know you. My

name is Paula. We have the same Dad, John. He was seeing both our mums for years, living a double life. One day he upped and left you and your mum, and moved in with me and my mum. It was because my mum had a bit of money. He was never very good to her. He used to go on about your mum and my mum saying they were both awful women. I didn't like him, and was scared of him, especially when he hit her. I used to hide in my room. Anyway, I thought you should know he has died. I found this address and this photo in his stuff. I didn't know about you before. If you want to come to the funeral, you're welcome, but if not it's ok, whatever you want to do.
Sorry if this is a bit of a shock.
Best wishes,
Paula

Enclosed with the letter was a photo Helena had never seen before: a little girl with long brown curly hair sitting on a young man's shoulders at the beach. On the back, in her mother's handwriting, it said, "John and Helena, day trip to Brighton." At the top of the letter Paula had written her address and phone number. Helena keyed in the address on her phone. She lived a few streets away. They had probably passed one another in the street, maybe even shared a glance.

She placed the letter and photo in her bag and packed the last of her belongings into a box borrowed from Cynthia's house. Her house. Actually, one of her three houses. She closed the door on her old life, and posted the keys back into the flat for the landlord to find. Walking towards the bus stop, she reflected again about the secrets people keep. Was her mum aware of Paula's existence? Did her dad love her after all? Did her dad hit her mum? Did he have other women? Other children?

'Helena, Helena, Helena. Stop. What matters now is… you've got a sister.'

Chapter Thirty-Two

Joan

Dear Jill,

It was very nice to meet you recently at the "Women's Achievements" event, and thank you for giving me your address. I don't know about you, but I find these things a little embarrassing. I enjoyed meeting new people, especially you, but I'm not really one for public displays of one's accomplishments. I was extremely interested to hear about your work with Dr McIndoe at East Grinstead Hospital. I had heard of him and his pioneering surgery with burns victims, as I mentioned to you: I had a girlfriend who needed surgery there due to a nasty growth on her face, and she talked often of all the "Guinea Pigs" as the chaps were known. She always held a torch for Dr

McIndoe, and talked about him often. There you were behind the scenes, quietly caring for them all and not losing a single man on your ward for the entire duration of the war. It was splendid they had several testimonies from a few of the men you helped, as it brought to life fascinating stories of your patience and skill, your unstinting support of the men from the minute they came out of the operating theatre. They said coming onto your ward was like coming home. How you managed to create such an atmosphere at a time of great suffering is remarkable.

It was touching, I admit, when they introduced us together at the event, saying how much we both contributed to the war effort. Me in Hut 8 and you on Ward III, doing different work, but with the same ultimate goal.

As you quite rightly said, we were only doing our bit, and working at Bletchley Park under The Official Secrets Act was the part I played. Many of the men and women felt quite bitter about not being able to discuss the work at Bletchley for such a long time. They believed we should be recognised earlier. I was lucky to receive the MBE soon after the war, although of course, I couldn't say how I had earnt it! Quite a few of the women died before the secrecy was lifted, including Margaret Rock, a great mathematician, while others lost their husbands before being able to tell them.

I didn't enjoy getting rounds of applause for being the only woman working on the Banburismus process with Alan Turing and for my cypher work. I found it all rather excruciating. It made me uncomfortable being applauded for being a woman doing these things. To me, it merely highlights the fact that it remains exceptional for women to achieve in academic fields such as science and maths. It's been a private bug bear of mine for a while. I wasn't awarded a degree at Cambridge because they didn't give out degrees to girls then, even though we had done all the same work as the boys. It was not until after the war that this changed. They told me I had a double first and I was allowed to say I had won a few prizes, but there was no formal recognition. Thankfully this didn't prevent me from getting the job at Bletchley. They sought young women with particular skills, and offered interviews and then jobs to girls on that basis, regardless of their background or level of education. They put us all on clerical duties to start with, then selected us for other work as and when we showed our aptitude for such.

At the event, they failed to mention the conditions for many of the "girls" as we were known. I suspect they thought we should be grateful women weren't allowed on the front line and could do our bit in relative safety. Nonetheless, inside the huts they were crammed in like sardines, with little light, working extremely long shifts day and night, keeping their spirits high through camaraderie and sheer determination. We should have had our own Sister Meally with us to build morale and make us feel more at home! You would have been a great addition to the team, with your caring nature and gentle humour.

Alan and others appreciated my contribution, but I earned considerably less than the men who did the same job. My sex prevented me from rising further in rank than deputy Head of Hut 8, and I must say a handful of the men were most disparaging about the presence of a woman code-breaker; one of them went so far as to declare that women weren't suited to such activities as we didn't have the aptitude for intellectual thinking.

I got to know Alan extremely well, and we were engaged briefly. I suspected he was a homosexual, and he confessed his tendencies to me the day after the proposal. Of course, it was illegal at the time, and we had to keep it completely hush hush. We carried on for a bit, but eventually he broke it off. It was plain awful, heartbreaking, the way he was treated. I was desperately sad when I heard he had taken his own life.

My eventual marriage was to John, and it was a happy one. He died a while ago, poor fellow. Nowadays, I amuse myself mainly with the study of coins. It's rather different from cryptology, but I enjoy the detailed work of studying and researching. It suits my character.

I would very much like to stay in touch with you, Jill. I feel we share a great deal in common with regards to our outlook on life. I do hope you agree. Perhaps we could meet if we are ever in the same area? If ever you and your husband are in Oxfordshire, do let me know.

Warmest wishes,

Joan Murray (nee Clarke)

It was peculiar to have finished reading all the letters, to have discovered all their revelations and to have met all these women. Helena had looked forward to reading each one, and there was a sense of loss at the realisation she would never again be reading one for the first time. This moment marked a supposed turning point. It was the end of reading as a passive participant and the beginning of what was meant to come next: the part where she had to try and be an active writer. What with one thing and another, what with recent seriously significant life events, Helena hadn't really paid much attention to the idea of writing.

Attached to the letter, as usual, was Clare's note.

Joan Clarke writing to Jill Meally. Both credited with saving lives in WWII. Neither sought the limelight, lived in the shadows of their more famous male colleagues. Illustrates how women were still competing for equality long after they got the vote. Notable campaigners in the UK included Mary Macarthur and Ellen Wilkinson. Mary Macarthur campaigned for pay for women chain makers and won them a minimum wage. Ellen Wilkinson, later a prominent MP, played a key role in the fight for the right to work in the 1930s. Even after WWII when women had clearly demonstrated their academic abilities, opportunities were limited. Similar in the US - Sister Mary Keller is an example. She managed to carve out a career in computer programming – her college made an exception to their men-only rule. She got her PhD in the 1960s.

Equal Pay Act in UK wasn't until 1970. Five years later The Sex Discrimination Act made it illegal to discriminate against women in employment, education, and training. Previously, married women weren't allowed to open a bank account without their husbands' permission. And as recently as the 1970s in Ireland, the marriage bar made it illegal for women to work in the civil service once they were married. So many women who might have gone on to achieve great things were forced to choose between a career or marriage and a family. Despite everything being stacked against them throughout history, many women broke the mould. Weave this in towards the end.

Once again, Helena got the impression that Clare's note had been written for her, even though Clare had no idea Helena existed. She put the letter and note back in their plastic home and reunited them with their companions.

Three months later, Helena and Alex decided to move in together. They kept a collection of Cynthia's belongings, partly as a reminder of her and her unbelievable decision to leave everything to Helena, and partly because they went perfectly with the house. Their house. Alex came into the lounge where Helena was arranging things on shelves. Sitting beside her was their little rescue dog, Lulu. Helena had never owned a pet, and now she had a limpet. A limpet shaped like a Yorkshire Terrier cross, but a limpet nonetheless, glued to her at every possible opportunity. For several days, the limpet didn't have a name. They considered naming her "Tray" after Mary Anning's dog, but Helena decided she would feel self-conscious calling out the name of a household accessory in the park. It would be akin to calling "Kettle!" or "Saucepan!" She briefly considered "Teacup" but eventually settled on Lulu. She bore a resemblance to Cynthia's dog; it felt fitting to give her the same name.

Summer warmth had stimulated garden growth. The roses were in full bloom and other flowers Helena couldn't yet name were also making their presence known. Alex had picked a small bunch of roses and placed them in a blue and green Moorcroft vase in the kitchen. Helena paused to smell them as she walked into the room to make a cup of tea and grab a quick bite while she decided how she might fill the rest of her day. The kettle boiled. She got a mug from the cupboard and was about to add the teabag when she changed her mind. She was going to do this properly. Out came the Clarice Cliff teapot and a cup and saucer, and she made herself a proper brew. To go with it, she prepared a tuna mayonnaise sandwich, taking time to mix and season the filling while the tea brewed in the pot. She put milk in the little jug. Then, she placed everything on a tray and carried it into the dining room, where she set it down on the little table next to Cynthia's chair. She sat down and poured, watching as the tea flowed from the spout into the cup, marvelling at the beautiful design of the objects, and contemplating the people who had used them before her. She was finally learning to savour simple moments.

The next few minutes passed in quiet contemplation as Helena savoured her lunch and allowed her eyes wander around the garden. They settled on the summer house. As she finished the last mouthful, a sudden rush of thoughts and words and ideas and themes and chapters and a beginning and a middle and an end appeared in her head, as if they were being placed there from an outside source. Helena left the lunch things where they were, dashed over to her laptop, shoved it under her arm, picked up her notebook, and ran across the lawn to the summer house. She threw open the door, and plonked herself down at the little table. Carefully, she moved Clare's typewriter onto the floor, replaced it with her laptop, and opened it. Words started appearing on the screen, and even though it felt as if it wasn't her writing them, they kept on coming. Was she finally becoming Clare's ghost writer, or was Clare her ghost writer, as she had been all along? Whatever, it didn't matter. It was happening.

Foreword

Dear Reader,

This is a book that someone else was meant to write, but for reasons I shall explain, the honour has become mine. Ostensibly, it is a book by a woman about another woman who was planning to write a book about women through history. Tragically, Clare Partridge, the woman who was going to write the book, was unable to complete it. The historical figures she intended to include were from different backgrounds and lived in different times and places. I have selected letters that particularly resonated with me. Each woman was notable in her own way and Clare's research on them offers a unique insight into their lives and the societies in which they lived. This is not a complete history of women. It is a selection of imagined letters bound together by a common thread: we are each on our own journey, and yet collectively, many of the issues we face are relatable, wherever or whenever we live.

On reading the letters alongside the context notes, I hope you will learn as I did about the roles women have played in society. Perhaps you will be encouraged as I was to do your own research on these women and indeed other women throughout history who have led interesting lives or made an important contribution.

The letters came into my possession through the most remarkable woman. I was working in my local library, a job I didn't like much. In fact, I was living a life I didn't like much. This was all to change when I became friends with Cynthia Partridge and got to hear about her brilliant daughter Clare. Cynthia encouraged me to write this book; I believe she saw a potential I was completely unaware of. For this, and for so much more, I am forever grateful.

One particularly cold winter's day, I reluctantly arrived at the library, and I was feeling miserable because I had a silly self-induced pain in my wrist…

Chapter Thirty-Three

Helena

A year and a half later

'Darling! They're here!'

Hearing the clunk of the front door shutting, Helena jumped up from the sofa where she had been reading the first online reviews for the last hour. She chose to do this alone in case they were awful. Remarkably, they weren't. She'd been worried as there had been a degree of backlash on social media about her writing a "women's book" that was "woke" and "anti-male." She'd never thought of it as a women's book and certainly didn't want to be considered anti-male. She didn't mind being called woke, after reading about its original meaning. She'd asked Chris for advice on how to deal with the backlash, and he had repeated his mantra: Believe in your own integrity. She'd decided not to respond to the nasty comments.

She went into the hallway, took the box from Alex, and carried it into the dining room where she set it on the table. It was a fitting place to open it, a full circle kind of moment. As she put it down, the twinge in her wrist reminded her she had an appointment the following week. It had been two years of discomfort now, which was quite enough. Anyway, that was for another day.

Amy brought in a pair of scissors from the kitchen and handed them to Helena, who cut open the box as they all three huddled in. A layer of brown crinkled paper separated her from the rest of the contents. This was one of those rare occurrences in a life, a pivotal beat that can never be captured again. A few days ago, someone in a factory miles away, possibly in another country, had packed this box. Did they consider the person it was being sent to, and did they have any idea of its significance for them? Helena savoured the feeling of butterflies in her stomach for a couple of seconds before gently lifting the brown paper and peering in. There they were. Two dozen author copies of her book, arranged into four piles, pristine. Perfect.

''Oh darling, they look fabulous,' said Alex.

'They do, don't they? I can't believe it,' said Helena.

She lifted three volumes from the box, and handed one each to Amy and Alex. They stood in silence briefly as they each handled a copy. The cover was simple: a dark teal background with a border of leaves, and an image of an old typewriter. Underneath the image was the name of the author: Helena French. And above it, the title of the book:

Women of Note

Inside was a dedication.

For Cynthia and Clare, who provided me with everything I needed to write the book, and for my family Alex and Amy, who helped me get it written.

Lily had done a brilliant job of formatting the manuscript ready to send out to potential publishers. There were so many people who had helped Helena get to this point. Not least, the lovely small indie publishing company who had taken her on. Their editing and emotional support through her inevitable bouts of imposter syndrome had been remarkable.

A couple of weeks later, Helena opened the front door to the last of the guests.

'Sue!' she exclaimed, and gave her school friend a hug.

'Let me look at you,' said Sue. 'Wow, you stunner!'

'Oh, I don't know about that,' Helena replied, blushing.

'She says that quite a bit,' said Alex, appearing from behind Helena. 'It's one of the many things I love about her.'

'Hi Alex!' said Sue. 'Yes, she has always said it.' Sue turned again to Helena. 'Wow, I love your dress, it really suits you. Vintage, yes?'

'Yes. I have quite the collection nowadays. Anyway, come in, come in! I'm so excited you're here.'

Helena introduced Sue to the other guests who'd gathered for the little book launch party. Food and drink were laid out in the lounge, including a range of home-made salads, quiches and dips. As she finished uncovering everything from its cling film, Helena joked about becoming a domestic goddess.

After ensuring everyone had food, drink, and someone to talk to, Helena leaned against the lounge doorframe holding a glass of bubbly. Sue came over, and linked arms with her as Helena surveyed the room.

'Can you believe this?' Helena said.

'Pretty awesome, Helena. You did good,' replied Sue, giving her a squeeze.

Over by the mantelpiece, Alex's parents listened to Lily talking about her favourite letters. Paula was with her family by the bookshelves, and was chatting to Rachel and Constance about father figures. By the piano, Carol was engaged in an intense conversation with Amy about musical influences. Helena noted to herself she might have to rescue Amy soon. Near the window, Colin was trying to persuade Chris to collaborate on a project together, researching the impact of book banning and book burning through history. Effia and Alex studied Alex's collection of African masks and other ephemera in the display cabinet.

Helena loved their eclectic a mix of different objects. In the cabinet alongside Alex's collection were things of Cynthia's they had kept, including the Lotz glass, Moorcroft and of course the Clarice Cliff. Amy's music awards were there too. Dotted amongst everything else were a little Peter Rabbit, a cigarette lighter in the shape of a beer bottle, a couple of *Whimsies* and an olive dish. Every item was special in its own way, and every item belonged there. A mix of photos on the piano reflected their blended family and its history: Amy with her degree certificate, Helena and Alex's wedding, Helena with her shadow Lulu, Cynthia and baby Clare taken by Clare's father Harry. On the walls were a portrait of Mary Anning with her little dog Tray, the print of Dido and Elizabeth at Kenwood, and a picture on papyrus in profile of Nefertari.

Helena handed out signed copies of the book to all her guests. Lulu patiently sat beside her, eyes fixed on Helena's face in case she was rewarded with a glance in her direction. Every now and again Helena would oblige, and a little tail would thump against the side of her leg.

Alex and Amy had nudged Helena to make a little speech, to thank people and to celebrate her achievement, they said. She had scribbled down a few ideas in the notebook that the library staff had given her but wasn't sure until the day if she would say anything. *Oh what the heck, you're among friends. Do it now before you change your mind.* She walked over to the mantelpiece and picked up the battered notebook. Flicking through its pages was a reminder of the agonising process that Helena had inflicted upon herself and those around her as she had struggled to begin writing.

She found the page she was looking for, and signalled to Alex, who tapped a fork against a wine glass. Everyone fell silent.

'Erm, hello. God, I am a bit nervous. Anyway, sorry to interrupt, but I wanted to say a few words. Well, actually I'd rather be sitting in the corner watching you all enjoying yourselves, but I've been persuaded this is a good idea. I will keep it brief. First of all, thank you all for coming. I really, really appreciate you all making the effort to be here. Ahem. Sorry. Those of you who've known me a long time will be very familiar with my ability to get choked up easily. Right, here we go. If you'd told me a couple of years ago I'd be standing here a published author, I would have laughed in disbelief. If you'd told me I'd be living in this lovely home, with my amazing family and my mad little dog and we'd all be here today, celebrating the writing of this book, I would have assumed you were mistaking me for someone else. I still feel in many ways it's Clare's book. I always will. Without her, it would never have been written. Well, without all of you actually. You've all made it possible.'

'Yes, but you wrote it,' said a voice from the other side of the room. 'None of us did!'

'Thank you Effia. Yes, that's true. Anyway, thank you all. Now, I'll need another project to get stuck into. Any ideas?'

'Write the second volume!' said Lily with enthusiasm.

'Here, here!' shouted Chris. A little titter rippled round the room, and several people nodded and clapped.

'Or come back to work in the library!' shouted Carol. 'There's a deputy role coming up soon, it would suit you down to the ground.'

'Or both!' said Alex. 'We'll all support you whatever you decide.'

'Thank you, darling, I know. Actually, as some of you are aware, I've applied for a job at the hospice. Constance, thank you for suggesting it.' Constance raised her glass.

'You'll be a godsend, dear,' she said. 'We're desperate for your organisational skills in our office.'

'Oh, I don't know…'

'Don't you dare!' yelled Sue.

'Do pop in to the library anyway please,' said Carol. 'I want you to see it now we've raised the funds and finished the refit. I hope you'll approve.' Carol cleared her throat. 'Actually, is it alright if I say a few words?'

'Yes of course,' said Helena.

'Thank you.' Carol hesitated. 'Excuse me, I feel a bit choked too. Yes... ahem. Thanks to your generous donation from Cynthia's estate, the History shelves have had a complete makeover. As a finishing touch, we've had a little brass plaque made in memory of Cynthia. It looks lovely against the dark, newly polished wood of the shelves. Pretty much everything else has been replaced, especially that awful carpet. Oh, and we've started having events. *Women of Note* is our book of the week soon, and we'd love you to come in for a "Meet the author" session, and to officially unveil the plaque.'

'Oh wow, really? Erm, ok, yes, lovely. That all sounds brilliant. Thank you Carol. I'd be honoured. As long as you don't mind me crying!'

'You won't be the only one,' said Carol, grinning through her own tears.

'We'll sort out a date soon, I promise,' said Helena. 'Right, before I shut up and let you all get on, I have to thank Chris for the book title. We were playing around with various ideas, and I suggested using the term "herstory", but Chris nailed it.'

'My pleasure,' said Chris. 'And I know I speak for us all when I say how incredibly proud we are of you, Helena.' Helena regarded the room with embarrassed wonder as it filled with cheers and claps and whoops. Once the noise had died down, Helena raised her hand to say a few final words, the hardest words.

'I... I wish Cynthia was here today. Dear Cynthia. She would have loved having you all here. Here's to Cynthia and to all she did.' She felt Alex's arm round her waist as her eyes misted over.

'Here's to YOU,' said Alex. Everyone raised their glass as they exclaimed in unison,

'To Helena!'

She closed the notebook while everyone applauded. It no longer shut properly, crammed full as it was, with her scribbles and angst. She held onto it tightly as she carried it through to the dining room, then released her grip to put it in the sideboard on top of the letters and notes. Closing the sideboard door with a satisfying click was like closing a chapter.

When she returned to the lounge, Alex went over to the mantelpiece and picked up an envelope. Helena opened it eagerly to find two tickets.

'Oh Alex! Egypt! Are you sure?'

'Absolutely. It'll be our belated honeymoon. It's mainly Luxor. You'll see Nefertari's tomb, and we can take your photo on Ramesses' foot. Also, I've booked a flight down to Abu Simbel.'

'Oh this is too much,' said Helena.

'No. No it isn't.'

Once all the guests had departed, Helena rose from the sofa and said she was popping outside for a quick breath of air. She took with her a copy of her book and her nice pen, and walked out over the lawns down to the summer house. She propped the door wide open with the typewriter. As a warm evening breeze swirled around her, she opened the book and began to write.

> Dear Mum,
>
> I thought you might like to receive a copy of this book. I can't quite believe it's me who has written it, but there you are, miracles do happen.
>
> I think of you often. I have become close with Dad's other daughter Paula, my sister. She and her family are decent, kind and friendly people. Paula has explained how Dad behaved towards her mum when they were together, and what she told me has made me reflect. I wonder whether he was

the same with you.

I had some counselling which helped me see things differently, and I am now mindful that perhaps life was tough for you, being abandoned by your husband, left with a child and little income. I have also come to appreciate I wasn't always the easiest or most understanding daughter. It's something I wish to rectify.

Things are going well for me at the moment after a rough patch. I am married, with a lovely step-daughter and a silly little dog. One day, you might meet them...

It has been a very long time since we saw each other, but I want to start again, if you agree. I'd like to get to know you again.

With love,
Helena xxx

Author's Notes

Women of Note was inspired by a visit to the Charleston Gallery in Lewes, East Sussex, during the summer of 2024. The exhibition was called "Dorothy Hepworth and Patricia Preece: an untold story," and I came away from it buzzing with ideas. The next week was spent researching their story and writing an imagined letter from Dorothy to Patricia. I had no idea I was going to write this book, but after doing more research on different women and writing several more letters, the project began to evolve almost organically. I was about half way through the letters when a storyline which could weave them together formed in my mind. Whilst all of the modern-day characters are fictional, all of the women whose letters have been imagined for this book were real historical figures. For the purposes of this story, some aspects of the women's lives have been embellished or fictionalised, although the facts presented about where and how they lived are all based on available evidence. My discoveries are very much mirrored in the storyline, in that the accounts presented by different historians can vary tremendously.

The letters are from women I had heard of and always been fascinated by, such as Nefertari, and from women who came from different backgrounds and times that I was not as familiar with, such as Susan La Fleche. Each woman's story was researched prior to the letter being drafted, and just as Clare and Helena both immersed themselves into their lives, so did I. Finding the different voices was a fascinating challenge – I wanted the reader to feel initially as though the letters might possibly be genuine, but at the same time, needed them to be readable and relatable, and aimed to hint that they couldn't possibly be original. I was able to find examples of some of the women's words, and for others, I had to rely on knowledge and research about how they might have expressed themselves. As Helena needed to, I must add a caveat that the language used in the letters is appropriate for the time the letter would have been written. In short, I tried to write the letters "in the style of" the women.

A comprehensive list of references is included for anyone interested to read more about the lives of these remarkable women. I found Wikipedia to be a good starting point in general, from where I could springboard into deeper research.

I owe special thanks to Bushey Museum in Hertfordshire for allowing me to use Lilly Gill's story. I volunteered at Bushey Museum in 2020, where I worked on their oral history project. When I listened to and typed out the transcription of Lilly's words, I commented at the time that someone should write about her life in a book, never thinking that someone would be me. Every time I came to her story during the editing process, it made me cry.

Thank you to all the women whose lives inspired this book, and to all the women who continue to campaign for equality and fairness around the world.

Thank you to UpLit Press for your wisdom and guidance.

Finally, thank you to H. Your quiet support and limitless patience is remarkable.

Em Buckman, December 2024.

About the Author

Born in the 1960s, MJ grew up in a mediocre town and lived a mediocre life, desperate to be liked and yet often feeling an outsider.

Moving to London to study speech therapy in the 1980s, she became immersed in gay culture which was thriving at the time, and learnt about difference and tolerance, but also about pain and injustice.

MJ stayed in London to pursue a career as a therapist, and then as a manager for disabled children's services. From there, she moved into community development and project management. She wrote professionally throughout her working life, and had a few articles published. At the same time, she brought up two sons with her first husband.

MJ spent much of her adult life creating and hiding behind a mask, presenting to the world a confident person, while inside she was often struggling. In her fifties, she finally came clean about who she is, warts and all, accepting that she has mental health issues. Her books delve into the lives of people who are or have historically been exploited, and explore themes she feels are important and relevant to this day: accepting ourselves, accepting each other, and celebrating difference.

Now retired, she lives on the beautiful south coast of England with her very patient husband, and enjoys a quiet life with their cool as anything cat and their anxious as anything little dog.

Also by M.J. Buckman

Bent Is Not Broken

References

Nefertari

Wikipedia website: **Nefertari**. Accessed 09.07.2024.

Wikipedia website: **Hathor**. Accessed 09.08.2024.

Mark J: **Women in Ancient Egypt** (2023). World History Encyclopedia website. Accessed 08.07.2024.

Wikipedia website: **List of pharaohs**. Accessed 10.07.2024.

Ancient Egypt Online website: **Queen Nefertari**. Accessed 10.07. 2024.

McDonald JK: **House of Eternity: The Tomb of Nefertari** (1996). The Getty Conservation Institute website. Accessed/Downloaded 11.07.2024.

Wikipedia website: **Karnak**. Accessed 11.07.2024.

History Skills website: **Who was Nefertari, the most famous ancient Egyptian queen?** Accessed 15.07.2024.

Habicht ME, Bianucci R, Buckley SA, Fletcher J, Bouwman AS, Öhrström LM, Seiler R, Galassi FM, Hajdas I, Vassilika E, Böni T, Henneberg M, Rühli FJ: **Queen Nefertari, the Royal Spouse of Pharaoh Ramses II: A Multidisciplinary Investigation of the Mummified Remains Found in Her Tomb (QV66)** (2016). National Library of Medicine website. Accessed 15.07.2024.

Lesko BS: **Nefertari (c.1295 – 1256 BCE).** Encyclodedia.com website: Accessed 15.07.2024.

Watson N: (2022). Wonderful Things Art website. Accessed 15.07.2024. Symbolism In The Art Of Queen Nefertari's Tomb

Osirisnet website: **The tomb of Nefertari Merytmut, QV66**. Accessed 15.07.2024.

Trung Tac

Gandhi L: How Two Vietnamese Sisters Led a Revolt Against Chinese Invaders—in the 1st Century (2021, updated 2024) History website. Accessed 09.06.2024.

Trung Sisters - Vietnamese rebel leaders. Last updated 2024. Britannica website. Accessed 09.06.2024.

Trung Sisters. Wikipedia website. Accessed 09.06.2024.

Trung Sisters. New World Encyclopedia website. Accessed 10.06.2024.

The Legend of the Trung Sisters: Vietnams Heroines. Where 2 go Vietnam website. Accessed 10.06.2024.

Trung Sisters (D.43 CE). Encyclopedia website. Accessed 01.06.2024.

Mawia

Monferrer-Sala JP: **'New skin for old stories' Queens Zenobia and Māwiya, and Christian Arab groups in the Eastern frontier during the 3rd – 4th centuries CE** (2014). Downloaded 11.06.2024. New_skin_for_old_stories_Queens_Zenobia.pdf

Denova R: **Constantine's Conversion to Christianity** (2021). World History Encyclopedia website. Accessed 12.06.2024.

Mark JJ: **Mavia** (2018). World History Encyclopedia website. Accessed 12.06.2024.

Encyclopedia Britannica: **Valens** (2024) Accessed 12.06.2024.

Wikipedia: **Mawiyya.** Accessed 12.06.2024.

Mayerson P: **Mauia, Queen of the Saracens? A Cautionary Note** (1980). Israel Exploration Journal Vol. 30,

No. 1/2, pp. 123-131 (9 pages) JSTOR website. Accessed 12.06.2024.

Theodora

Wikipedia website: **Theodora (wife of Justinian I)**. Accessed 01.08.2024.

El-Abbadi M: **Library of Alexandria** (2024). Encyclopedia Britannica website. Accessed 01.08.2024.

Wikipedia website: **Antioch**. Accessed 01.08.2024.

Britannica website: **Theodora, Byzantine empress [died 548]** (2024). Accessed 02.08.2024.

History Vista website: **Exploring the Blues and Greens: Political Factions in the Byzantine Empire.** Accessed 02.08.2024.

Medieval Women website: **St. Theodora, Byzantine Empress, 497-548.** Accessed 02.08.2024.

Wikipedia website: **Corpus Juris Civilis**. Accessed 0 2.08.2024.

Shvangiradze T: **Byzantine Empress Theodora: The Legacy of a Powerful Woman** (2023). The Collector website. Accessed 02.08.2024.

Hellenica World website: **Theodora (6th century)**. Accessed 02.08.2024.

New World Encyclopedia website: **Theodora (sixth century)**. Accessed 02.08.2024.

Wikipedia website: **Justinian I**. Accessed 02.08.2024.

Wu Zhao

Ting Lee Y: **Wu Zhao: Ruler of Tang Dynasty China** (2015). Asian Studies website. Accessed 03.08.2024.

Fitzgerald CP: **Wuhou, Empress of Tang dynasty** (2024). Britannica website. Accessed 04.08.2024.

Morris S: **Empress Wu Zetian: the only woman to rule China, and who would be hated for it** (2023). History Extra website (official website for BBC History Magazine). Accessed 04.08.2024.

Encyclopedia.com website: **Empress Wu (Wu Zhao)**. Accessed 04.08.2024.

Dash M: **The Demonization of Empress Wu** (2012). Smithsonian magazine website. Accessed 05.08.2024.

Ende

Gu W: Ende: **The First Documented Spanish Female Manuscript Illuminator** (2024). Daily Art Magazine website. Accessed 05.08.2024.

Wikipedia website: **Ende (artist)**. Accessed 05.08.2024.

James Barry

Du Preez M and Dronfield J: **Dr James Barry: the Irishwoman who fooled the British Empire** (2016). Irish Times website. Accessed 07.08.2024.

National Archives website: **Dr James Barry, Why was he significant in 19th century medicine?** Accessed 07.08.2024.

Ortenberg R: **How History Keeps Ignoring James Barry** (2020). Science History Institute website. Accessed 07.08.2024.

Wikipedia website: **Medical Act 1858**. Accessed 07.08.2024.

April Ashley

Wikipedia website: **April Ashley**. Accessed 07.08.2024.

Wikipedia website: **Arthur Corbett, 3rd Baron Rowallan.** Accessed 07.08.2024.

Iglikowski-Broad V: **April Ashley: The legal battle** (2023). National Archives UK website. Accessed 08.08.2024.

Wikipedia website: **Georges Burou**. Accessed 08.08.2024.

Hildegard of Bingen

Hopkin O: **Hildegard of Bingen: life and music of the great female composer.** Classic FM website. Accessed 30.06.2024.

Classic FM website: **Hildegard of Bingen (1098 – 1179)**

Wikipedia website: **European witchcraft.** Accessed 30.06.2024.

Delahoyde M (Dr): **Hildegard of Bingen.** Washington State University website. Accessed 02.07.2024.

Gentile N: **Texts and Translations of Hildegard von Bingen's Gregorian Chants.** Healing Chants website. Accessed 02.07.2024.

Newman, B: **Hildegard of Bingen: Visions and Validation** (1985). Church History, 54(2), 163–175. . JSTOR website. Accessed 02.07.2024.

Britannica website: **St Hildegard, German Mystic.** Accessed 03/07/2024.

Franciscan Media website: **Saint Hildegard of Bingen.** Accessed 03/07/2024.

Britannica Website: **Humour, Ancient physiology.** Accessed 03/07/2024.

Howell J: **Hildegard of Bingen: medieval mother of science.** UCCF Christian Union website. Accessed 03/07/2024.

Mark J: **Hildegard of Bingen** (2019). World History website. Accessed 03/07/2024.

Wikiart website: **Hildegard of Bingen – 18 artworks**. Accessed 09.08.2024.

Christine de Pizan

Mark JJ: **Christine de Pizan** (2019). World History Encyclopedia website. Accessed 29.09.2024.

Wikipedia: **Christine de Pizan**. Accessed 29.09.2024.

Wikiquote website: **Christine de Pizan**. Accessed 2 9.09.2024.

Britannica website: **Christine de Pisan**. Accessed 29 .09.2024.

Brooklyn Museum website: **Christine de Pisan**. Accessed 29.09.024.

Rodriguez D: **Christine de Pizan: Her Works**. A Medieval Woman's Companion website. Accessed 29.09.2024.

Alice Kyteler

Wikipedia website: **Alice Kyteler**. Accessed 19.07.2024.

London Walks website: **London's Red Light District Laid Bare.** Accessed 21.07.2024.

Pavlac BA: **Lady Alive [sic] Kyteler Found Guilty of Witchcraft** (2004). Salem Press website. Accessed 22.0 7.2024.

Kenny S: **Witchcraft in Medieval Kilkenny, Kilkenny's medieval witch – Dame Alice Kyteler** (2003). Irish Identity website. Accessed 22.07.2024.

Seymour S-J D: **A.D. 1324 Dame Alice Kyteler, The Sorceress of Kilkenny** (1913). Irish Witchcraft and Demonology Chapter Two. Sacred Texts website. Accessed 23.07.2024.

Wikipedia website: **Petronilla de Meath**. Accessed 24.07.2024.

Historic Kilkenny website: **Alice Kyteler**. Accessed 24.07.2024.

Williams B: **The Sorcery Trial of Alice Kyteler**. History Ireland website. Accessed 24.07.2024.

Atteberry T: **Dame Alice Kyteler of Kilkenny, Ireland: A poisoner? Quite likely. A witch? Perhaps. A fighter? Absolutely.** Gothic Horror Stories website. Accessed 24.07.2024.

Mingren W: **Alice Kyteler: The Kilkenny 'Witch' Who Ran While her Servant Burned** (2018). Ancient Origins website. Accessed 24.07.2024.

Dido Elizabeth Belle

Wikipedia website: **Dido Elizabeth Belle**. Accessed 11.08.2024.

Historic England: **Slavery and Justice at Kenwood House**, Part 1 (PDF). Historic England. Archive.org website. Accessed 11.08.2024.

Wikipedia website: **Lady Elizabeth Finch-Hatton**. Accessed 12.08.2024.

English Heritage Website: **Dido Belle**. Accessed 12.08.2024.

Little NK: **Biography of Dido Elizabeth Belle, English Aristocrat** (2019). ThoughtCo website. Accessed 12.08.2024.

Mary Anning

Eylott M-C: **Mary Anning: the unsung hero of fossil discovery**. Natural History Museum website. Accessed 15.08.2024.

Lyme Regis Museum website: **Mary Anning.** Accessed 15.08.2024.

Rafferty JP: **Mary Anning**. Britannica website. Accessed 16.08.024.

Britannica website: **Sir Henry Thomas De La Beche.** Accessed 16.08.2024.

McKie R: **The untold tale of the woman who dug up ancient sea monsters** (2019). Guardian website. Accessed 16.08.2024.

Oxford University Museum of Natural History website: **Mary Anning's Ichthyosaur.** Accessed 16.08.2024.

Dorothea Dix

Dix DL: **Memorial of Miss DL Dix; in relation to the Illinois penitentiary** (1847). Internet Archive website. Accessed 02.06.2024

Bill of Rights Institute website: **Dorothea Dix, Memorial to the Legislation of Massachusetts** (1843). Accessed 05.06.2024.

Dix DL: **Memorial of Miss DL Dix to the Hon, the General Assembly in behalf of the insane of Maryland** (1852). Accessed 05.06.2024.

Norwood AR: **Dorothea Dix** (2017). National Women's History Museum. Accessed 05.06.2024

Wikipedia: **Dorothea Dix**. Accessed 05.06.2024.

Disability History Museum website: **Senate Debates On The Land-Grant Bill For Indigent Insane Persons** (1854). Accessed 07.06.2024.

Mental Health Matters website: **Lunacy Act 1845**. Accessed 07.06.2024.

The National Archives: **Asylums, psychiatric hospitals and mental health**. Accessed 07.06.2024.

Truong, Alexander H. M.D., M.A.; Maguire, Gerald E. M.D.; Maguire, Gerald A. M.D.,*. **A history of psychiatry in the United States of America**. Taiwanese Journal of Psychiatry 34(2):p 59-66, Apr–Jun 2020. | DOI: 10.4103/TPSY.TPSY_12_20 (

19th Century events and developments website: **Understanding Mental Health in the 19th Century: A Historical Perspective**. Accessed 09.06.2024.

Susan La Fleche

Mathes VS: **SUSAN LAFLESCHE PICOTTE, M.D.: NINETEENTH-CENTURY PHYSICIAN AND REFORMER** *Great Plains Quarterly*, vol. 13, no. 3, 1993, pp. 172–86. *JSTOR*, .

LISC website: **Susan La Flesche Picotte: A Pathbreaking Doctor from Indigenous America**. Accessed 19.06.2024.

History website: **Dr. Susan La Flesche Picotte becomes the first Native American woman to graduate from medical school** (Updated 2024). Accessed 27.06.2024.

National Library of Medicine website: **If you knew the conditions…" Healthcare to Native Americans. Susan La Flesche Picotte (1865-1915) First Native American Woman M.D.** (Last reviewed 2024). Accessed 27.06.2024.

Vaughan C: **The Incredible Legacy of Susan La Flesche, the First Native American to Earn a Medical Degree** (2017). Smithsonian mag website. Accessed 27.07.2024.

American Masters website: **The First American Indian Doctor.** Film transcript. Accessed 27.06.2024.

Wagner SR: **How Native American Women Inspired the Women's Rights Movement.** National Park Service website. Accessed 28.06.2024.

Speer G: **Disease & Death Comes to the Plains Indians.** Legends of America website, Accessed 28.06.2024.

Edith Smith

Wikipedia website: **Edith Smith (police officer).** Accessed 05.07.2024.

Wikipedia website: **Nina Boyle.** Accessed 05.07.2024.

Knowles B, Finn C, and Sterry D: **Edith Smith, Britain's First Warranted Policewoman** (2018). The Oxton Society. Booklet accessed online 06.07.2024.

Woodeson A: **The first women police: a force for equality or infringement?** (Original article 1993, published online 2006). Taylor and Francis website. Accessed 07.07.2024.

Jackson Dr LA: **The First World War and the first female police officer** (2014).History of Government website. Accessed 07.07.2024.

BBC website (BBC Sounds): **World War One At Home – Grantham, Lincolnshire: First Policewoman With Powers to Arrest.** Accessed 08.07.024.

Nina Boyle

Wikipedia website: **Nina Boyle**. Accessed 22.08.2024.

Simpkin J: **Nina Boyle** (updated 2021). Spartacus Educational Website Accessed 22.08.2024.

Briffett E: **Flappers, sanitary pads and public drinking: was the 1920s a time of increased liberation for women?** (2022). History Extra website. Accessed 22.08.2024.

Laybourn K: **Introduction: Twenties Britain (part one), Decade of conflict, realignment and change? The National Archives website:** Accessed 22.08.2024.

Gillett F: **Women's suffrage: 10 reasons why men opposed votes for women** (2018). BBC News website. Accessed 22.08.2024.

Brown E: **The Anti-Suffrage Anomaly: Gertrude Bell and the question of privilege** Newcastle University website. Accessed 22.08.2024.

Gertrude Ederle (Trudy)

Wang J: **The true story of "Young Woman and the Sea: "Fact-checking Daisy Ridley's Gertrude Ederle biopic** (2024). Yahoo News website. Accessed 13.06.2024.

Little B: **The First Woman to Swim the English Channel Beat the Men's Record by Two Hours** (2018, updated 2023). History website. Accessed 13.06.2024.

Britannica website: **Gertrude Ederle**. Accessed 13.06.2024.

Wikipedia website: **Gertrude Ederle**. Accessed 13.06.2024.

Channel swimming Dover website: **Miss Gertrude Ederle and Jabez Wolffe, failed attempt.** Accessed 13.06.24.

Waxman OB: **The True Story Behind Young Woman and the Sea** (2024). Time magazine website. Accessed 17.06.2024.

Channel swimming Dover website: **Jabez Wolffe, Champion Long Distance Swimmer.** Accessed 13.06.2024.

Dover Museum website: **Jabez Wolffe Biography.** Accessed 13.06.2024.

Wikipedia website: **Jabez Wolffe**. Accessed 13.06.2024.

Homeblown website: **The Benefits Of Using Grease For Cold Water Swimming** (2021). Accessed 15.06.2024.

Lives of the first world war website: **We remember Jacob Jabez Wolffe.** Accessed 16.06.2024.

Wikipedia website: **Bill Burgess**. Accessed 17.06.2024.

Denman E: **SWIMMING; A Pioneer Looks Back on Her Unforgettable Feat** (2001). New York Times Website. Accessed 17.06.2024.

Lilly Gill

Bushey Museum and Art Gallery: **Lilly Gill** (written transcription of audio interview conducted with the artist).

Smith J: **Bushey Artists** (2020). Bushey Museum and Art Gallery.

The Rowntree Society website: **Tessa Rowntree, 1909-1999: Caring Humanitarian and 'Tough Girl'** Accessed 24.08.2024.

Art UK website: **Karel Vogel**. Accessed 25.08.2024.

Dalyell T: **Obituary: Sir Nevill Mott** (1996). The Independent website. Accessed 25.08.2024.

Dorothy Hepworth

Nicholls-Lee D: **The Truth About Dorothy Hepworth and Patricia Preece** (2024). Sussex Life Magazine. Accessed online 01.06.2024.

Elliott V: Lives **Laid Bare / The second wife of the British painter Stanley Spencer who wouldn't live with him – and it turns out she didn't paint her own pictures** (1998). SFGATE. Accessed online 01.06.2024.

Black H: **Artists of Artifice** (2024). World Of Interiors. Accessed online 01.06.2024.

Griffiths V: **Dorothy Hepworth and Patricia Preece: and untold story** (2024) Sussex Bylines. Accessed online 01.06.2024.

Hodges M: **Why Stanley Spencer tore apart his family for a lesbian muse** (2018). Radio Times. Accessed online 01.06.2024.

Wikipedia: **Patricia Preece** Accessed 01.06.2024.

Wilcox DJ: **The Secret Art of Dorothy Hepworth AKA Patricia Preece** (2024). The Court Gallery.

Joan Murray (nee Clarke)

Scientific women website: **Joan Clarke.** Accessed 28.08.2024.

Kerry Howard (You Tube): **My Engagement to Alan Turing by Joan Clarke (later Joan Murray).** Accessed 28.08.2024.

Lesser Known Faces (You Tube): **Joan Clarke - WW2 Enigma Codebreaker.** Accessed 28.08.2024.

Wikipedia website: **Women in Bletchley Park.** Accessed 28.08.2024.

Wikipedia website: **Joan Clarke.** Accessed 28.08.2024.

Miller J: **Joan Clarke, woman who cracked Enigma cyphers with Alan Turing** (2014). BBC News website. Accessed 29.08.2024.

East Grinsted Museum website: **Sister Meally – Ward Sister on Ward III – Queen Victoria Hospital – 2nd World War** (2023). Accessed 29.08.2024.

McKay S: **The Secret Life of Bletchley Park** (2011 edition). Aurum Press

Other references

Kenyon O: **800 Years of Women's Letters** (1995 edition). Alan Sutton Publishing

Tate: **Now You See Us, Women Artists in Britain 1520 – 1920** (2024). Tate Publishing

De Vries S: **Great Pioneer Women of the Outback** (2005). Harper Collins

UpLitPress.co.uk

Publishing books that make you glad to be part of the human race.

Get a free anthology when you join our mailing list

www.ingramcontent.com/pod-product-compliance
Ingram Content Group UK Ltd.
Pitfield, Milton Keynes, MK11 3LW, UK
UKHW040050030625
6199UKWH00003B/225